Anne Wilson

Governing Body

THE SECOND SARA KINGSLEY MYSTERY

First published by The Women's Press Ltd, 1997
A member of the Namara Group
34 Great Sutton Street, London EC1V 0DX

This is a work of fiction and any resemblance to actual persons living or
dead is purely coincidental.

British Library Cataloguing-in-Publication Data
A catalogue record for this book is available from the British Library

ISBN 0 7043 4557 9

Typeset in Bembo 11/13pt by The FSH Group Ltd
Printed and bound in Great Britain by Caledonian International

*To hard-working teachers everywhere —
you have my admiration and respect*

Acknowledgements

Thanks to my family and to those friends – you know who you are – whose loving support makes it possible for me to write fiction. Special thanks to Joanne, who helps with all things psychotherapeutic, and to my agents, Gregory and Radice, who keep the whole thing on track.

Chapter One

It was the most difficult group Robin and I had ever worked with. The air crackled with tension; words which seemed innocuous to us had an electric effect on the group.

'I think the fence on the south side of the playground is a priority,' said Tony, with authority. 'It's the only way to stop the vandalism.'

Bridget's thin lips hardened into a straight line and she looked at Mona. Mona stared back, then turned away and covered her mouth with her hand, resting her elbow on the other hand. Rajesh tapped the floor with his foot. No one spoke.

'Sounds like a sensible idea,' put in Robin brightly. 'Does anyone have any feelings about that – either way?'

I half expected them to hiss demonically at him, the hostility was palpable. My heart sank. I had a baby-sitter who was eight months pregnant, who had to be home and tucked up in bed by ten thirty. It was already nine o'clock. The baby could be born and weaned by the time I got back.

'I have a suggestion.'

1

All eyes turned towards me.

'I suggest we abandon this – ' I held up the piece of paper with the pre-prepared agenda on it – 'and get down to the real issues.'

There was a collective holding of breath. I turned to my left. 'Mona.'

'Yes?'

'How do you feel at the moment?'

I hardly needed to ask. Mona's fine features were disfigured by anger. Her dark brown eyes were dull and dangerous; her normal dignified manner had gone. She was like a swan poised to break an arm with its wings.

'Very angry,' she said softly. She turned and glared significantly at Tony.

'Why do you feel angry, Mona?'

'Ask her why she – '

'Tony!' I interrupted him sharply. 'Let Mona finish.'

Mona took a deep breath and chose her words carefully. 'Racism is never easy to deal with – ' she began.

'She's paranoid,' muttered Tony.

'We're getting sidetracked again,' sighed Bridget, folding her arms. 'Why can't we stick to the point, which is that – '

'Please!' Robin held up a hand. 'Let Mona finish.'

Bridget's mouth snapped shut and she sighed extravagantly through her nose. Cynthia's eyes flicked over towards Mona and her full lips turned up into a secret smile.

'Let's try again,' I said, turning to Mona. Then, to the group, 'Everyone will get their chance to talk.' And we'll all be home by morning, I added to myself.

When Mona had first asked us to come and help break the deadlock among the governors of Arkwright High, I could hardly believe her account of the backbiting, the bitching and betrayals, the allegiances and double-crosses which had preceded our intervention. It sounded more like a multi-national company than a secondary school. But then, that's just the sort of approach the government wanted. Mona had had the misfortune to be made head at the time when Local Management of Schools was just coming in and middle-management mini-Hitlers were queuing up to show those lefty teachers a thing or two about how to manage a budget. Suddenly, heads, teachers, politicians, business people and parents were supposed to work together as a body to make all the major decisions about a school. It was a recipe for disaster.

Tony Thornley – chair of the governors – was the joint managing director of a small company in Park Royal. He was a small, stout man of forty-five or so. His face was square, with an iron jawline and a strong, wide mouth. His nose was slightly upturned, which might have given his face a more cheerful look had it not been for the hard, sunken eyes on either side of it. The other two men were parent–governors – Brian Farrell and Rajesh Patel. Mona had said that there should have been more, but it was hard to get them to come since Tony became chair. Brian was stocky, like Tony, and prematurely balding. His shiny pate was plastered with two thin strands of hair that he kept smoothing down nervously. He was Tony's sidekick, nodding eagerly even before Tony had finished what he was saying. Rajesh was tall and well groomed, the only one of the three men who was wearing a suit. His allegiances within the governing body were ambiguous. He claimed that being an accountant, he was only prepared to comment on financial matters, but that didn't seem to stop him throwing in the odd inflammatory remark. The other people at the meeting were all women – Mona; Maggie, the school administrator who was there to take the minutes; Bridget Scudder, the deputy head; and Cynthia Marsh, a governor appointed by the Local Education Authority. Bridget was tense and combative, challenging everyone, including Mona; Cynthia clearly disliked Bridget; and all the women were at odds with Tony Thornley. Quite a happy bunch.

Mona had approached us because she knew Robin in a

professional capacity – they both advised a local authority subcommittee on youth services – and she knew our centre sometimes took on as clients different groups in the community to help them work together better. The Acton Counselling Centre is funded by a mixture of health authority money, social services, charity donations and fees from clients who can afford to pay. It's a hand-to-mouth existence, especially with the annual threat of losing our official grants, but somehow we manage to make ends meet. We mostly work with individuals, giving practical, down-to-earth counselling to get people out of a rut so they can see their problems in a different way. Our referrals come from GPs, schools and child guidance clinics – usually the hard-to-handle clients everyone else has given up on – but sometimes groups, like the governors, approach us directly. Occasionally people walk in off the street, but more often either they've mistaken us for the dentist up the road or they just want somewhere warm to sit.

'You,' quivered Mona, pointing an accusing finger at Tony, 'have mounted an unrelenting attack on me ever since you became a governor. You have questioned every decision I have made, you have sullied my name with my staff, you have taken every opportunity to put obstacles in my path and now you are mounting a campaign to opt out of the local authority when there is every indication that the majority of parents and staff oppose it. Why?' It was a rhetorical question really. Mona knew why. Her eyes flashed dangerously and she raised her chin in eloquent defiance. 'Because you hate women, and black women in particular. Mr Thornley, you are a bigot!'

I turned to face Tony, who was sitting back in his chair, legs apart, apparently unmoved by her outburst. He stared at her impassively and stuck out his lower lip.

'Tony,' I said evenly, 'your turn.'

He turned his eyes in my direction and I noticed again how small and deep-set they were.

'My feelings are well known,' he said crisply. 'I believe

opting out raises school standards and improves the morale of pupils, parents and staff. In financial terms – '

'Feelings, Tony,' I reminded him firmly. 'We're talking about your feelings. Is it true that you resent Mona? Do you find her threatening? Do you find it difficult to work with a group like this?'

Tony pressed his lips together and fixed me with a cold, beady gaze. Eventually he asked, 'May I ask what your qualifications are for being at this meeting?'

Maggie, who was sitting beside him with her notepad clutched tightly in her hands, whispered, 'Oh, dear,' and shifted nervously on her moulded plastic chair.

'I think we covered this ground at the beginning of the meeting. Robin and I are trained counsellors who work with all kinds of groups to help them work together more effectively. You agreed as a group to ask us to work with you because you seemed to have reached deadlock on certain issues. How do you feel, Tony?'

'I'd prefer you to call me Mr Thornley,' said Tony. 'What shall I call you – Doctor something, is it . . . ?'

I smiled. Nice try, Tone. 'Sara will do fine. I see you feel safer if there's some distance between you and other people, Mr Thornley. How does the group feel about that, I wonder?'

Ten blank faces gawped at me. Rajesh resumed his foot-tapping.

'Yes, Cynthia?'

She was dressed in a smart tailored suit with a jacket that ended at the waist, with a tight-fitting top underneath. She was expertly made up, with subtle shades of cream and gold that matched the highlights in her hair. She licked her lips and said in a smooth, controlled voice, 'I think I speak for most people when I say that the more distance Tony puts between himself and this governing body, the better.'

There was a momentary silence while everyone absorbed the full nastiness of the remark.

'Thank you, Mrs Marsh,' snapped Thornley. 'Helpful as ever.'

He glanced at his watch to emphasise his impatience. Cynthia's lip curled with displeasure. Mona raised her eyebrows and looked at Bridget. Rajesh started drumming his fingers on the back of his chair. I fantasised about mowing down the lot of them with a sub-machine gun.

The meeting lurched from tension to tension for the best part of an hour. Robin and I struggled to get a dialogue going, but however many layers of bitterness we uncovered, there were always more underneath. Tony, as well as being part of the loony racist fringe, also clearly resented Mona's intelligence and authority. Mona felt cornered by everyone, even Bridget, a member of her staff, who agreed with her views but in an overbearing way which seemed to owe more to her dislike of Tony and her obsessive concern for children with 'special needs' than loyalty to Mona. Brian seemed to support Tony on principle – he clearly believed in boys sticking together – but otherwise contributed very little. Cynthia seemed to be at the meeting predominantly to put down Tony Thornley and took little notice of anyone else. Mona had told us before the meeting that she was an LEA governor with ambitions to become a local councillor. She seemed to regard Thornley as an arch rival. Rajesh watched it all with an air of amused detachment, but I noted the sharp attention of his narrowed eyes and the shrewd way he said just enough to make it seem as if he was participating without committing himself to any particular faction.

Robin and I agreed afterwards, it was a highly complex matrix of conflict, and Tony Thornley was at its centre. No one liked him, but everyone took notice of him. Except perhaps Rajesh, whose attitude was difficult to fathom. At the end of an hour, I called a halt; we weren't making progress and Robin and I were both under time pressure. I called for feedback, but got none, except from Mona, who thanked Robin and me for our efforts. I wound up the session by saying that at the meeting the following month, we would address items one to five on the agenda. I asked everyone to come prepared both to talk and listen. I wanted to add that a bit of human decency wouldn't go amiss either.

As it turned out, the meeting never took place. A couple of weeks later, my eye caught the headline of a local paper, one of those free weekly rags that is posted, irritatingly, through the door:

Local Businessman Stabbed To Death

Tony Thornley's name leapt out at me.

> Tony Thornley, managing director of Thornley Veneers, was fatally wounded outside Arkwright High School on Thursday night in a frenzied attack. He was stabbed fifteen times in the stomach and chest. He had been attending a governors' meeting at the school and was attacked in the playground as he walked to his car. Thornley leaves a wife, Frances, and a fifteen-year-old son. A close friend of the family told the *Acton Reporter*, 'His wife is in a state of shock. Tony was very well known and respected locally – it's a tragedy.'

I scanned the rest of the article, torn between the ungenerous thought that he would be little missed by the Arkwright governors and distress at the idea of any life ending so violently. But when I reached the last line, I almost choked: 'Mona Pearson, the headteacher of Arkwright High, is currently helping police with their inquiries.'

★ ★ ★

'Mona Pearson is not a murderer!' Robin cried. The nostrils at the base of his aquiline nose flared outwards, bright red. His cheeks were flushed, brows knitted in outrage, a stray lock of hair having flopped behind his small round glasses. He was towering over me, standing in a shaft of sunlight, leaning on

7

my desk. I hoisted my feet off the desk and mentally shook myself out of the reverie I'd been enjoying involving indecent acts on a Hawaiian beach. I shaded my eyes to look at him. He's normally utterly unflappable, with twinkling eyes and a ready wit. I found it rather unsettling to see him so wound up.

'Have a seat, Robin.'

He fumbled distractedly, then parked his tall frame on a seat by the bookcase. I got up from the desk and went over to sit on the couch, opposite him. Nine thirty on a Monday morning after a weekend mothering two kids with chicken-pox – I felt like a slot machine waiting for someone to put the coin in.

'I think we should at least make sure she's got good legal advice, don't you? Christ knows what the police are doing to her.'

I gawped at him; it was like watching a film when you've missed a crucial part of the plot.

'You have heard about Mona?' demanded Robin, his eyes blinking rapidly behind his glasses.

'Yes. It's shocking. But I don't see what it has to do with us.'

'Sara! Mona's our client, she's black and she's innocent.'

'Is Mona a friend of yours, Robin?'

'What? I don't see what that has to do with – '

'Is she?'

'I . . . she . . . ' He faltered, lifted his glasses and rubbed his eyes to cover his awkwardness. 'Sort of.'

'Are you involved with her?'

I braced myself, ready to berate him for counselling a group when he knew one of the people intimately. Robin shook his head vigorously.

'There's nothing between us now.'

I looked at him questioningly. He stopped fidgeting and met my gaze.

'I was infatuated with her for a while, about three years ago. A crush. It went no further than that.' He jutted out his chin. 'I didn't see it as a reason not to work with the Arkwright group.'

That was a matter of opinion – Robin knew it was

completely unprofessional to work with a group where you knew one of the members – but this didn't seem like the right time to discuss it.

I went over to the small table at the side of the room and poured myself a cup of coffee. I offered one to Robin; he shook his head. I sympathised with him about Mona, but I felt reluctant to get involved. The police would be at our door soon enough, wanting to hear about the meeting we had attended and get our opinion of Mona's state of mind. We'd do her more good by staying neutral and telling them exactly what we knew. I sipped the dark Italian coffee and went back to sit on the couch. At last, I was beginning to wake up.

'Have they actually charged her?'

Robin frowned and nodded. He stood up and started to pace the room, rubbing his hands together anxiously.

'Thornley and Mona were the last to leave. The caretaker heard Thornley's screams, searched the playground and found him bleeding to death by the dustbins. As he ran to call the police, he came across Mona standing just outside the door holding a knife.'

I stared at him, dumbstruck. Had Thornley finally tipped Mona over the edge? Where did she get the knife? Surely she didn't carry one.

'The knife came from her office,' said Robin, as if reading my thoughts, 'confiscated from a kid earlier in the week.'

'How do you know all this?'

Robin ducked his head in embarrassment. 'Pathologist – friend of my dad.'

Robin normally plays down his influential connections, but they can be mighty useful.

'The police knew she hated Thornley. She said she wasn't sure what happened. She went after Thornley to tell him something and found him collapsed on the ground. She was going to get help and then ran into the caretaker. They didn't believe her. She was standing there, knife in hand, and that was enough for them.'

I blew out my cheeks. It was probably enough for me too.

'Mona didn't do it!' exclaimed Robin, catching my train of thought again. 'She's incapable of hating someone that much.'

The cynical part of me countered that everyone is capable of hating someone that much, but I didn't say it. Robin's passionate defence of Mona moved me. There are five of us who work at the centre, and Robin is normally the most calm and rational of everyone. Clancy, who works predominantly with the elderly, is bossy and volatile – qualities she puts to great use in the groups she runs, such as 'You Can Do It' (sex and the over-seventies) and 'Speak Out' (how to be assertive – and annoy your middle-aged children). Greg, who like me works with a range of ages, is aggressively working class and very opinionated; I'm well known for my intolerance. Mel, our children and families expert, is reasonable and soft-spoken, but prone to irrational outbursts if you threaten any of her sacred cows. Robin is our voice of reason and sound judgement; until now, I had never known him let his heart rule his head. I had always thought of him as a bit of a cold fish where women were concerned.

'Couldn't you ring round some of your police contacts?' pleaded Robin. 'At least find out what's going on. Whether she has a good solicitor and whether she's likely to get bail.'

I wanted to warn him not to get involved, not to do something silly, like standing bail unless he was sure of his facts, but looking at his face I knew it was useless.

'I'll make some tentative inquiries,' I promised. 'In the meantime, why don't you get in touch with some of Mona's friends or her family? Does she live with anyone?'

He looked away, preoccupied and worried. 'Not as far as I know. I remember her saying once that she had no close family at all. And friends – I'm not sure. She's a bit of a lone wolf.'

I could see he needed to do something. 'Start with Bridget at the school and see what she knows. You can at least make sure Mona's got some support.'

He nodded pensively. 'I'll do that.'

After he had gone, I hovered by the phone and wondered

who to call first. Our work at the Acton Counselling Centre involves a fair bit of contact with the police – mainly through young people who fall foul of the law – and generally relations are not too bad. I tried ringing a couple of people I knew in the right area, but got nowhere. Finally, I decided to call Barry, a detective inspector I know in Chiswick. He was in the wrong area, but at least he could get my name right and he had the good grace to return favours. Barry was in a rush, but he listened to my garbled account – Mona's arrest, Robin's doubts and the vitriol of the governors' meeting. His cynicism crackled down the line, but he promised to find out as much as he could and phone me back in the next few days.

Steve – an actor, who lives round the corner – arrived bang on time to baby-sit. I dawdled getting ready, feeling guilty about leaving the children, especially knowing the kind of evening I had planned. Steve was my best friend and normally I confided in him about everything, but this was something I didn't want to share. Steve sensed that I was holding back and – master of tact that he is – he asked no questions, but I knew my secrecy worried him and he wondered if I was hiding something that could harm either me or the children. He watched me applying my lipstick with an unspoken question on his face. I worked slowly, with a hand mirror held close to my lips, grimacing in a set pattern. I have a wide mouth, well shaped, with sensuous lips – it's one of my few good features – so I often put on lipstick. But as my glistening mouth took shape under Steve's scrutiny, self-doubt crept over me like a stealthy insect. Was my skirt too short? Was this shade of lipstick too lusciously red, too obvious? I looked myself in the eye as I massaged my lips together, and told myself that keeping this relationship to myself was a sign of maturity, that I had confided too much in Steve about my previous boyfriend, John, and should have been more circumspect. Still, at the back of my mind I knew it was a mixture of guilt and embarrassment that held me back this time.

*

John was a guy who worked for Customs and Excise whom I had met the summer before. We had been seeing each other for the past nine months, but, looking back, it had never felt quite right. We were too similar. John was analytical, a thinker and a talker; although he could be funny, he could also be over-serious and intense. He wanted to know everything, to pull everything apart to reduce it to its constituent parts and then put it back together. He was the kind of guy who took apart washing machines and car engines for fun, but he also did the same thing with people.

Over the past few weeks, the relationship had been foundering and I wanted to call it a day. I didn't think it was going anywhere – it was too heavy-going, too much like wading through mud. I had tried to end it without causing too much hurt, but John refused to let go without picking over the carcass of the relationship, for reasons, reasons, reasons. I was tired of justifying my desire for the split.

Now, dressed to kill, yet obviously not going out with John, I hovered in the hallway, hoping to get Steve's blessing for leaving two sick children and going out to claim a purely selfish pleasure. It was a forlorn hope when Steve didn't even know where I was going.

'I'll be back by eleven thirty.'

Steve shooed me towards the front door. 'Just go!' he boomed, exasperated.

I said a final goodbye to Hannah and Jake, who were clinging onto Steve's legs – red-spotted faces turned upwards, pestering him for a story – and dashed with relief out of the front door.

It was balmy night for early spring, giving a hint of summer evenings to come. I decided to drive, even though I wasn't going far. I turned my Vauxhall Chevette out into Churchfield Road, where the evening buzz was just beginning. Petty criminals making for the Weaver's Arms; the drivers outside Doogie's minicabs, yawning and hitching up their trousers, clocking on for work after having slept all day. The Indian takeaway was just starting to get a few customers and in the small grocer's shops, like Hari's, I glimpsed a couple of harassed mothers with buggies. Just home from work, I bet, with kids they had picked up from the child-minders. They were probably telling themselves they were shopping for the kids' tea, but ten to one they would give in and stop at the chippy on the way home. Ask me how I know – I've been a single mother for nearly four years now and for the first six months I practically kept the local chippy in business. I thanked my lucky stars I was out for the evening, free from mothering and domestic drudgery. I cut down a side street to the Uxbridge Road and headed down towards Shepherd's Bush.

The house was in a dead-end street off the Uxbridge Road, a few hundred yards from the Bush, a nondescript place which had been made into dingy bedsits. I pressed the bottom bell and waited, nervously smoothing down my skirt. The doubts I had felt in front of Steve returned. Was I too old for this? I ran one hand over my mass of frizzy hair in a half-hearted attempt to smooth it down, but changed my mind mid-gesture and shook it out with my fingers. May as well go the whole hog. He had hardly opened the door before we were kissing hungrily, tongues exploring each other's mouths. We stopped briefly to exchange a greeting, then moved into his room, shut the door behind us and started again. As we kissed, I moved one hand round to his stomach, slipped it under his T-shirt and marvelled for the umpteenth time at his flat midriff and smooth skin. I felt myself relaxing, anticipating the pleasures ahead. Suddenly, he drew back.

'Sara . . .'

My hand was getting ready to unbutton his jeans.

'Sara – wait.'

'That's the problem, Pete,' I whispered. 'I just can't wait.'

I undid the first button and moved down to the next.

'Sara!'

It was half sigh, half groan, a pleading sort of sound. He

pulled back, one hand on each of my arms, and held me gently away from him.

Startled, and not a little annoyed, I stared at him. 'What's the matter?'

'Just – just hang on.'

I looked at his face for the first time and saw that he was grimacing, struggling to find the right words. I felt a terrible rush of irritation. Why was he so slow to say what he wanted to say? Why didn't he just get on with it?

Finally, he stuttered, 'H–how come we never talk?'

'What?'

'Talk. Why don't we talk?'

'What do you mean, talk? About what?'

He gestured desperately. 'Anything.'

I ran my hand through my hair and sighed. Oh, do me a favour! I had come wanting, expecting, sex with no strings attached. The last thing I wanted was a cosy chat. In my job, that's all people ever do – talk. With a rush, I realised how sick I was of talking, sharing, communicating. Clients talking about their feelings, colleagues talking about their problems, John talking about 'us', Hannah and Jake talking all the time about everything. Words, words, words. Isn't this better? I wanted say. Isn't it better just to express how you feel, just get on with it, without all the angst and soul-searching?

I tried not to sound as irritable as I felt. 'What is there to talk about?'

'Us. For a start.'

My heart sank further. 'Us?' I sounded like an echo.

He looked like a little boy, his trousers undone, his T-shirt rumpled. And in a way, he was a little boy – twenty-three years old. Not quite, I reminded myself, young enough to be my son. When I first laid eyes on him, in a pub where I had gone to drown my sorrows after an argument with John, I was dumbstruck by his beauty – a Greek god with cut-glass cheekbones, smooth olive skin and shining black eyes. My first thought was to wish desperately that I was a beautiful, blonde twenty-year-old so that he would chat me up. But it turned out, miraculously, that he had grown tired of nubile, fair-haired women throwing themselves in his path. He was quite taken, thank you very much, with a slightly drunk, curly-haired Jewish woman with a big nose and dome-shaped breasts. My sassy one-liners made him smile, a wide unaffected smile; not for him the self-conscious smirk of the shaving-commercial model. He laughed at my jokes – another miracle – and when he laughed, he opened his mouth and threw back his head so that the muscles on his neck stood out. He was that rare breed, the good-looking young man who has moved beyond the 'let-me-just-check-my-hair-in-the-mirror' stage. His body was as good as his face – spare and well toned, with hard thighs that came from manual work rather than preening sessions in the gym. His only vanity was his hair – a thick, black mane – which he kept long, tied back in a pony-tail.

My first instinct now was to gather up my things and run away. But thirty-four years of guilt-producing Jewish upbringing got in the way. A man was upset – I had to stay and make it better! If I'd been a smoker, I would have lit up. Instead, I opted for a different drug.

'Have you got a drink?'

'Got some lager somewhere.'

'That'll do.'

He did up his jeans and produced a couple of cans from under the bed. We sat there side by side and punched in the tabs with a synchronised hiss. I reflected ruefully that that was probably about as close as we would get all evening to a simultaneous orgasm.

'I've been thinking.'

Shit. The one thing I counted on Pete not to do was think. I took a pull of lager and waited.

'I was thinking – why we don't do anything together except – you know – this? I know you've got kids and maybe you don't want me coming round, but we could see a movie, have a meal. Go to the theatre.'

'The theatre?'

'Why not?' His brow darkened. 'What do you think? That I'm a moron?'

'Of course I don't think you're a moron.'

I couldn't think of anything to add that wouldn't sound patronising. It just hadn't crossed my mind that he would be even remotely interested in going to the theatre.

'You don't think I'm good enough for you, do you?'

I heaved a sigh. 'What do you mean?'

'Just because you went to college, you think you're better than me. Well, I've got friends who went to college – we go out, we do things. How come you don't want to do those things with me? How come you don't want me to meet your kids?'

Whatever I'd expected, it wasn't this. I closed my eyes for a moment, begging for it not to be real. How did this happen? Surely it was possible, sometimes, for life to be simple and for me to pick a man who was exactly what he seemed.

'Pete – listen.'

I pinched the bridge of my nose between finger and thumb, trying to muster patience and honesty in equal measure. I opened my eyes and sought eye contact. He had eyes to die for – the shape of almonds, the colour of melted treacle, set atop those angular cheekbones.

'When we met, there was an instant attraction.' I could feel it as I spoke – the sight of him still turned my knees to jelly. 'You asked me if I had a boyfriend and I told you the truth: that I was seeing someone, but wanted to end it.'

If I remembered rightly, I told him I was sick to death of a relationship where you couldn't choose a pizza together without causing a major international incident.

'With you, I just followed my instinct. I told myself not think about it, just do it.'

'So we've done it. A lot. We've done it from the back, from the front, on the floor, on the table – '

'Don't you like it?'

'Course I like it. But what I mean is — can't we do something else for a change?'

I laughed. 'I never thought I'd hear a twenty-three-year-old man say that.'

He didn't smile. 'That's it, isn't it? You get off on it. The age difference.'

'Pete — '

'You're always on about it. "At your age", "You're such a baby." You're on some age thing and this makes you feel good.'

'Yes.'

'Eh?'

'I'm thirty-four and it makes me feel good to be going out with a twenty-three-year-old man. I like you, I like your body. Full stop. End of story. Is that so bad?'

He shook his head. 'You're a bitch, you know that?'

I gaped. 'What's your problem? Most men I've ever known would kill for this situation. A willing female, no ties, no commitment — '

'Maybe I'm different!' he shouted. 'Ever thought about that?'

It was like a slap in the face.

'No,' I admitted softly. 'I've never thought about that.'

It was awful, but true. I had to face it. Up to that moment, I had been thinking of him as a body, not a mind, not even a real person. A fantasy come true. I allowed myself to believe that the ego trip and the great sex could go on and on without changing or progressing, or turning into something else. I knew he wanted more from me, but I resisted it. I never asked him questions about himself and fobbed him off with flippant answers whenever he asked about me. I knew now why I felt so guilty and why I hadn't wanted to discuss the relationship with Steve. My admission lay like a spiked wall between us.

'Get out,' he said flatly.

I looked at him. A man feeling exploited, his feelings hurt. I wanted to write it off as a quid pro quo for all the times the roles had been reversed, for all the times I had been strung along emotionally when all the man wanted was sex. But I knew life didn't work like that.

'I'm sorry,' I began.

'Just fucking go.'

I wanted to say something. Something that told him how much I fancied him, how grateful I was for his sexual attention, but no words came. I wondered if I would ever grow up where men were concerned and stop getting myself into messy situations. However I tried to break the cycle, it always ended up the same way. I picked up my jacket from the floor and turned to go. With my hand on the door handle, I turned back.

'Pete?'

'What?'

'You're a great lay,' I said meekly. 'The best I've ever had.'

'God!' he expostulated, throwing up his hands. He looked up and our eyes met. His mouth, sullen and down-turned, twitched, widened and then he laughed and shook his head. 'You're sex mad – you know that?'

'I day-dream about you.'

He raised his eyes to the ceiling, embarrassed. 'Get away.'

'I do.'

'Yeah, well, I do about you too.'

I laughed at that. What did he have, a mother complex?

I moved towards him and crouched down in front of him, leaning my elbows on his knees. We kissed briefly.

'Next week, we'll have dinner, okay? Do you like Indian?'

He shrugged. 'You can't get round me that easily.'

'Who's trying to get round you? Simple question – do you like Indian food?'

'I know a good one in King Street,' he admitted.

'Great. We'll go there. Have a chat. Get to know each other a bit better. Not an Aries, are you? That could be a problem – '

'I'm Gemini. You're Aquarius. You told me when we met.'

'Of course.' How could I forget? Another direct hit in the foot. I stood up. 'I'd better go.'

He looked up mischievously and my stomach flipped in automatic response. 'Stay for a bit.'

'A bit?'

'Of this.'

He drew me towards him and lay back on the bed in a single action.

'I thought you wanted to do something else for a change.'

'You persuaded me. Got your evil way with me again.'

I smiled and kissed him slowly, smoothing his eyebrows with my fingers, but I felt cautious. Was it an ambush? Had the clouds really passed so quickly, or would we start making love only for him to stop again to jab words, like spokes, into the wheels of our lovemaking? The eager response of his mouth reassured me; his tongue probing and exploring, a much better use for it than talking. He had said what he wanted to say; now he was willing to wait and see if it made any difference. I took heart from noting that he wasn't a sulker, that my meagre promise had satisfied him for now. Perhaps, I thought grudgingly, the relationship could survive the odd meal out without sliding into deep psychoanalysis. I felt his rising excitement and pushed aside the thought that I should be more responsible. I knew I shouldn't stay until I had thought the whole thing through, but my desire for him had not diminished one iota. As he pressed his lips to my neck and tugged at my jumper with his teeth, a voice inside me whispered, 'Do it now, think later.' And, bad girl that I am, I listened.

I left almost immediately afterwards, telling Pete the truth, that my kids were ill and I wanted to get back early. What I didn't tell him was that I found the dingy bedsit depressing and that I wanted to avoid the possibility of starting up a 'meaningful dialogue' about our burgeoning relationship. I knew the talking had to come, but I wanted to put it off for as long as I could. I had intended to drive around for an hour to give myself space to think, but as I turned the car out into the Uxbridge Road the sad yellow lights and dismal late-night grocery stores made the prospect seem so unappealing that I drove straight home to take guilty refuge in the bosom of my family.

When I opened the door I could hear Steve's voice coming from the living room. 'How could you do it? Murder your own child in cold blood and think you could get away with it?' Luckily, I knew that he was auditioning for a plum role in a revival of a late-nineteenth-century melodrama – Steve is a stage actor, who does the occasional telly. He was keeping his voice low so as not to wake the children, but the sound still carried well into the hall. I went into the living room and smiled at the familiar sight – Steve leaning back in his favourite chair, outstretched hand holding the script, reading it through the half-glasses perched on the end of his nose. He acknowledged my arrival with a wave and carried on reading – he doesn't like to break the flow when he's learning lines.

I slumped down on the sofa and waited for him to finish. Absently, I watched his face, changing shape as he mouthed each sentence. He's no teen idol – he's forty-three, with a rapidly receding hairline and more than a hint of a paunch – but his face is full of character. His good humour shows in the raised curve of his eyebrows and the crinkled laughter lines around his eyes; but the pout of his lower lip betrays a certain discontentment with life, betraying the bad times – like when his marriage to Nicole ended and he thought he would never see his son, Eric, again.

When he had finished, he peered curiously at me over the top of his glasses. I must have looked a sight.

'Want to talk about it?'

I shrugged. I wasn't proud of myself. Steve can be hard on me sometimes – I wasn't ready to let him delve into my motives for getting involved with Pete.

'Nothing to talk about.'

'Please yourself.' He started to gather up his papers. 'When did you last see John?'

Good old Steve. Straight to the point.

'Three weeks ago.'

'Miss him?'

'No. And yes.'

'He rang tonight.'

'Really?' I couldn't hide my interest. 'What time?'

'I thought you didn't miss him.'

'I said I did and I didn't.'

'He rang about nine. I told him you were out. No message.'

'Is he going to ring again?'

Steve put on a camp voice. 'Well, now, we had a good natter about that. "Should I phone her again, Stevie?" And I said to him, "Well, dear, the last time she mentioned you it was to call you an over-dependent wanker – "'

I put up my hand 'Okay! Okay! So he doesn't confide in you.'

John liked Steve, but always treated him warily. He felt Steve knew too much about 'us'.

Steve stuffed the script into a duffle bag and drained the last of a can of beer. 'Your son asked me this evening where electricity comes from.'

I grinned. 'What did you say?'

'It was a challenge. I decided to leave out fossil fuels and energy released through combustion and concentrate on power stations and the national grid.'

I was impressed. 'And?'

'He listened to the whole explanation and then told me – in a very sniffy tone – that I was wrong. "'Lectricity comes out of there, Steve" – he points to the socket – "and you mustn't touch it, 'cos it's hot."'

We laughed.

As I saw him out, he brushed his lips lightly over my cheek.

I hugged him. 'Thanks, Steve.'

He squeezed my shoulder. 'Give him a ring.'

'Yeah,' I said. 'Maybe.'

I didn't exactly wait up for the phone to ring – I had a few vital tasks, like folding socks and pacing from room to room. John didn't ring back. At midnight, I gave in and went to bed. I dropped into a dreamless sleep, surfacing only briefly as a small spotty body crept into my bed and snuggled into the small of my back.

Chapter Two

I had wanted to pee since nine thirty, but didn't manage it until twelve thirty, stopping at the downstairs loo on the way to the kitchen to throw together a sandwich. It was that sort of morning. I had just seen a young woman who had been raped two months ago. She was due to get married in two weeks' time. She hadn't reported it to the police and she hadn't told her fiancé. The man who raped her was her future husband's father. She didn't want to embarrass him. She thought that if she kept quiet and tried to forget it, the pain and humiliation would go away. She cried for an hour, curled up on my couch, and asked if she could come back tomorrow. I hoped I could persuade her to go to the police, but somehow I doubted that I would manage it. I was going to have to talk to Clancy about that one later in the day – rape counselling was an area I found particularly hard. Before that, I had two young parents and their screaming baby – she postnatally depressed and he unable to understand why. I had a fairly good idea of why a nineteen-year-old with a colicky baby might be depressed, living as she did in a shabby bedsit on a busy road with her boyfriend on night shifts. But at least he came with her to see me – unlike the cowardly shit who raped the woman his son was about to marry.

The kitchen is at the back of the clinic – a large, white room with a pine table, a microwave oven, a coffee maker and an outsize fridge. It's the place where we tend to congregate in rare moments of calm – at lunchtime, or at the end of a busy day – to meet and exchange a few words over a microwaved lasagne.

'A black, single woman in a position of authority – what more can I say?'

It was Clancy speaking, leaning her large frame against the counter and waving a can of cut-price cola in the faces of Greg, Mel and Robin. It was a full house, apart from Doreen, our stalwart support staff, who was talking calmly into the phone in reception. Clancy was in full flight – eyes glittering with indignation, head flung back, nostrils flaring. A single plait had fallen across her face, giving it an extra-wild look.

'What more can you say? Why, Clancy, that she's beautiful, intelligent, sensitive, eats like a horse and is a dab hand at geriatric karaoke.'

They looked at me blankly. I smiled and gestured towards Clancy.

'A black single woman, in a position of authority. Who else could it be?'

Clancy glared at me, and Greg said gravely, 'We were talking about Mona Pearson.'

'Oh.' Feeling sheepish, I flipped the switch on the kettle.

'Does she have a good solicitor?' asked Mel.

'When I talked to her on the phone yesterday, she said she didn't want to see anyone,' Robin's voice was low and earnest. 'Except Sara.'

'What?' This was news to me.

'Mona has asked to see you,' said Robin. 'I hope you'll go.'

His eyes were so anxious, I could hardly stand to look at them. I stalled by opening the fridge and staring into the shelves. That Cheddar, surely, had been there for weeks.

'There's a visiting session between two and four this afternoon,' continued Robin. 'Mel says her meeting with you could easily be postponed until tomorrow – '

'Whoa! Hold on a minute.' I whirled round from the fridge and stared at them all.

'I haven't committed you to anything, Sara,' said Mel. 'I merely – '

'Why on earth would Mona want to see me?'

'Yeah,' agreed Clancy pensively. 'You'd think she'd want to see another black woman at a time like this.'

'She wants to see a white, single woman in a position of authority,' quipped Mel.

'She doesn't need me, she needs someone who can give her good legal advice.'

'Maybe she just wants to talk things over,' Mel said reasonably.

'But why me?'

'She trusts you,' said Robin.

'I think you should go,' declared Clancy.

'Okay, okay!' I raised my hand in mock defence. 'I'll go. But, Robin, I think the most likely reason she wants to talk to me is to send a message indirectly to you. So brace yourself and, whatever it is, don't shoot the messenger.'

'She didn't do it, Sara,' said Robin firmly. 'But I hear what you're saying.'

The conversation switched to other things and, after a minute or so, the others wandered out of the kitchen, leaving just Robin and me sitting at the table. I was clutching a stale cheese sandwich; he was staring into a dark brew of coffee, still looking uncharacteristically distracted.

'I spoke to Bridget Scudder last night,' he said.

'What did she say?'

The words 'last night' were like a stab in the chest – a reminder that Pete and my feelings towards him were another problem to be solved, sooner rather than later. Hoping to find some comfort in food, I took a large bite of my sandwich. It was dry and disgusting, but I chewed it anyway.

Robin paused, choosing his words carefully. His eyes, behind his glasses, looked keen and attentive. He has a polite, public schoolboy manner, but it is mostly a cover; he is actually a keen observer of humanity who picks apart people's motivations with a sharp mental scalpel. He questions closely, misses nothing and can be as tough as any situation demands. I knew he would have tried to get as much as possible out of Bridget, in his own peculiar way.

'She was certainly shocked about Mona's arrest, but her dislike of Mona is so intense that she can't disguise a certain amount of glee.'

I raised my eyebrows questioningly.

'It's obvious that Bridget resents Mona's popularity with the staff,' continued Robin, frowning. 'Mona is a person who likes to delegate, to get the staff involved, whereas Bridget favours a more dictatorial style of management. Reading between the lines, I'd say Mona has to strike a balance between not undermining Bridget's authority as deputy head and keeping her on a tight rein so that she doesn't bully the rest of the staff.' He smiled. 'Mona's an operator. She's one of the few people who could pull it off.'

He seemed to know an awful lot about Mona and the internal politics of Arkwright High.

Robin pushed up his glasses, keen to continue. 'Bridget couldn't stand Thornley.'

'Join the club,' I murmured.

'She said he'd done a lot of damage to the school – undermined the staff, lowered morale . . . '

It was a catalogue of obstructive behaviour, most of it politically inspired. Thornley sneered at the selection of library books. Mona and the staff insisted that all modern fiction should be non-sexist and non-racist; Thornley tried to whip up parental support over 'censorship', although he failed to get it. The staff devised a sports day based on co-operative team games. Thornley objected – he wanted blood and guts, individual winners and losers and medals. Mona got her way on every issue in the end, mainly through explaining her methods and ideas, patiently and continuously, to staff and parents. Bridget was critical of Mona's low-key style, preferring a more bullish approach.

Bridget's main objection to Thornley was his attitude to children with 'special needs'. She believed that one of the main reasons Thornley wanted the school to opt out of local authority control was so that it could practise back-door selection, screening out the 'difficult' children. This was Bridget's big obsession, and Robin waxed lyrical with a theory about why she homed in on it so much, based on a few meagre crumbs he had gleaned about her childhood.

'She obviously has a strong identification with children who have learning difficulties, and yet she comes across as a bully. She is a very angry woman who deflects attention away from her aggression by championing the cause of the weak and vulnerable. I'm convinced she had a cold, authoritarian father and a weak, passive mother, probably non-tactile, who – '

'Robin?'

'Yes?'

'What else did she say about Mona?'

'Ah, right.'

Robin does tend to get sidetracked. Luckily, he isn't offended when you steer him back to the main point.

'I wouldn't say she was being supportive. The reverse, if anything. I'm afraid she might try to turn the staff against Mona. I asked her whether Mona had seemed her normal self recently – whether she was depressed, withdrawn or anything like that. Bridget didn't have much to say on that count, except that Mona was always aloof, kept her home life separate and never gave much away.' Robin paused, as if he were about to say something, then changed his mind. 'She is fairly secretive,' he added finally.

I decided to seize the moment to tackle him.

'Why has this upset you so much, Robin? Was it serious between you and Mona?'

He hesitated before saying crisply, 'It was a crush on my side which wasn't returned. My pride was hurt, that's all.'

His tone warned me off probing any further.

'I still admire her, although I feel I don't know her that well. There's something about her I find fascinating — a certain sadness behind her super-achiever perfectionism.'

I knew what he meant. Mona was a very controlled person, but you could sense that behind the well-constructed mask was someone sensitive and emotional.

'She may have killed him, Robin,' I reminded him quietly. 'Thornley may have said something or done something that pushed her over the edge — '

'I know,' he conceded. 'But whether she did it or not, she's a proud, independent woman who doesn't ask for help easily. Let's at least give her a hearing.'

I couldn't argue with that and assured him I would do my best. A quick glance at my watch then told me that my next client would arrive in two minutes. I hurled the remainder of the cheese sandwich into the bin and belted upstairs to face my afternoon appointments.

* * *

Mona clasped my hand and held onto it without speaking. Her eyes were full of pain. I sat very still and kept my grip firm, saying nothing. Finally, she let go, raised her chin and said in a dignified voice, 'Thank you for coming, Sara.'

'Thank you for having me, Mona.'

The riposte made her laugh, as I had meant it to, and it broke the tension. I felt relieved. I can't help cracking a joke in that sort of situation — it's my way of coping. Mel assures me that a counsellor needs to have a sense of humour, but it can be a drawback on occasions.

Mona and I leaned towards each other across the table and

tried to screen out the drab room, the other desperate conversations between inmates and visitors, and the heavy presence of the prison warders.

'How are you doing?' I asked.

'I'm managing,' she replied stiffly.

I had little to offer her except my presence. I could give no reassurance about how supportive her friends and colleagues were being, nor could I talk to her like a counsellor. I had come to see her because she had asked for me, as a fellow human being, because she was in trouble. I could feel myself tensing with fear as I thought myself into her situation. What must it be like to be locked up for the first time in your life, to be watched and controlled by uniformed authority twenty-four hours a day? Many of the women in the room, though younger than Mona, looked hard and tough, in that way women are when they have already done a stint inside. It does something to you, doing time, robs you of your self-respect and gives you a protective shield of cynicism and deviousness. Though I did not know Mona well, I knew instinctively that, for her, prison would be harder than for most. She was used to politeness and respect; used to running things her own way. She earned a good income and probably lived in a comfortable flat in a quiet street in west London.

'I don't expect you to believe what I'm about to tell you,' said Mona flatly. 'I know my solicitor doesn't. I think she doubts my sanity.'

Mona paused and shook her head. I had never seen her with such a forlorn expression – she was normally so erect and sure. Her hair, though still holding its short Afro shape, looked dull and limp, and her caramel skin had tinges of grey.

'I thought if I could tell you what happened, it might help people to understand . . . '

By 'people', I assumed she meant 'Robin', for who else would I tell? Certainly none of the parents and teachers at the school. I nodded, but I still didn't quite know why I was there.

'I'm listening.'

Mona took a deep breath. 'After the governors' meeting, Tony Thornley came to my office. We spoke about one or two things and then – ' She locked her eyes onto mine. They were clouded with bitterness. '. . . He made a pass at me. It was disgusting.' Her voice went up a notch in tone. 'I have never been so angry in my life!'

'He made a pass at you?' I was surprised, but not that surprised. 'You mean, out of the blue – just like that?'

'No, Sara, not just like that. He built up to it by making suggestive remarks.'

I tried to imagine it and found that the images came quite easily. I pictured Thornley's face – his sunken granite eyes and his wide, lecherous mouth, smiling with anticipation. The more I thought about it, the more it made sense. It was a classic. A white man feels threatened by a black woman, so he tries to defuse it in the only way he knows how – by treating her as sexually available. Why, then, had Mona let it get to her so much? Strong, independent Mona, who treated Thornley with polite and well-disguised contempt; who had patiently batted back every lousy ball Thornley had ever pitched at her – why did she flip her lid when Thornley came on to her? It was the perfect opportunity for her to discredit him.

Mona sighed, as if reading my thoughts. 'Everyone believes I am this calm, strong person, with no emotion, no vulnerability. But there are some things that I cannot – have never – been able to handle. With men.'

I tried to suspend disbelief. 'He made a pass at you . . . Did he actually touch you?'

Mona nodded. 'He came round my desk to where I was standing. I backed away, but he grabbed hold of me and tried to kiss me.' She shuddered. 'I have never felt such rage before.' Her eyes were burning, imploring, willing me to understand. 'Could you believe that such a man – a blatant racist, a politically motivated troublemaker who doesn't give two hoots for the education and welfare of children would have the arrogance to threaten me, to think that I would let him touch me – '

I leapt on that. 'He threatened you. What with?'

Her eyes slid away. 'Not a weapon. Vague threats. The threats of a bully.' She opened her hands in exasperation. 'Don't you see? It was simply another attempt to intimidate me! But this time he went too far.'

I still didn't get it. Thornley made a pass at her – a big 'yuk' definitely, but so what? Any woman who had known him five minutes would guess that 'sexual harassment' was his middle name.

Charily, I asked, 'Did you call out, or try to run away?'

'I said something teacherish.' Mona smiled bitterly. 'Something like, "Don't be ridiculous, Tony," and I pushed him away. He bumped into the side of the desk, but came for me again. This time I – I – ' Mona bit her lip. 'I spat in his face.'

I tried to picture Mona spitting, but that image wouldn't come.

'What did he do?'

'He slapped me.'

I chose my next words carefully.

'The man was a bastard, Mona. You knew it, I knew it. You could have exposed him. Why didn't you just walk away?'

'I told you – it made me so angry. I wanted to hit out at him.'

I watched the irate glitter in her eyes fade into weariness.

'Anyway, it would have been my word against his.' She brushed her hand across the table, sweeping away a path of non-existent dust.

It seemed a very strange story. I wondered what she wanted me to do with it. Was she hoping I would tell Robin, and anyone else who would listen, that Mona Pearson had killed Tony Thornley because he tried to kiss her and she had a problem dealing with sexually aggressive men? It was unpleasant, certainly – unpardonable on his part – but a reason to murder someone? Hardly. I knew she hadn't told me the whole truth, but I was reluctant to probe. There wasn't the time and she wasn't my client. I stole a surreptitious look at the clock.

'What happened next?'

She hesitated. Having noticed me checking the time, she emulated the glance and saw that we had only three minutes left. A wave of panic passed over her face. She knew that she had just three minutes to reveal the real reason she had asked me to come.

I encouraged her gently. 'Did he leave?'

She leaned over, her eyes cast low, and she said, quietly but distinctly, 'He left. And I stood there in my office and – I – wished – him – dead.'

She enunciated the words with an eerie precision. There was murderous passion in her voice.

My stomach lurched, but I took her hand and murmured back, 'Wishing is not the same as doing, Mona. Did you have a knife? Did you follow him?'

'Everything is blurred. I followed him – yes, but just to talk to him. To shout at him, to tell him he couldn't threaten me. The knife – I don't remember having it until I held it in my hand, covered in blood.'

I took a deep breath. 'Did you kill him?'

She didn't reply immediately. She sat in agitated silence, chewing hard on her lower lip. Her answer came at the same time as the prison officers calling time. Over the din and the scraping of chairs, her grip on my hand tightened. She squeezed her eyes shut and two tears burst out from under her eyelids and splashed onto her cheeks.

'I don't know,' was her anguished reply. 'That's the trouble, Sara, I can't remember. I just – don't – know.'

'It's okay, Mona. It's okay.'

A prison warder was approaching. 'Come on, Miss. Time to go.'

I squeezed Mona's hand and stood up. She opened her eyes to look up at me and her face was twisted with torment.

'Please – come back soon. I need to talk. I think I'm going mad.'

I felt a chill of foreboding as I prised her hand out of mine.

'I'll come as soon as I can,' I promised. 'Any messages – for Robin or anyone?'

Mona bowed her head.

'Just tell him what I've told you.'

I tore myself away from her, upset that I couldn't offer any comfort, or even give her a quick hug. I made my way back to the prison entrance with her words ringing in my head – 'I just don't know!' – and a desperate, lingering image: a formerly proud woman being led away to a cell, her head twisted back towards me, her eyes full of dread. She would have all the time in the world to fall prey to the fear of madness.

Later that evening, as I read a Thomas the Tank Engine story to Jake, I thought about what Mona had said. This is a common gift among parents, to read a book with all the proper inflections and every appearance of giving it your full attention, while thinking about something completely different. My instincts told me to be cautious, to resist getting involved, yet I had to admit that Mona's story both moved and intrigued me. Was it a case of selective memory – that she had killed Thornley, but blotted it out? Or was she stringing me a line in the hope that I would help her in some way?

'Why, Mummy, why?'

'What?'

My cover was blown. Jake had detected that my mind was not 100 per cent on Daisy the Diesel Engine.

'Not "what", Mummy, "pardon".'

'Jake – '

'Why is Daisy a girl? Is it because she's silly?'

So much for my commitment to non-sexist children's books.

'Of course not. The writer is just pretending she's a girl engine, that's all.'

'Has she got a vagina?'

'No, but – '

'Then she can't be a girl, can she? Has Thomas got a willy?'

'Tank engines don't have willies, Jake.'

33

'Then how can he be a boy?'

Sighing, I took up the challenge. Sex education always comes at the worst possible times – in the car, in swimming-pool changing rooms, with a hundred ears listening, or at the end of the day when all you want to do is sit quietly with a glass of wine and pursue your own thoughts.

I made it downstairs half an hour later, exhausted from the effort of deflecting the pile-driver logic of a four-year-old. Hannah, luckily, was in the grip of the Famous Five, which she read by torchlight under the bedclothes. All she required was a good-night prod and a reminder to clean her teeth.

Just as I sank into a chair to gather my thoughts and decide what to make for dinner, the doorbell rang. Cursing, I remembered that Robin had asked if he could come round to hear about my visit with Mona. I opened the door and greeted him with finger over lips, indicating the children upstairs – the last thing I wanted was two children clamouring downstairs to say hello to him. He nodded knowingly and followed me into the kitchen.

'I brought dinner,' he said. 'I hope you like scallops.'

My chilly welcome warmed by several degrees. Do I like scallops? Is the Pope a Catholic?

'You didn't have to do that,' I said, unconvincingly. 'I'm sure I've got some fish fingers stashed away somewhere. We could have had them flambéed.'

Robin gave me his typical smile – a restrained, lopsided quizzical look, while exhaling through his nose. It wasn't exactly a laugh, more of an expression of indulgence. Robin doesn't quite know what to make of me sometimes.

He dumped two Sainsbury's carrier bags on the counter. 'Do you mind if I take over your kitchen?' he said, looking around the small room with its cluttered surfaces and tell-tale signs of small children – a plastic hippopotamus, a crumbling wax crayon and an accumulating pile of letters from school about head lice and cake sales.

Not at all,' I lied. 'Sharp knives are in there, pans in the cupboard – oil, butter, garlic, onions. Anything else you need, just say. Would you like a glass of wine?'

'Not while I'm cooking, thanks. But you have one.'

I grinned. 'I will.'

I sat at the table and watched him move round the kitchen, peering into cupboards and humming to himself. I reflected that, considering Robin and I had worked together for two years, I hardly knew him at all. I knew him professionally, of course. I knew that he had a degree in social policy, had done a stint as a residential care worker, then trained in social work and counselling. I knew he came from a well-off family, that his father was a consultant cardiologist and his mother rushed around doing voluntary work in the village where they lived. I knew that he had been through psychotherapy in his early twenties. Robin was a good counsellor – thorough, professional and committed – but as to what he did at weekends – his pastimes, his passions – I didn't have a clue.

I watched him unpack his groceries and start to scour the kitchen for ingredients. His long limbs were ill at ease in my small kitchen – two paces and he had crossed the room. His elbows bumped on protruding cupboards and his head seemed in permanent danger of hitting the low doorframe. I couldn't help but contrast him with John and feel a pang of regret. John was methodical and fastidious; he worked with a quiet purposefulness which I found extremely restful. Robin, on the other hand, was clearly not used to cooking in front of an audience – especially one as critical as me – and was thrown by the unfamiliar kitchen. I busied myself with uncorking the wine, to help restrain myself from taking over.

Robin, looking flushed and flustered, leafed through a recipe book he had brought with him. He started to chop an onion, then stopped, unwrapped the scallops and asked where I kept my measuring cups.

'Measuring cups?' I tried not to laugh. 'I don't use them.'

'Scales?'

'Nope.'

Robin's face fell. 'Oh dear.'

'What do you need them for?'

He tapped the book with a knife. 'It says I need a quarter of a cup of butter.'

I took the knife from him and cut off a piece.

He frowned. 'Are you sure that's right?'

'Trust me. I was raised by a woman who could make latkes in an air-raid shelter, blindfold, with one hand tied behind her back.'

He smiled uncertainly, took the saucepan of butter to the stove and lit the gas under it – too high, I couldn't help but notice. I followed him and, as soon as he turned his back, lowered the flame. As he turned, we bumped into each other. We both apologised politely.

'Look, Robin, since you've brought dinner, why don't I cook it?'

'It *is* rather a small kitchen.'

'It helps if you know where things are.'

'Do you know how to cook scallops with lime?'

'I can follow a recipe. Sit down and have a drink.'

Gratefully, he dropped into a chair and poured himself a glass of wine.

'So?'

'So?'

'How is Mona?'

I considered the question for a moment and my perplexity came seeping back.

'She's managing,' I said darkly. 'Just about.'

I skimmed the recipe. It all seemed fairly straightforward – scallops, garlic, mushrooms and a smattering of prawns, fried in butter; then add the rind and juice of a lime and single cream to make the sauce. Wonderful, provided you didn't think about the calories. As I put on water for the tagliatelle and lifted a lettuce out of the bag, I pondered how to convey Mona's story to Robin.

'The whole thing seemed rather odd to me,' I began.

Robin listened intently as I repeated Mona's story of how Thornley had behaved and how she had felt furious and unable to deal with it. I told him how despondent she seemed, how unlike herself. I simply couldn't work out what it was she was trying to communicate. Robin made a tut of disgust at Thornley's behaviour, but otherwise sat quietly, trying to interpret the encounter.

'Why did you think it was odd?' he asked. 'What did you expect?'

I finished washing the salad, dropped the pasta into the water and started heating the butter again for the scallops. Robin followed my movements like a man watching a tennis match. My speed seemed to rather alarm him, but I cook so much, I work automatically; thoughts of what to do next slip through without touching the sides.

I stopped cooking for a moment and turned to face him. 'It's ten o'clock at night and you've just had a governors' meeting. You go into your office to collect your things and Thornley follows, banging on about some aspect of the budget. Then, all of a sudden, he starts making suggestive comments – says you're looking sexy tonight, your short skirt really suits you, whatever. What do you do at that point, if you're Mona? Stand there and take it? Of course not. You're a woman of the world, you know where it's leading. If you're me, you tell him he's a dirty, disgusting old man and he should know better; if you're Mona, you make a polite excuse and leave, making a mental note never to leave your female staff alone with him. I cannot believe that Mona stood passively, waiting for Thornley to get to the point when he actually made a pass at her.'

'She said he threatened her.'

'With what? A gun? A knife? He didn't have one. The only explanation she can give is that she has a particular problem telling men she isn't interested.'

Robin's eyebrows shot up and pushed his glasses up his nose.

'That could be true,' he said awkwardly.

37

'Come on, Robin! Mona deals with the suggestive remarks of sixteen-year-old boys every day. Perfect training, I would have thought, for fending off an adolescent bully like Thornley.'

Robin was thoughtful; his calm expression was one I knew well from case meetings.

'She says she doesn't remember what happened?'

'She followed him, but after that – she says she's not sure.'

'If the situation stirred up something for her, it might affect her memory of the event.'

'It might – or it might not.'

The delicate aroma of scallops sizzling in butter wafted through the kitchen, reminding me that my only sustenance so far today had been a stale cheese sandwich. I reached for my wine and took a sip. I drained the tagliatelle, arranged it on a large oval plate and decorated it with parsley. I always serve food to look attractive, even if it's just for me and the children.

'She wants you to go back,' said Robin. 'Perhaps she'll trust you enough to tell you the whole story.'

I made a face. 'I don't think I want to hear the whole story.'

'You're right. We have to think through the professional implications of this.'

The meal was delicious. The scallops were fragrant and tender, their sweet, subtle flavour set off perfectly by the lime. After we had both savoured a mouthful and praised each other appropriately – him for the choice of recipe, me for my culinary talents – we turned our attention back to Mona.

'You went to see Mona out of kindness,' began Robin.

'I went to see Mona because you lot would've made me feel a shit if I hadn't,' I corrected him.

'The point is, you went to see her as a friend. Is she asking you now to give her professional counselling? I don't think so. I think she's asking to see you again because she's still shocked to be in prison and disturbed by the fact that she can't remember what happened.'

'Mona's most pressing problem is a legal one. She's been accused of murder, for God's sake. We never take on a client under these circumstances. It opens up all kinds of issues about what we're trying to do.'

'I agree. But my point is that Mona is simply asking for human contact, not counselling. And you are the person she wants to see.'

Lucky old me.

'I want to help her, Robin, but I won't go unless I'm clear about what I'm offering.'

Robin let that hang in the air. Subtext: only you can know what you're offering, Sara.

'Her solicitor will suggest a psychiatric assessment,' I said, thinking aloud. 'The prosecution might ask for one too.'

'And since we all know how frequently black people are labelled mentally ill,' said Robin looking at me significantly, 'she's going to need all the help she can get.'

Thanks, Robin, I thought as I scooped up another scallop with my fork. Thanks a lot.

Chapter Three

'Bridget who?'

Doreen's message that Bridget Scudder was waiting in reception took me by surprise. I glanced at my watch; I had half an hour before I picked up the children from Yasmeen, my child-minder. I had intended using the time to catch up on some paperwork. Doreen repeated the name and the penny dropped – as did my face. Bridget Scudder was Mona's colleague. It was two days since my visit to Mona in prison and I had been trying to avoid thinking about the fact that I would soon have to visit her again. I half considered telling Doreen I was busy and asking her to get Bridget to make an appointment, but then thought better of it. At least I could truthfully say I only had half an hour to spare.

'Send her up please, Doreen,' I said.

My impression of Bridget from the governors' meeting had been of a large, overbearing woman with about as much charm as your average military dictator, but I'd met her in exceptional circumstances and so was prepared to change my mind. She knocked on the door of my office – a good start, plenty don't – and then strode in and took my proffered hand. She was tall and solidly built – a high brick wall of a woman, dressed in a navy blue suit and a blue floral blouse. A soft cushion of hair, which had once been blonde but was now a light grey, was swept back from her face and held fast with a clip at the back. Her eyes were blue, set closely together, giving her a rather intense stare. I indicated a chair and she took it. Her manner was brisk and polite; she thanked me for seeing her and said she would not keep me long.

'How can I help you, Bridget?'

'The staff are extremely concerned about Ms Pearson – Mona – so I rang your colleague to see if he had any news. I understand you went to see her.'

My hackles rose. 'Why don't you go and see her yourself? I'm sure she'd appreciate a visit.' I knew Mona had said she didn't want any visitors, but they could at least try.

'I've told the staff I don't think it's appropriate.'

I wondered if I had understood her correctly. 'Not appropriate that you should see her, or not appropriate that other staff should?'

'Both.'

'Why?'

Bridget took a deep breath. 'Mona is accused of murdering the chair of our governors – '

'Accused, but not found guilty – '

'Yes, but we have to think of how it looks for the school. We can't be seen to take sides.'

'I hardly think visiting a colleague in prison is taking sides.'

'And we have Tony's son to consider. He's one of our pupils.'

'Is he?'

I hadn't known that. I knew Thornley had a son, but somehow I assumed he would be at a private school. Some uncharitable instinct told me that Thornley was just the type to use the state system as a political springboard while sending his own little darlings to a safe haven with rugger in term-time and white-water rafting in the hols.

41

'He was at Browning Grange – ' Aha! An expensive boarding school in Sussex. 'But he joined us last year.'

'Why?'

'He had had some behavioural difficulties,' Bridget explained, 'but he's been doing very well with us. Poor lad. I'm not sure he'll be able to stay with us after this. He's had a very difficult time.'

The fierce line of her brow softened and for a moment I glimpsed her gentle side – protector of children who were friendless, or weak or difficult. I felt a surge of sympathy towards her. I imagined Bridget as a plain, awkward ten-year-old with pigtails who was picked on mercilessly by older children, whose only way to fight back was by becoming a bully among her peers. I thought back to Robin's guess about her background. What had he said? 'She probably had a cold, authoritarian father.' A man, in other words, just like Tony Thornley.

Then she asked, 'Do tell me – how is Mona?'

'She's distressed and shocked. And feeling abandoned by everyone.'

Just the answer Bridget didn't want to hear. The lines around her mouth pulled tight again.

'The staff are right behind her, you know. It's just – '

'Mona needs to know that,' I said firmly.

We stared at each other for a moment.

'How is everyone taking it at the school?' I asked.

'They're very shocked, naturally. But life must go on. The governors and the local authority have asked me to take over as acting head. We've told the children not to believe everything they read in the press, to be sensitive to Richard Thornley's feelings – he's still attending for the moment – and to try not to discuss the matter among themselves. We may use it in some classes to look at the British legal system.'

I scanned her face to check that she was serious. She was. I could have launched into a diatribe about how the children and the staff might be feeling about losing a much-loved and much-respected head, and how those feelings were best brought out rather than squashed or denied, but I held back. I'd learned late in life to stick to my father's maxim: 'never give advice unless you're asked for it.' My mother, unfortunately, did not agree with my father on this and continued to dispense advice, unasked for, on every aspect of child-rearing, from nits to knitwear.

'I don't know Mona that well,' I said. 'Tell me about her. Is she good at her job?'

Bridget crossed her legs and clasped her hands together. Her face took on a guarded look. 'She's certainly well liked.'

It was an ambivalent reply, and there was a criticism lurking in it somewhere.

'Some of the staff almost hero-worship her.'

Did I detect the teensiest hint of jealousy?

'Is she a good administrator?'

'I think so. If I had to criticise Mona on something, it would be that she takes too much notice of what other people think.'

'In what way?'

'In taking decisions. Mona tends to have endless consultations with junior staff before deciding anything. My style is rather different.' Bridget gave a grim smile. 'I believe that if you give strong leadership from the top, the rest will follow.'

I'll bet you do, I thought. The idea of Bridget's brand of strong leadership made my knees knock.

'How do you two manage to work together?'

Bridget's chin went up a degree. 'I think we are both professional enough to cope,' she said brusquely.

'Did Mona appoint you?'

'No, I predate her. I've been at Arkwright for fourteen years.'

And you probably expected to be head by now, I thought. Quite a disappointment.

I could see the time ticking away, but I couldn't resist asking Bridget about the governors' meeting on the night Thornley died. She said the subject had been one close to her heart — children with special needs. Much to Thornley's annoyance, they had recently agreed to admit two extra children to the school who had statements of special educational need. The discussion was about how much money should be spent on support for them – so-called Section 11 staff. In the midst of her explanation, Bridget suddenly became heated.

'I cannot understand Mona's position on this! She claims to have the interests of the children at heart, yet she will not spend the proper amount on Section 11 support. She feeds into Thornley's hands.'

'What would you do?'

'I would crack down on those members of staff who are avoiding mixed-ability teaching. I would take money from areas like IT and increase support for children with special needs.' Her eyes narrowed. 'If it had been left up to me, I would have taken Thornley head on, fought him to the last – not negotiated and gone round him the way Mona did, desperate for a consensus. I wasn't afraid of him.'

'Was Mona?'

'I always thought she was too soft on him. But in view of what has happened, perhaps I was wrong, after all.'

I wasn't sure I liked her intimation. I told Bridget I had to cut short our chat and go home. I would have to drive like a maniac not to be late. I shook her hand.

'Please contact Mona,' I pleaded. 'As a friend if not as a colleague.'

'We all do as we think fit, Ms Kingsley,' she said primly.

Poor Mona. How on earth did she manage to work with such a woman? Her talents as a diplomat and a tactician must be awesome.

The journey home was a nightmare – pissing rain, crawling traffic – and I arrived at the child-minder's house stressed out and ten minutes late. Luckily, Yasmeen is fairly flexible about timekeeping. I picked up two delightful, smiling children, who turned into two whining, wailing monsters as soon as Yasmeen closed her door. It always amazes me how children manage to store up every whinge, whimper and moan in order to dump it on their exhausted mother as soon as she puts in an appearance. Quite natural, of course, but bloody irritating.

When we got home there were three messages waiting for me on my answering machine. I listened to them with an inane Postman Pat video in the background and, in the foreground, the low mutterings of Hannah as she complained about her day to her Barbie doll.

The first message was from my police contact, Barry, asking me to call him when I got a chance. He sounded clipped and official and was undoubtedly ringing from the Division. Then came an inarticulate but sweet message from Pete. 'Just saying hello, babe . . . finking about ya, know what I mean? Can't stand these machines – they make me go all – never mind. Anyway – see ya!' The third was from John, sounding calm and sensible, and asking me to ring him when I got in.

I wanted to ring John first, but I reined myself in and rang Barry instead. He cut short the preliminaries – he was busy. 'Things don't look good for your friend.'

'She not exactly my – '

'There's been no post-mortem yet, but everyone we've interviewed thinks she had good reason to kill him. Pleasant little bastard, wasn't he?'

'Charming. What about the wife and son?'

'The son was out with friends; the wife was playing bridge with the Townswomen's Guild. She's convinced Pearson did it.'

'Why?'

'Because "they" are more likely to lose control of themselves, aren't "they"?'

'Black women, she means?'

'Exactly.'

'Terrific.'

And if Thornley's wife was playing the race card, how many police officers were doing the same?

'Sorry I can't be more helpful. If I hear anything, I'll let you know.'

'Thanks, Barry.'

Just as I was about to hang up, I had a mental flash – then a terrible sense of dread.

'Barry?'

He grabbed the receiver again. 'Yes?'

'Who's working on this?'

He answered cautiously. 'Detective Superintendent Clarkson is heading it.'

'Who's the Detective Sergeant?'

He hesitated only a beat. 'Gould.'

'Gould!'

It came out as a screech, my worst fears confirmed. How could I have forgotten that the most racist police officer I've ever met just happened to be in that area?

'Barry, Mona is a black woman – '

'And Gould is a good police officer,' countered Barry, his tone defensive.

Gould was well known locally for his outspoken views on ethnic minority involvement in crime. He was also something of a hero on his Division because of his terrier-like pursuit of petty criminals.

Barry lowered his voice. 'I'll keep my eye on it, okay? But it's not my area – '

'You're a DI now – '

Barry had been promoted a few months before – partly as a result of his work on a drugs case involving a prominent MP, on which I had given him not a little help.

'That's irrelevant. There's a good team on the case, Sara. Give them a fair chance.'

'Of course I will, Inspector. But will they do the same for Mona?'

I put the phone down with Barry's reassurances ringing in my ears and slapped my hand hard on the table. 'Damn!'

Poor Jake jumped out of his skin. I went and absently planted a kiss on the back of his neck and stroked his head. Postman Pat and his pesky cat had stopped for yet another cup of tea on their way to take a package to Granny Dryden. Lazy devil. No wonder people have turned to e-mail.

Deciding there was nothing I could do for the present about the Met's poor choice of investigating officers, I took the phone into the kitchen and dialled John's number. I felt jittery as I did so — we hadn't spoken for three weeks. He answered on the second ring. It was good to hear his voice again.

We talked about nothing for a while as I moved around the kitchen, making the children's tea. After the first pangs of hearing him say my name, which gave me an almost physical ache to touch him, I was aware of the familiar feelings creeping back. The heavy thud of frustration; irritation that he took everything so seriously; an overwhelming sense of hopelessness as I assessed the huge gulf between us. He said how much he missed me, but then launched into an analysis of our communication problems. He said that if we got back together again we should redouble our efforts to tell each other every burp, fart and hiccup of our feelings. I couldn't have disagreed more, but I murmured noncommittally, too tired to hop onto the familiar merry-go-round of argument.

Finally, with Hannah and Jake jumping up and down howling for their tea, John told me that he had been asked to apply for a job in Manchester — a promotion which would entail the undercover work he liked so much. He wanted to go for the job, but he also wanted us to get together again. I knew this was my cue to say something encouraging — to beg him to stay in London so that we could move in together, or to take us to Manchester with him, but I didn't.

'Sounds like a good move,' I said carefully.

The words hit home; I could hear the hurt in his voice.

'It will mean being further away from Sam.'

Sam was his son, a bubbly five-year-old; John doted on him.

'You can still see him every other weekend, surely? And he can stay with you for holidays, just like he does now.'

'It sounds like you want me to go.'

My stomach churned with a mixture of bitterness and

inadequacy. Why was he dumping this on me? Why should I take responsibility for his happiness? With a pang of nostalgia, I remembered how, when we first met, we used to have fun together. But quite early on, the hard work had overtaken the light-heartedness.

'John, it's your decision. It has nothing to do with me.'

'But Sara – '

'John, we both know – ' I knew what I was going to say but hesitated, dreading the moment. 'Neither of us wants to admit this, but it's – it's over between us.'

I had said it before, but this time we both knew it was for real. There was a long silence. In my mind's eye, I could see his face, the smiling eyes behind designer glasses, the warm, full mouth, and I could almost smell his wonderful male scent . . .

Hot, stinging tears welled up and trickled down my cheeks. Hannah and Jake had both stopped jumping up and down. Jake was strangely engrossed in fiddling with the top of a ketchup bottle and Hannah was staring up at me, her brow puckered with anxiety. What sort of mother had emotional telephone scenes with a boyfriend right in the middle of making tea?

Finally, John and I said goodbye, both knowing it was for the last time, and I sat down to blow my nose and wipe my eyes. As I stemmed the flow of tears, Hannah stood beside me and put her arms round my neck; Jake crept onto my knee and tried to burrow into my lap.

'Even mummies cry sometimes,' I reminded them pathetically.

They didn't say a word. Of course, they knew it only too well.

★ ★ ★

'Okay, here it is. "Amnesia can be related to an emotional trauma." Yeah, we know that – blah, blah, blah. "Amnesia can be localised, selective, generalised or continuous."'

Clancy was sitting cross-legged on the chaise longue in my

office. Robin, always relaxed in Clancy's company, straddled one end, like a gawky cowboy riding a docile nag. They were both ignoring the fact that I was trying to write an extremely difficult reference, explaining why I thought sixteen-year-old Kevin McDonald was ideally suited to a job for which he had not one of the required qualifications.

'What's another way of saying self-motivated?' I wondered aloud.

'Ripe for exploitation,' squawked Clancy, deliberately accentuating her Manchester accent.

Robin laughed. I continued to chew my pen.

'Very funny, but not that helpful.'

'Self-managing,' suggested Robin.

I shook my head. 'Maybe I'll just put "self-motivated" and add a bit more about his reliability.' If anyone deserved this job, Kevin did. 'I hope this at least gets him an interview.'

Robin turned back to Clancy, whose head was still buried in my biggest psychology reference book.

'Try "localised amnesia",' said Robin.

It was Friday morning and they were raiding my bookshelves to see what they could come up with to explain Mona's inability to recall what happened that night at the school. It was a prelude, I knew, to persuading me to go and see her that afternoon.

'"Localised amnesia",' read Clancy, '"is when specific features, or events, from the time around the trauma are lost – that is, they fail to be both accessible and available for recall."'

'That could be it,' said Robin.

Clancy tapped the book with her long finger, tipped with pink nail polish. 'My guess is, Thornley did more than just make a pass at her. He tried to rape her.'

'Or Mona *thought* he was about to rape her,' put in Robin. 'I think the fear of rape could be enough of an emotional trauma to trigger localised amnesia.'

I wasn't sure I agreed, but I kept my head down, not wanting to encourage the discussion.

'So how would you work with that?' asked Clancy, giving me a meaningful look. 'To try and unlock the memory?'

'You wouldn't,' I said, still writing. 'If you're a counsellor, you leave that sort of thing to a psychiatrist.'

'I mean *theoretically*.'

I know from experience that the word has no meaning for Clancy. Her acceleration rate is nought to psychoanalysis in fifty seconds.

'You'd have to find out more about what the experience meant for the person concerned,' said Robin. 'What exactly Mona felt when Thornley tried to kiss her.'

'Sick, if I had to hazard a guess.'

'Was he a large man? Powerfully built?' asked Clancy.

'Not tall,' said Robin, 'but fairly strong, I suppose.'

Clancy tossed back her plaits and frowned contemplatively. 'So Mona pushed him away the first time, then spat at him when he came at her again. She remembers that part. If it were *me* talking to Mona as a *friend* – ' another look in my direction – 'I'd be trying to get her to think about where that knife was, whether she picked it up, whether or not it she remembers going out of her door holding it. I wouldn't try to press her about what happened after that.'

'If I were going to see Mona as a friend,' said Robin, 'I wouldn't try to get anything out of her, I would simply listen.'

'Hear, hear,' I said.

Clancy and Robin both looked at me witheringly, then got back to the books. Sometimes I wonder if my co-workers have a true appreciation of my wit.

For a quiet life, and because I couldn't get her out of my mind, I went to see Mona that afternoon. This time, her face looked thinner, her eyes red-rimmed and bloodshot. I asked her about the food and whether or not she was sleeping, but she brushed aside the small talk with a gesture like sweeping chess pieces off a board. She was desperate to talk.

'I still can't remember anything!' she whispered fiercely

across the table. 'Yet I think of nothing else! They want me to see a psychiatrist.'

Her fear was infectious, but I kept my voice deliberately calm.

'Who wants you to see a psychiatrist?'

'My solicitor.'

'So see one. It may help. What are you afraid of?'

The tears spilled easily this time – though against her will – splashing from her cheek onto the Formica table. She wiped them impatiently with her hand.

'I'm afraid that I shall find out I did kill him,' she whispered. 'And that I'm going mad.'

I decided the only way I could be of any use to Mona in such a short time was to talk some plain common sense. 'Listen, Mona, I've seen quite a few headcases in my time and you aren't one of them.'

The tears stopped; she was listening.

'You're a calm, effective person who has a good grasp on reality. You're excellent at your job. Right now, you are rational and articulate. There could be a number of explanations as to why you can't remember exactly what happened that night. Stop panicking about losing your sanity and use the opportunity of seeing a psychiatrist to find out more about them.'

My bossy homily seemed to calm her. There was a hint of upturning at the edges of her mouth.

'You don't think I'm mad?'

'No, but I do think you need to talk to someone about it.'

She blew her nose and took a deep, calming breath. She looked at me, then looked away and bit her lip. I stayed still and said nothing. I knew she wanted to tell me something and was deciding whether or not to trust me.

At the next table, a woman of about my age leaned towards her daughter, relating an argument. 'I told 'er to fuck off – said I couldn't do nuffin' abaht it – fuckin' bitch . . . .' Her daughter rocked back on her chair, arms folded over her shapeless body, vacant eyes staring, not caring, not wanting to hear.

When Mona started to talk, she spoke in a low monotone that was so quiet I had to strain to hear it. 'I want to tell you something,' she said. 'I don't know if it's relevant, or even if it will help my case.' She sighed. 'Psychiatrists always ask about your childhood, don't they?'

She paused for an answer, so I nodded mutely.

'I spent most of my adolescence in care.'

'In care?'

She nodded. 'I've always found it difficult to stand up to men,' she said. 'It started with my father. I was the eldest of three girls. My mother died when I was nine. My dad looked after us for a year or two, but couldn't really cope. He didn't earn much – he was a bus driver – and after a while, he started drinking and beating us up.' She suddenly became self-conscious and her smile was apologetic, self-deprecating. 'But you're a counsellor. I expect you've heard a million like this one.'

'Every story is different,' I assured her.

I was surprised on two counts already – that Mona had had an unstable childhood and that she came from relatively humble origins, neither of which you would have guessed from her accent or demeanour. But counsellors are good at hiding surprise, and other emotions. I rested my chin on my hand and touched her arm. 'Go on.'

'Once, he beat me so badly, I had to go to hospital. After that, we were all taken into care. I was fourteen years old – my twin sisters were seven.' She stopped. It was a staccato speech, delivered robotically, devoid of emotion. Her eyes had a faraway look. I waited for her to continue. 'I was glad to be away from my father, but I didn't like the home. Have you ever been inside one?'

'Many times.'

When I was a social worker, I placed quite a few children in a bright, modern home in West Ealing. However nice the home, the cutting sadness of abandoned children still permeates the atmosphere.

Mona stared past me at the wall. 'I behaved appallingly – ran amok in my room, cut my wrists, kept running away. The staff did their best, but they were young themselves and didn't seem to know what to do. Someone always found me and brought me back.'

I tried to imagine calm, serene Mona trashing her room and acting out, but I couldn't. Her manner, her accent – do people change that much? Doubter that I am, I wondered if she might even be making it up – a desperate sob story to help her case. It wouldn't be the first time I'd sat listening to a completely invented childhood.

'Were your sisters there too?'

'At first they were. But there was such an age gap, and they were better fostering material than me. They went to a foster family together and were adopted later. I – I've lost touch with them.'

It was a cruel and sad story. I looked into Mona's dark brown eyes, looking for a glimpse of a motherless girl, the abandoned teenager longing to be loved, but could not find it. If it was there, it was deeply buried.

'When I was sixteen, I ran away for good and moved in with my boyfriend,' Mona continued, in the same automatic way. 'He was older than me – twenty, twenty-one – and he seemed like a man of the world. He claimed to be a poet. It was the time of Bob Marley and reggae and we lived a bohemian life, staying up all night, smoking ganja, eating and drinking at strange times.' Now her face started to register emotion. Her lower lip trembled and her hand flew up to her temple. 'I – I worshipped him. For the first time in my life, I felt loved by a man. But then he – ' Mona paused, and ducked her head. 'He changed. He was bored, or perhaps he was put off by my intensity. He became violent and got into serious drugs. He needed money, so – ' Mona glanced self-consciously at the other people next to us. 'He encouraged me to go with men, then made them pay, or stole from them.'

I kept my eyes fixed on her face and wondered where this was leading.

Mona's voice dropped even more. She was almost whispering now, and I had to lean nearer to hear what she was saying. Our heads were almost touching as she rasped, 'I did it, Sara. I'm ashamed even to talk about it now. It was a terrible time in my life. I had no one, no adult to guide me.'

Strange how the abandoned little girl emerged when she was talking about her boyfriend, not her father.

'I tried to get away, but he always found me. He threatened to kill me.' Mona's eyes, which had strayed away from mine, sought them again and she smiled bitterly. 'Some poet, eh? For a few months, I did what he asked. Mona Pearson, thirty-nine years old, head teacher, pillar of the community, was on the game in Ladbroke Grove. Surprised?'

'Very.'

Suddenly the bitterness ignited into anger. 'No you're not!' Her eyes flashed. 'It just confirms your stereotype of black women – that we're all sluts at heart, however middle class we seem! Isn't that what you think?'

I could have denied it, but I stayed silent. It was not a personal attack. I knew why she was angry. I felt the same way about Jewish stereotypes – it was like a noose around your neck which could hang you before you even noticed. I let her anger pass and tried to tell her with my eyes that I understood it.

After a moment, I asked, 'How did you get away from him?'

Mona breathed out and closed her eyes to calm herself. 'I'm sorry.'

'For nothing,' I said. 'You have every right to be angry.' I paused, then returned to my question. 'What happened next?'

She opened her eyes again. 'I had the good fortune to meet a woman called Doris Lavender – a feminist writer and teacher from Jamaica. She was an inspiration – she opened my eyes to the way I was being exploited, made me believe in myself. I started reading books, going to evening classes. I was bright, underneath it all, so I did well, and it gave me confidence. But the only way I could forget what I had been through was to reinvent myself. Doris didn't approve of that, but I think she understood it. I taught myself to speak nicely, to dress well. I made up a new background – a father who was a university lecturer, mother a nurse who died when I was in my teens. Eventually, I went to college and did a degree. Doris supported me through it all – spiritually and, to some extent, financially. She gave me a home to come back to. I decided to be a teacher, did the training, and got my first job at a time when they were crying out for black teachers. I got promoted – ' She stopped suddenly, aware of time passing, and her tone became brusque, more like the Mona I recognised. 'The reason I'm telling you all this is because I want you to understand what it meant for me when Thornley stayed behind after that meeting last Thursday and said that he had found out something about my past that the Arkwright governors would be very interested to hear. Something that wasn't on my CV.' Mona stopped talking and closed her eyes again. Her voice was holding, but only just. 'I couldn't heal myself without breaking completely with my past. Now it's caught up with me – as I always knew it would.'

I didn't know what to say to that. I didn't even know if I believed her. So I stuck to practicalities.

'How did he find out?'

'He wouldn't say. I've racked my brains to find a connection, but there is none that I know of.'

'What did Thornley want? Money?'

'No.' Mona opened her eyes and smiled. 'Me,' she said softly. 'Isn't that nicely ironic? Tony wanted to go to bed with a black woman in return for keeping quiet about my brief career as a prostitute.'

Could it be true? Would Thornley stoop to that sort of blackmail?

'What did you say?'

Mona's eyes were cold. 'I said no, of course.'

'And then?'

She turned her face to the side, not wanting to meet my

eye. 'He seemed surprised, told me to think it over. Said he would talk to me again. Then everything happened as I told you. He tried to kiss me, I pushed him away. He tried again and I spat at him. Then he left.' She paused. 'I stood by the desk in my office, shaking. I don't know for how long. I wept a bit and wondered what would happen to me. All the work, everything I cared about, just thrown away. I hated him.'

So you killed him, I finished silently, and your mind erased the memory of what you did.

I wondered fleetingly what would have happened if Mona had called Thornley's bluff and let him expose her past.

'Do you have a criminal record?' I asked.

She shook her head. 'I wouldn't have got my first job if I did. Police checks are rigorous these days. But don't fool yourself – if a head loses the respect of parents and the community, her career is finished.'

So the stakes were high. Mona knew that Thornley could, and would, ruin her. It was as good a motive as any for murdering him.

'You think I killed him, don't you?' Her hands dropped into her lap and her shoulders drooped.

I was sorry to be so transparent, but I also felt burdened by her confidences. I hadn't asked for them; I didn't want them.

'I don't know what to believe, Mona,' I told her truthfully. 'It's a strange story.'

I thought about the localised amnesia – a loss of memory triggered by emotional trauma. If Mona had buried her feelings about her father's violence towards her for so long, it was not inconceivable that Thornley's threats had revived them. His sexual advances may have given Mona enough of a shock to make her unable to recall what had happened next. That I could believe. What none of us knew was whether or not she had actually killed him.

Mona looked at me, and her expression was hard to read, 'I appreciate you coming here Sara.' The words were warm, but the tone was cold.

56

'I want to help you, Mona. We all do.' I laid my hand on her arm. 'You must tell the psychiatrist everything you've told me. What happened with Tony Thornley could well have reawakened painful memories about your father. That could explain why you can't remember what happened afterwards.'

In her eyes I could see hope and mistrust. 'Do you think so?'

'Localised amnesia,' I said, with more confidence than I felt. 'It's certainly a possibility.'

I remembered what Clancy said about unlocking Mona's memory. I do listen to Clancy, although I try never to let on. 'Think back to when you were standing in your office.'

She nodded thoughtfully.

'What about the knife?'

'The knife?'

'Where was it?'

'In the drawer of my desk.'

'You took it out?'

'No.'

'Are you sure?'

She frowned and squeezed her eyes shut. Then snapped them open. 'I'm sure. I did not take out the knife.'

'You moved towards the door of your office, to follow Tony, to yell at him . . . '

'That's right.'

'Was the knife in your hand then? Think hard, Mona!'

She blinked and her eyes moved round, and from side to side, as if following the scene in her mind's eye.

'I can't remember holding anything.'

'Where was the knife?'

'I don't know. In the drawer, I suppose.'

'When was the last time you saw it?'

'The last time I opened the drawer. I keep petty cash in there, so I may have seen it earlier in the day.'

'Do you keep the drawer locked?'

'Of course. And there are only two keys. I have one and Maggie, the school administrator, has the other. I'm very careful to lock it after I – ' Mona stopped suddenly and the blood drained from her face. She turned to me in horror. 'Oh, God! Oh, my God!'

'What?'

Her hands trembled with agitation. 'I told the police the drawer was locked. Oh, why didn't I think of this before?' Mona cried. 'That afternoon – after the bell – Maggie came in and said she had no change to give a parent who had bought a school sweatshirt. Then the phone rang – one of the kids had had an accident – so I had to rush away and Maggie took the money out herself. As I was crossing the playground, I remember thinking, "I must check to make sure the drawer is locked when I get back to the office" – but I don't know if I did. Oh, Sara! What if she didn't lock it? What if someone else took the knife?'

We both sat thinking about that one. What if they did? I wondered if we could ever find out who and, if so, whether anyone would believe us.

Once again, the prison officers called time. Mona hugged me and kissed my cheek – hers felt wet and cold against my skin. I felt desperate to get away.

'Thank you. You've given me hope,' she said.

I murmured a reply, but in my heart I was begging her not to put too much store by what I'd said. Whether she killed Thornley or not, I knew it would be an uphill struggle to put together a believable defence based on automatism.

I asked her if I could share what she had told me with my co-workers at the clinic, with the assurance that it would go no further. She said I could tell whomever I liked – before long, she said sadly, her life story would be common knowledge.

Chapter Four

'So here we are.'

I grinned stupidly and dipped a poppadum into hot lime chutney, just for something to do. I knew from the moment I walked into the restaurant that this was going to be a disaster. It was an upmarket Indian place on King Street – nice decor, good menu. The only problem was that we were the only people in it.

'A drink for you, sir, madam?'

'A beer please.'

'Mine's a pint. Cheers, mate.'

The waiter bowed and backed away. I cringed inwardly and felt an instant pang of guilt. So Pete wasn't used to restaurants. So what? He looked different in a suit, his body confined in a shirt collar and tie, and a jacket that was slightly too tight.

'So you're – '

'Where do you – '

We had both spoken at once, then politely asked the other to go first. I won – and opted for him to go first. He wanted us to have this dinner, so he could do most of the talking. Sloe-eyed, his gaze was fixed on me, his hair pulled tightly back from his face into a pony-tail, so that, from the front, it looked very short. With his smooth Mediterranean skin and high cheekbones, he reminded me of one of the sons from the film *The Godfather* – I couldn't remember which one. All he needed was a pair of sunglasses and he would be perfect.

'You're some kind of shrink, aren't you? That's your job.'

'I'm a counsellor.' I explained the difference, slowly, and found myself deliberately avoiding words of more than two syllables. God, was I patronising! Why couldn't I just act naturally?

'Sounds interesting,' said Pete blandly, when I had finished.

'It is,' I agreed, 'interesting.' There was an awkward silence. Was this the same man with whom I had enjoyed wild and wicked sex? 'What do you do?' Apart from picking up older women in pubs and giving them the green light into your knickers, I wanted to add, but managed to hold myself in check.

'I work in security. Security and handyman. At a company in Park Royal.'

'What sort of company?'

'They make panelling – for shopfitting and stuff.'

'I see.' I didn't. I didn't really want to see. 'Do you eat here often?'

'Here, yes, quite often.' He put on an affected voice and his face clouded. 'Or at the Savoy, or I might eat at the friggin' Ritz – '

'Pete – '

'Oh, for Chrissake, Sara!' he hissed. 'Loosen up! What's your problem?'

I stared at the poppadums and avoided meeting his eye. What was my problem? He was my problem. Men were my problem.

'Sara – '

'What?'

'We like to fuck, okay?'

'Shhhh! Keep your voice down.'

The waiter behind the bar was studiously ignoring us. Pete drummed his fingers on the table. His nails were cracked and torn, but clean – rough, practical hands.

'I like you, you like me. We fuck – make love. We have a good time. We go out for a meal. I ask you about your day, you ask me about mine. That's not so fucking hard for you, is it? Is that so hard?'

That wasn't so hard, no. Now that I thought about it.

Pete waved his hand at me, exasperated. 'So you start off. "How was your day, Pete?"'

'How was your day, Pete?'

'Not bad, thanks, Sara, not bad at all. Production manager told me I done a good job helping them out with a big order yesterday. Girl in accounts with the big tits give me a nice smile and asked me if I'd like to see her software – '

'Oh, yes?'

'Yes. See? Some people know a good thing when they see it.'

'I know a good thing when I see it,' I protested. 'And I know how to use it.'

'Dirty girl,' said Pete. He was relaxing now, getting in control. 'And to make an okay day into a good one, someone murdered one of me bosses. How was your day, Sara?'

'You're joking!'

'Nope. Only it wasn't today, it was last Thursday. Knife in the gut – wham! – well dead. Wicked, eh? Anyone get murdered down your place this week?'

'No, but I was sorely tempted.' A little light switched on in my head. 'This boss – it wasn't Tony Thornley, was it?'

Pete looked slightly deflated. 'How did you know?'

'I knew him – vaguely.'

It was not such a coincidence when you thought about it. There were only a handful of businesses left in our area and most of those were in Park Royal, not far from where I lived and worked.

Pete raised his eyebrows. 'So you knew Thornley too. Well, we all have our crosses to bear.' He turned to look at the waiter, hoping to hurry him with the drinks. When he looked back, he resumed the set-piece conversation. 'So what did you do today, Sara?'

The question caught me unawares – I was still trying to process the fact that he worked at Tony Thornley's factory. I wanted to find a witty reply, so I searched through the images which came tumbling through my mind. The first frantic hour of the day . . . a seven o'clock battle with Hannah over the pink socks, which she hates; the green turtle socks, her favourites, were in the wash. Packing their bags for going to their father's, worrying about whether Jake was really well enough to go, still off-colour from the chicken-pox; Weetabix and Shreddies, burnt toast and spilled jam, the desperate search for reading books, which *have* to be in on Fridays, otherwise 'Miss' gets cross; the last-minute tears because Jake couldn't find his Thunderbird 4 model for 'show and tell'. All that before arriving at the clinic to get news of the suicide of a former client – a girl of eighteen – no merry quips to be made about that; the effing and blinding of a boy who hasn't been to school for two years; meetings, phone calls, endless form-filling; the woman of about my age who is going through a messy divorce; the depressed fifteen-year-old who may or may not be bulimic. Then the dash back home to two tired children, pizza with tomato sauce, an apple crumble made in record time, a phone call from my mother. What had I done today? The jokes eluded me for once.

'Not a lot,' I told Pete wearily.

Without any preliminaries, he reached across the table, lifted my hair with one hand and with the other massaged the back of my neck. It was a gentle, instinctive gesture – a purely intuitive response to my tiredness. I felt oddly embarrassed. I was caught off guard, not used to any touch from Pete except sexual ones, not used to being caressed so tenderly across a table in an empty restaurant.

Despite my shyness, it felt rather good, so I let him carry on. There was an easy sympathy and comfort in the way he did it, far more than he could have conveyed to me in words. It seemed as if he was telling me that it was okay, that he understood. He knew there was more to me than the smart-arse joker he'd picked up in a pub; he knew I was a working single mother as well as a lover, and a playmate, and he accepted it, welcomed it even. I wondered how such a young man could respond like that.

When I saw the waiter approaching with our beer, I pulled away and he withdrew his hand. I sipped my drink and Pete lifted his chin and took a long draw from his pint glass. His Adam's apple bobbed as the beer went down and the ropes of muscle in his neck strained against his shirt collar. He put down the glass and grinned at me. I grinned back, suddenly feeling more at ease in his company. Maybe it was possible to forge a relationship out of an extended one-night stand; maybe the evening would not turn out to be as dreadful as I had feared.

A profusion of dishes arrived all at once — samosas, chicken korma, rogan josh, bengan bhajee and basmati rice.

'We've ordered too much,' I told Pete, but he shook his head and began to eat, shovelling the food by the forkful into his mouth.

I hadn't seen him eat before — not at a table, only snacks in bed. He ate with the typical abandon of a ravenous young man who knows he will burn up every calorie as quickly as he eats it. I love food and I'm greedy, but I've learned to be cautious. I put on weight with an ease which increases with every passing year. I took pleasure in watching his mad fuelling, and took one mouthful for every six of his.

As we ate, we listed our favourite foods and talked about cooking. It was superficial chitchat, which I usually hate, but I found it relaxing with Pete, because there seemed to be no subtext to it — no hidden agenda which would emerge later like a bear from behind a rock. The subject of cooking brought us on to families. His parents were Italian, and they ran a coffee and sandwich shop in Luton. He had three older brothers and one younger sister. Two of them helped in the shop, but the rest had left home and now lived in London.

When the first pangs of his hunger began to recede – about 2,000 calories later – he went back to the subject of Tony Thornley.

'How do you know him?'

I said I knew him through my work with Arkwright High School. I didn't go into detail.

'The school where the head's been arrested?'

'That's right.'

'Before they pulled her in, the talk at work was that the wife did it.'

'Thornley's wife? Why?'

He raised one eyebrow and said drily, 'I thought you said you knew him.'

I smiled. 'There are plenty of Thornleys whose wives think they're God's gift to women. Believe me – I see them. They "fall downstairs" a lot.' I waggled my fingers to indicate the inverted commas.

'I don't think he beat her – not that I heard. It was the way he went after women.'

Mona's face leapt into my mind, taut and disgusted as she described Thornley's kiss. I tried not to get too intense.

'Bit of a ladies' man, was he?' I said casually.

'He thought he was,' said Pete. 'He was the one at the Christmas party putting his hand up women's dresses. They never complained because he was the boss.'

Thornley Veneers was a family company, inherited, on their father's retirement, by two sons, Tony and Geoff. The brothers were polar opposites: Geoff, a quiet, practical bloke who knew the business, and how to manage people; Tony, older, louder than his brother – the bad guy who gave the reps a hard time about sales targets and cared only about the bottom line. Tony liked money and power. He wanted to be a big, successful businessman; he wanted to go into politics. The company was doing well, according to Pete, mainly thanks to Geoff. When the sons took over, Geoff had reorganised the production process and now they were starting to reap the rewards.

'Geoff likes these Japanese companies where they don't have production lines, they make the stuff in small groups. When the old man retired, he got rid of all the supervisors and put everyone in groups. When I first got there, everyone was moaning about it, but you never hear that now.' Geoff Thornley was something of a hero in Pete's eyes.

I had imagined, when Pete said he was a security guard, that it was just a job he did for the money because he couldn't find anything else. As he talked, it dawned on me that I had made yet another middle-class assumption – if it isn't a 'profession', it must be mind-numbing. Pete really enjoyed his job and took a pride in it.

'Geoff doesn't put himself above you. He listens to what you have to say. Like, I told him I thought there should be shutters on one of the office windows – it's a gift for burglars. He says thanks very much and gets me to organise getting a bloke to do it. Says he'll give me a little budget. There's plenty of bosses don't like suggestions from the security guard. They tell you it all costs money and you're paid to make sure they don't get burgled.'

Pete took some naan and mopped up the rest of the chicken. It disappeared in seconds.

'Did the two brothers get on?' I asked.

'They had their ups and downs, but they got along okay. If you're thinking Geoff may have bumped him off, you're wrong – he was on a business trip.'

'So what's your theory?'

'Could've been another woman.'

'Who?'

Pete shrugged impatiently. 'I don't know! I'm not psychic!' Then, when he saw I expected an answer, he admitted, 'According to the girls at work, there was a woman he took on business trips, but I don't know who she was.'

I tried to imagine the sort of woman who would be attracted to Tony Thornley. It wasn't as hard as it should have been. A young, impressionable employee would be a pushover – bludgeoned into submission by him pulling rank. There were plenty of older women too who would turn a blind eye to the overbearing manner and spreading paunch and see only the sleek black Porsche and a wallet full of credit cards.

We refused the sweets and went on to coffee. We both ordered cappuccinos, which tasted like treacle with frothy milk on top. Pete, apparently, felt we had talked enough about Thornley's murder.

He tapped his coffee spoon. 'This bloke of yours – are you still seeing him?' he asked abruptly.

'No.'

I dipped a finger into the chocolate-speckled surface of my coffee and sucked it. I hoped this was not the start of the dreaded conversation about 'us'. Pete leaned back and loosened the waistband of his jeans, then smoothed back his hair. I waited for the opening fire; I suspected that the key words would be 'girlfriend', 'serious' and 'love me for myself'.

Nothing happened. When I risked looking up, there was a mischievous gleam dancing in Pete's eyes. He leaned forward.

'You know something? You remind me of my mother.'

I began a howl of protestation and Pete laughed, and grabbed playfully at my hair.

'I knew that would get you going.'

'What is it – the wrinkles round the eyes? The spreading waistline?'

'You watch what you say about my mum! No, I think – ' he inclined his head and scrutinised my face – 'it's the big, soulful eyes. And the way you make jokes when you get emotional. My mother does that too. And the way your face changes when you laugh – very warm. Beautiful. You give people the feeling that they could tell you anything.'

I wriggled with embarrassment. I wrestled with the

inclination to ask whether his mother also screwed around with young men — anything to ruin a romantic moment.

'Why don't you like it when I look at you and talk about you? Most women like it.'

Women, in my case, not girls.

'You speak from vast experience, I suppose?'

He continued to gaze at me. 'I've had few girlfriends, but nothing serious.'

Bingo! Two key words in one sentence. I put on my best therapist manner. 'So, stuck in the Oedipal phase. You're still in love with your mother?'

'I was,' said Pete laconically, 'but now I'm in love with you.'

The statement hung in the air like a bubble blown by a child — just asking to be popped. I couldn't let that go — I had to deal with it. I would tell him that I wasn't ready for commitment, that I didn't think we were suited to each other, that I had to think about the children. With a sigh of resignation, 'Pete — ' I began. But he stopped me, deliberately or not, I couldn't tell — with a long kiss. As I tasted the salt and spice of his lips, I panicked. I don't even know what 'being in love with someone' means. Love, in my eyes, is a soap opera concept that is barely related to everyday life. When the kiss ended, Pete swivelled round until he made eye contact with the waiter.

'Can we have the bill? Cheers, mate.'

'Hang on. Shouldn't we talk about this?'

'Talk about what?'

'What you've just said?'

He was genuinely surprised. 'What's there to talk about?'

'Aren't I supposed to say I'm in love with you?'

'Are you?'

'No.'

'Not much to talk about then.'

'But I thought the whole idea of this meal was to talk.'

He stared at me as if I had grown two heads. 'So we talked! We've had a night out together for once — good meal. I've enjoyed it. Have you enjoyed it?'

Was this a game? Had I missed something?

'Yes. I've enjoyed it.'

'Good.' He scratched his head. 'Right then.' We sat awkwardly as the waiter placed the bill between us. I reached for it, but Pete got there first. 'My treat.'

'No, Pete, I – '

'Yes.'

'Okay.' I didn't have the heart to argue. 'Thank you.'

'You can get the next one.'

The next one? He honestly believed that this would become a habit? I searched his face for some trace of irony, but saw none. All I saw was the simple, perfectly proportioned face of a handsome young man who said he was in love with me, but who didn't have an inkling of the selfish, self-analytical, over-intellectualising, over-verbalising, up-her-own-bottom woman he had taken on. I felt the evening had been oddly anticlimactic – no scenes, no tears, no drama.

Pete paid the bill, cheerful and jokey with the waiter, and then went off to the loo. I stood up to put on my coat. There were several tables occupied now, though I had hardly noticed people coming in. A voice from behind me said, 'Sara! Dahling.' I turned to see a bejewelled, heavy-set woman, with a Dallas hairstyle and painted nails, sitting at a table behind us. My heart sank as I recognised a cousin – distant, on my mother's side – one of the loudest and brashest women in my family. She was sitting with a balding, paunchy man, looking like Lady Macbeth in a version set in modern-day Finchley.

'Judy, you're looking well.'

'We've been to the Lyric,' she said confidentially, misinterpreting the horror in my face for curiosity. 'I saw you earlier, only I didn't want to disturb you.' She winked. I smiled weakly.

Pete had emerged from the back of the restaurant; Judy gave a stage whisper, 'I won't tell if you won't!' She indicated her companion – he wiggled his hand in greeting – and I recalled my mother telling me that Judy had just separated from her husband. Her eyes flicked up to Pete approaching the table. 'Introduce us, dah-ling – he's so young. Where do you get the energy?'

'Pete – Judy.'

Pete smiled and held out his hand, which Judy took eagerly. I almost had to prise them apart.

'Sorry, got to rush. Lovely to see you.' I hustled Pete out as fast as I could.

'Who was that?'

'Friend of my parents.'

I couldn't bring myself to own her as a relative. I just hoped he didn't see any family resemblance. I wondered how long it would take her to relay a full description of Pete to my mother. She would probably be on the mobile phone before I even reached my car.

We stood outside, in the chilly April air, and kissed.

'Are you coming back to my place?'

He managed to keep his tone casual, but I knew he wanted me to say 'yes'. The idea of going back to Pete's bedsit held little appeal. I thought fleetingly of inviting him back to my place, but rejected that idea too. Having dinner together seemed to have put the relationship on a new plane. Until Pete's tantrum, I saw our relationship as a brief fling which would die a natural death in a week or two. Now, I was having to change the way I looked at it. I stalled my answer for a moment, imagining the luxury of having Pete's body snuggled up against me all night, waking up in the morning and making love slowly, but my natural caution intervened.

'I have to get back,' I lied.

Pete didn't question it and for the umpteenth time I felt guilty. We kissed goodbye and arranged to meet the following week.

When I got home, the house seemed cold and lonely. I went to bed, unsettled and dissatisfied, and dreamt of a house with square rooms and plain colours and battered old furniture. I dreamed that, just beyond the part where I was living, the house became a castle with rich oak panelling, elaborate stairways, towers and turrets, and rooms with fantastical adornments. This beautiful place was there, behind the door, just waiting to be explored, but something was holding me back. I felt vulnerable, exposed, afraid of venturing out alone and getting lost. I stood for hours, torn between trepidation and longing. My hand stayed on the door handle, and when I awoke to the dark of my bedroom, I had the feeling of being trapped inside the four walls of a familiar room.

★ ★ ★

Clancy's face was thunderous; her manner, dangerously calm. She is a formidable presence, even when sitting down. If I had been the two policemen facing her from the sofa in my office, I would have been thinking of making a will. The young DC on the left was blushing and uncomfortable; but DS Gould, on the right, did not even bother to hide his contempt.

'I am merely pointing out,' said Clancy, fanning out the fingers of both hands, 'that there have been suggestions in the press recently of racism on your Division. I am asking for reassurance that Mona Pearson will be treated fairly.'

'Everyone is equal in the eyes of the law,' smiled Gould. He picked a speck of dust off his trousers. 'Now, if you've finished— '

Clancy stood up. She seemed to tower over the room. She looked down her nose at Gould with barely concealed contempt. 'My colleagues have given you their full co-operation,' she said icily. 'I hope it has been helpful.'

'Very helpful.'

Gould got up and the constable followed. Their heads were about level with Clancy's shoulders. Robin rose also. He was the same height as Clancy.

'We shall follow this case very closely,' said Robin. 'We always maintain an interest in the welfare of former clients.

Especially those from minorities, who might be vulnerable to weak points in the system.'

'You do that, sir.' Gould's lip curled. 'But as far as I am aware, there are no weak points in the system.'

'I've met one or two in my time,' I said, raising my eyebrows, 'naming no names.'

Gould threw me a withering look. The two detectives left and Robin followed to escort them off the premises.

When the door shut on them, I expected to see Clancy erupt. I had been considering which furniture to hide behind for protection. Clancy is a large woman and her wrath is usually proportionate to her size. Instead, she moved over to the window and stood very still. When I approached her, I saw a solitary tear slipping over the surface of her smooth brown skin. I had known Clancy a long time and had seen her cry only once or twice. I slipped an arm round her waist (I couldn't reach her shoulders) and gave her a reassuring squeeze. She bit her lip and brushed the tear away with the back of her hand.

'It's the frustration.'

'I know.'

For every Gould you discredited, another would come along and take his place. Whether or not Mona killed Thornley was not the issue – it was a question of whether the facts of the case would ever get to court. The closely woven fabric of police procedure was shot through with threads of racism, impossible to unravel. A small interpretation here, a slight fabrication of evidence there . . .

I didn't offer any words of reassurance about it – I had none to offer. Instead, I said, 'You know what this case needs? A black single woman in a position of authority.'

Clancy's beautiful, wide mouth twitched into a smile. She lifted her chin.

'I could be that woman,' she intoned, in her best Bible-belt accent. Then she sighed heavily. 'Seriously, it's so depressing. The questions he asked!' Clancy mimicked Gould's robotic delivery. ''Did Miss Pearson seem emotional in governors' meetings? Did she seem upset with Mr Thornley?"'

'We didn't fall into any of the traps,' I reminded her gently. 'We made it plain that Mona acted professionally throughout. We told them about Thornley's offensive remarks and the feeling that he was universally disliked.'

'I know, but did he listen? Did he hell! I saw what he wrote down. "Emotional", "Called victim a bigot".'

'We can only do so much, Clancy. It's up to Mona's solicitor and counsel to expose any police bias.' Even as I said it, I felt unconvinced of Mona's chances.

As we stood together in glum silence, Robin came back into the room, ushering in Mel and Greg just in front of him, and then shut the door with calm precision.

Dressed in a crumpled shirt and baggy cords, Greg shambled towards a chair, looking, as usual, as if he had just been dragged out of bed. Mel – a complete contrast to Greg in her dainty size-eight jeans and hand-knitted cardigan – tucked a wisp of hair behind her ear and looked up at Robin, her grey eyes full of concern. Robin adjusted his glasses; his cheeks were flushed with anger.

'I've asked Mel and Greg to join us because I want all four of you to know my position. I am not prepared to stand by and let Mona be set up for a crime she did not commit. I shall be doing everything I can to make sure the police conduct a fair investigation. I am not doing this under the auspices of my work at the clinic. I am doing it out of affection for Mona and a . . . a . . . ' Robin blinked and reverted to his usual sheepish style. 'I don't want to sound pompous, but I want to see justice done.'

'A-all RIGHT!'

We all jumped at Clancy's exultant shout, which she accompanied with a great slap on Robin's shoulders. He was forced to take a couple of steps to help absorb the blow.

'I'm with you all the way, Rob. Let's get TO IT!'

Mel and I exchange cautious looks.

'I agree with Robin's sentiments,' Mel said calmly, 'but let's not jump to conclusions. Just because a racist policeman is investigating Mona's case, it doesn't automatically make her innocent.'

'I didn't say that,' protested Robin, 'but you're right – I do have a gut feeling that she didn't kill Thornley.'

Mel laid a gentle hand on his upper arm. 'I understand how you're feeling, Robin, but we can probably help Mona best by staying objective.'

'I agree.' I was touched by Robin's faith in Mona's innocence, but I couldn't share it. She had a good reason to kill him and she was found with the knife in her hand. She might not be able to remember doing it, but she was still the most obvious suspect. 'If we get involved at all, it should be to try and make sure she has a fair trial – not to decide whether or not she killed him.'

Robin, with uncharacteristic abandon, wanted to launch an immediate campaign to declare Mona's innocence and work for her release. Mel and I argued that the clinic couldn't support that and urged him to be more cautious. Clancy reluctantly agreed with Mel and me. There were plenty of things we could do without committing ourselves to Mona's guilt or innocence. If Mona had been traumatised into memory loss, we could monitor the sort of help she got, come up with names of good expert witnesses who would be convincing in court. Robin and I could talk to a few more people – Maggie, the school administrator, Bridget Scudder and the other governors. If we turned up anything that might help Mona's case, we could hand it over to her solicitor. Greg put in, 'They're right, y'know,' adding enigmatically, 'as usual.' He then put his dirty feet up on my sofa and closed his eyes.

Robin resisted our arguments initially, but he came round in the end. Finally we agreed that he and I would do more digging at Arkwright High, while Clancy would cast a wider net to get more background on Thornley. She has impressive contacts in local government and all sorts of community organisations. Mel and Greg would have no direct involvement – just as well, given Greg's current energy level – but Mel, at least, said she was willing to help if there was something specific she could do. I felt better about the whole thing with Mel on board. She was good at setting limits and helping us to keep things in perspective.

'We're like the Famous Five,' I said, looking round at four sombre faces. 'What's the password, chaps?'

Only Greg laughed – he wasn't really asleep – and I thought I glimpsed an irreverent twitch of a smile on Mel's lips. But Clancy and Robin ignored me, and launched straight into an intense name-swapping session – listing the people they knew on local authority subcommittees who might have heard of Tony Thornley.

As luck would have it, Robin and I both had relatively clear afternoons the following day. We arrived at Arkwright at four o'clock, just after classes had ended for the day. I had been there only once, for the governors' meeting, and never in daylight. I had no idea the place was so vast. The main building was a low brick structure on two levels which ran on all four sides of an inner square, with an additional protruding arm. It was probably built in the early 1970s. Adjacent to the main building were two more recent additions – a tall building with high windows that was probably a gym and a grey brick, two-storey block which could easily have been the home of a design company.

Robin and I strolled around the concrete walkways looking for the way in. Being used to Hannah's ancient primary school – where the main door is obvious from the playground and is still marked 'Boys' Entrance' in Edwardian stonework, Arkwright seemed rather daunting. At the primary school too, the children are small enough to trip over. The students who passed us at Arkwright – jostling each other and talking loudly – seemed enormous. Is it my imagination or does puberty, like spring, come earlier each year? Is the greenhouse effect ripening our children prematurely? The twelve-year-olds looked at least fifteen and the fifteen-year-olds were going on twenty-five. Was I hallucinating, or did that boy running out towards the playing fields with a football have a moustache?

Finally, we found the front entrance and stepped inside. It was clearly a busy time. Students were milling everywhere, chatting in corners, hugging bags bulging with books, rushing off after each other down corridors reverberating with the sound of voices. The smell of the place – a heady compound of wooden floors, paint and sweaty bodies – reminded me uncomfortably of my own school days, which I look back on with mixed feelings.

My sister and I had gone to a small, snobbish private school – all girls – with eccentric and largely untrained teachers. The chemistry teacher spent most of her time searching for missing test tubes, complaining about her fellow teachers, and giving us lectures on astrology, which was something of a hobby. For the privilege of such an education, my parents made great sacrifices and they never allowed us to forget it. My father believed that giving us a good English education would somehow protect us from the curse of anti-Semitism and give us the credentials to fit into English middle-class life. It didn't work. My sister left as soon as she could, to marry a good Jewish boy and go shopping with my mother. I got involved with a bad lot at a Jewish youth club and spent my entire school career on the verge of being expelled for rebellious behaviour. When I finally left for university, both the headmistress and I breathed a sigh of relief – and to this day I have not been able to bring myself to set foot within ten yards of the place.

Robin and I got lost almost as soon as we were inside the school and ended up in the library. After asking directions of a rather frightening youth who looked like a crack addict but spoke like a TV presenter, we found our way back to the school office, where Maggie Molloy was expecting us. The place was buzzing. With the phone ringing and a printer noisily spewing out pages, it seemed more like the office of a busy company than a school.

Maggie greeted us, then motioned us to chairs. She was a soft-spoken woman in her early fifties, smartly dressed in a beige woollen jacket and a black and tan skirt. Her hair might have been naturally grey, but she had chosen to keep it a subtle honey colour, which suited her complexion. I watched her patiently questioning a gawky boy who was in a desperate hurry for her to take a brown envelope full of money. ('Wait a minute, Dean. What's it for?' Dean waved his arms about, as if trying to shake them free of his oversized hands. 'It's the *money*, Miss – for the *thing* next week!') There was a smaller boy, dressed unaccountably as a parrot, who wanted to know the way to the Learning Support Unit, and a teacher, admirably containing an irate father, who wanted Maggie to make an urgent appointment for him to see Bridget.

'Sorry about all that,' said Maggie, as she approached us, smiling. 'How can I help?'

I asked if we could have a chat somewhere quiet. After exchanging a few words with one of her assistants, Maggie led the way down the corridor and opened a door marked 'Head'.

'Bridget is using Mona's office for the time being,' she said, with a hint of disapproval in her voice. 'But she's taking Computer Club at the moment, so we should be all right in here.'

It was a light, airy room, calm and well ordered and strongly stamped by Mona's professional persona. On the shelves, the books were graded by size and you knew instinctively that if you opened the filing cabinets you would find everything neatly and logically arranged. Though tidy, it was far from clinical. On the walls, there was a beautiful framed African batik of a woman carrying her baby, done in black, red and burnished gold; a still life of a market stall piled high with fruit, obviously done by some talented pupil; and a framed fabric collage spelling out the school's name. The desk was superficially cluttered, piled high with papers and files – evidence of Bridget's occupancy? – but this was unmistakably Mona's room.

As we moved to the cluster of chairs round a coffee table near the window, I looked over to the desk and tried to imagine the scene on the night Thornley died. The Venetian blinds had probably been closed, and the desk lamp turned on. I imagined Mona standing behind the desk, her proud face lit from below, her cheekbones sculpted by shadows. Thornley, corpulent and bold, taking her by the arms and trying to press his mouth onto hers – a revolting thought. Then Mona pushing him away, Thornley staggering back and coming at her again. Mona spitting in his face. Somehow, being in the room made the sense of violation more real. This room represented the apotheosis of Mona's career – an acknow-ledgement of the obstacles she had overcome, of her hard work and dedication. On that evening, in the space of a few minutes, she had to face the prospect of losing everything to an unprincipled, mean-minded bully. Just as her early life had been snatched away from her by the loss of her mother, so, out of the blue, a man she despised was threatening the identity she had so carefully constructed for herself. She would have to be inhuman not to react in some extreme way.

'We're still in a state of shock,' said Maggie, when we were settled in our chairs. 'We're trying to keep everything as normal as possible, for the sake of the students, but what with the press and the TV people – ' She shook her head. 'Bridget is doing her best, but she's not the most sensitive person. She's trying to make changes before we've even got to grips with Mr Thornley's death and Mona's arrest. It's been dreadful.'

We made sympathetic noises.

With a glance at the door, as if she almost expected Bridget to be listening outside, Maggie asked, 'How is Mona? You said on the phone you'd seen her.'

'She's bearing up, but she knows that things don't look too good for her.'

'I wanted to go and see her, but Bridget doesn't seem to think it's wise.'

Bloody Bridget, I thought, should try a night or two in the

slammer herself and see how she liked it.

I said between gritted teeth, 'I'm sure Mona would appreciate a note at least.'

Maggie's face lit up. 'Will it get to her?'

'It certainly should.'

'It's a good idea. Perhaps I'll suggest it to one or two of the staff as well. They've been asking if there's any news.'

She stopped talking and waited for us to take the lead. She had a bright, open face that seemed to be smiling even in repose.

'May we ask you something, Maggie?' ventured Robin.

'Of course.'

'Do you think Mona . . . um . . . had anything to do with Tony's death?'

Maggie clutched her hands together on her lap. 'Everything points to it, but it's so out of character. That's my opinion, and most of the staff agree with me, though they wouldn't necessarily say so in front of Bridget. You should see Mona with some of the youngsters – the language they use! Yet I could count on the fingers of one hand the number of times I've heard her raise her voice. As far as I'm aware, she doesn't have a violent bone in her body.'

Robin nodded and glanced at me. Maggie obviously spoke from the heart – but did she really know Mona? Did anyone?

'She's never married, never had kids,' continued Maggie. 'She's put her whole life into this job. Look – five years ago this was a sink school, no one wanted to send their children here. Now we're over-subscribed. Mona has a way of making people feel part of something, so they don't want to let her down. From the very first, she believed in the potential of Arkwright to be a really good community school. She believed it could be a school that got the best out of every pupil, no matter what their background, and everyone responded to that belief – staff, students and governors. Until LMS came in, that is, and Tony Thornley got his hands on the governing body.'

Robin told Maggie that the counsellors at the clinic were worried that Mona's guilt was being taken for granted and that the police weren't asking enough questions. He said that Mona was having difficulty remembering what happened and that she was particularly worried about the whereabouts of the knife on the day Thornley was murdered.

'Do you remember unlocking the drawer that afternoon?'

Maggie frowned with concentration. 'I didn't unlock it, Mona did. But I did take out some money while she was on the phone. Why?'

'Did you lock it again?'

'No.' Maggie looked puzzled. 'I probably closed it, but I didn't have my key with me. Didn't Mona lock it?'

'She thought you did.'

'I left the room just before she got off the phone. I assumed she would lock it.'

'She meant to check it when she got back, but she forgot.'

'So the drawer – '

'May have been left open. Exactly.'

'Oh, my goodness! Should we tell the police?'

I said I thought we should. Robin folded his arms and said nothing. I knew he was convinced that telling the police anything which supported Mona's innocence was a waste of time.

'Whose knife was it?' I asked.

'A boy in Year Ten. It was confiscated on the Monday morning.'

'Who else knew it was there?'

'It's hard to say. Mona, of course . . . myself, the staff, and all the governors, because there was some talk of the boy being excluded. I'm sure lots of students knew that a knife had been confiscated and that it would probably be in the head's office somewhere. Even some of the parents might have been aware of it. Rumours spread like wildfire in a school.'

'So, theoretically, anyone could have come into Mona's office between, say, four o'clock in the afternoon and nine o'clock at night and removed the knife?'

'I suppose so, yes.'

We asked her if she had any theories about the murder. She said she did not; she preferred not to think about the kind of person who might do such a thing. Then she hesitated, one finger tapping meditatively at the corner of her mouth.

'There is one thing that's bothering me though. I tried to tell this to the police, but the young man didn't seem that interested.'

'Yes?' said Robin, a little too eagerly.

'I'm afraid it's a conversation I wasn't meant to hear.' Maggie blushed, showing up a light dusting of powder on her cheeks. 'In itself, it was nothing. It's the way it was said. I was coming up towards the staff room one evening and I heard Mr Patel and Mrs Marsh talking. She was quite heated. "I'll kill Tony" she said. "If I don't get that money, I'll kill him." I'm sure she didn't mean it literally, but she sounded furious.'

'When was this?'

'A few weeks ago. Before you came to that governors' meeting.'

'Have you any idea what money they were talking about?' I asked.

Maggie shook her head. 'I don't think it was anything to do with the school. I wondered if it was to do with the Conservative Association – they're all members. Mr Patel told her to be patient. "It hasn't happened yet," he said. "You're jumping the gun." "He promised," she said. "I'll be after him if he tries to slide out of it."'

Robin looked at me. I shrugged. It meant nothing to me.

'Was there a business connection between Cynthia, Tony and Rajesh?' I asked.

'Mr Patel was Mr Thornley's accountant, I think. But Mrs Marsh has her own business. No connection with Thornley's as far as I'm aware. I've puzzled over it since, but I'm none the wiser. I hope you don't think I'm a gossip. I didn't mean to eavesdrop . . .'

'Not at all,' soothed Robin. 'It might be important.'

It might be, but I doubted it. Most people who knew Tony Thornley had probably felt like killing him at one time or another. Maybe he had promised some funds for the party, but hadn't come up with them. Or maybe he had borrowed money from her. It could be anything. Whatever it was, though, the information was unlikely to help Mona.

We thanked Maggie for her help and said we thought it would be best if she informed the police about the drawer – at least she could corroborate Mona's story. We also asked if we could speak to the caretaker, Mr Breeley, but Maggie said he was on compassionate leave for a few days.

'He was the one who found Mr Thornley, as you know. He was quite shaken up, what with talking to the police and everything.'

As we wound up our conversation, the door opened and Bridget walked in. She looked less than delighted to see Robin and me.

'Are you waiting to see me?' she asked. Then, accusingly, she said to Maggie, 'You should have come and got me.'

Maggie was soothing. 'It's all right. It was me they wanted.'

The comment had the opposite effect to the one intended. Bridget was peeved not to have been included. She moved quickly behind Mona's desk. 'If you were talking to Maggie about Mona, you should have consulted me first.' She spoke imperiously, as if to a couple of thirteen-year-olds who had been caught snogging behind the bicycle sheds. 'In future, if you wish to question my staff regarding sensitive matters to do with the school, please go through me.'

'I'm sorry you feel like that,' I said. 'We assumed you would have no objection to us talking to Mrs Molloy directly.'

'We'll talk about this later, Maggie.'

'No harm done,' said Maggie, evenly. She ushered us out.

'I hope we haven't got you into trouble,' said Robin.

Maggie smiled and seemed unperturbed. 'Not at all,' she said, waving the idea aside. For which I read: despite my benign exterior, I can look after myself, thank you. 'Is your car parked at the back? I'll show you the way out.'

We followed Maggie from the front of the school, where Mona's office was, down several corridors, towards the back entrance. The school was quiet now and almost empty. In some of the classrooms, teachers were marking books, clearing up or putting out equipment for the next day. Occasionally, the echo of a young person's voice reached us from the bowels of the building, like the call of a bird from a distant tree.

As we turned the final corner, we came upon a boy leaning up against a multicoloured wall. He was dressed in the battlegear of his chosen tribe – baggy trousers, huge trainers and a distressed T-shirt showing the face of a rock star who was, as Pete would say, 'well dead'. There was a cursory nod at school uniform in the form of a baseball cap with the Arkwright High logo on it. His lounging back was slumped against a mural on which the emaciated figure of Munch's *Scream* had been copied in a variety of horrific postures, accompanied by captions like, 'Drugs: know the score.' I thought back to the grey school uniform and grey walls of my own schooldays and felt about a 100 years old.

As we approached, I noticed that the boy was staring at us with an odd intensity. I met his gaze as we got up to him and saw the resemblance to Tony Thornley immediately. He had Tony's big bones, his turned-up nose and thick lips; his eyes, though, were bigger and more soulful, perhaps inherited from his mother. His skin was red and blotchy, especially round the nose and mouth. I instantly wondered about drugs, although it could just have been acne. His hair was cut extremely short, with some sort of design razored into it; one ear was discreetly pierced – less discreetly, so was one of his eyebrows.

'Hello Richard,' said Maggie brightly. 'Are you staying for homework club?'

He blushed and shook his head, scuffing the skirting board with one foot.

'Nah – goin' home in a minit. Jus' wai'in' for Rory an' Aaron.'

The abundance of glottal stops was, I supposed, an essential acquisition for a public schoolboy who was clawing his way into the pecking order of a tough, local high school. His manner was tortuously self-conscious. My heart contracted with sympathy for him. It must have been hard enough to deal with whatever problems had got him excluded from his previous school, without then being faced with a bereavement.

As we were about to move off, he raised his head and jabbed a finger in my direction. 'I've seen you before,' he said, grinning. 'You do sex talks.'

When he smiled, a row of small white teeth appeared, and you got a glimpse of the little boy he must have been five years ago, with apple cheeks and a toffee-smeared mouth. I grinned back and nodded – I didn't think I had ever seen him before, but I was pretty sure I knew what he meant by 'sex talks'. Twice a year, I do a session at a local youth advisory service where youngsters submit questions anonymously to a panel of health professionals. The questions are not just about sex, but, of course, those are the ones that everyone remembers – and I usually get to answer the graphic ones like 'What is a blow job?' and 'Is anal sex harmful?' The service invites young people who are currently in counselling to the sessions, although they can also bring friends. I wondered if Richard Thornley had been seeing a counsellor at the service, or whether he went along with a friend.

'I don't remember seeing you, I'm afraid. Did you learn anything?'

'Nuffin' I din' know already!'

'That's what they all say. But you'd be surprised what people don't know.'

He shuffled uneasily, as if he had something particular to say to me, but couldn't quite find the words. He had clearly volunteered the information that he knew me for a reason. I wondered if he was interested in the advisory service – perhaps felt the need to speak to someone – but didn't quite know how to phrase it.

'Do you know the Market Street YAS?' I asked Robin. Of course he knew it — he helped start it. 'It's a good place. You can just walk in, you don't have to be referred.'

Robin nodded.

'This is Richard Thornley,' said Maggie unnecessarily.

I turned back to the boy. 'I know. I recognised you from knowing your father. I'm so sorry. This must be a very difficult time for you and your mother.'

His forced grin was more like a grimace. 'I 'ated the bastard,' he said boldly, hoping to shock. 'I'm glad he's dead. And so is she.'

Maggie shifted uncomfortably and made a tentative gesture to usher us forward, but Robin laid a gentle hand on her arm, silently asking her to wait for a moment. I chose my words carefully.

'All the same,' I said evenly, 'it's very hard to lose a father.'

'Not one like him,' he countered. 'You knew him, did you?' The smile twisted suddenly into a snarl. 'Not another one of his women, are you? Nah — you're too ugly.'

'Richard!' said Maggie, appalled.

'Nice to meet you, Richard,' I said quietly.

His eyes were shooting from side to side, looking for an avenue of escape. Just on cue, a boy came out the classroom opposite.

'Yo, Aaron!'

The big lad with a bag slung over his shoulder swivelled round.

'You off? Me too,' said Richard.

The boy shrugged. 'Come on then.'

Tossing an impressive scowl in our direction, Richard marched off down the corridor. His heavy trainers made him walk as if he were weighed down by concrete blocks.

'Sorry about that,' said Maggie.

'Is he seeing a counsellor?' I asked.

'He has little chats with Bridget, I believe.'

I met Robin's eye. As usual, his response was discreet.

'Could I send you some YAS leaflets? We've just produced a new one.'

'I'll make sure he gets one,' said Maggie. (Message received and understood.) 'Poor lad. He's had it tough. Mind you, it's hard to feel sympathetic. He's such a charmless character. Terribly moody.' She lowered her voice. 'Bridget's given him one of her drugs lectures, but I suspect it hasn't done much good.'

We said goodbye to Maggie at the door and thanked her for her help.

'Keep in touch,' she said. 'And give my regards to Mona.'

When we were halfway across the car park, I looked back at the school. It seemed blind and impersonal, like a silent witness who had seen everything but refused to get involved. Surely someone saw something the night Thornley died. I resolved to speak to Mr Breeley, the caretaker, as soon as I could.

'Mona is stamped everywhere on this place,' said Robin, standing just behind me.

'I expect she'll be back someday,' I said.

It was more a wish than a prophecy.

Chapter Five

When I say that Steve is my best friend, I mean that he is the person I turn to when things go wrong in my life, and the person for whom, if he is in trouble, I will drop everything to help. I trust him utterly, but I try not to take him for granted. We have seen each other at our worst, but also at our best – we are equally at home sitting on the floor, watching TV or weeping over a slushy rented video and meeting at the party of a mutual friend, spruced up and superficial, being smart-arsed and witty to impress a new lover. I have heard it said that men and women can only say they are just friends if they can imagine their friend in bed with someone and heartily wish them a good time. I think that's only true up to a point. I can't say I don't fancy Steve, or that I never feel jealous when he is wrapped up in a new girlfriend; it is simply that to experience him as a lover would be to lose him as a friend, and as I get older I am beginning to value friends more highly than lovers.

It was Wednesday night and I had just talked Steve through a problem he was having with a particularly difficult director. The director was well known and brilliant, and it was considered a privilege to work with him. He was also a bumptious, egotistical maniac with mood swings that went from high camp to serial killer in the course of morning coffee. He seemed to have it in for Steve that week, criticising his work continually and making snide remarks in front of the rest of the cast. I suggested a few techniques to deflect his attacks, but in the end Steve knew the only answer was to stay cool and hope the guy switched to persecuting someone else sooner rather than later. We must have looked a sight: me in jogging pants and an old shirt, stretched full length on the settee; Steve in jeans and a T-shirt, lying on his side on the floor, lightly holding a pint glass of beer balanced on his rump. A couple of middle-aged deadbeats relaxing in a midweek stupor. When it was my turn to air my thoughts about life and the universe, I decided to tell Steve about Mona and Thornley. I knew I could rely on his discretion and I wanted to see what he made of it.

Steve was intrigued.

'You mean Mona can't remember whether she put the knife in or not? How strange. Do you believe her?'

'I believe Thornley threatened her,' I said. 'But I have no idea whether or not she actually killed him. The way she described her childhood bothered me – almost glibly, like something she had read in the paper. But that could be because she's so disconnected from the emotion of it.'

'What about the amnesia?'

'The trauma, the suddenness of it – yeah, I could buy it. But I could also buy the idea that Thornley made her so furious that she grabbed the nearest weapon and stabbed him.'

'Weird.'

Steve took a sip of beer and scratched his stomach. I looked fondly at his paunch, and at the trace of downy hair, glinting golden, as his T-shirt crept up.

'But even if she didn't do it, you think the police will nail her,' he added thoughtfully.

'Put it this way – I don't think Gould will be falling over himself to pursue other suspects. Anyway, the case could take a year to come to trial. She'll do time whether she's guilty or not, unless something happens in the meantime to make them drop the charges.'

We sat in silence for a while, thinking it over.

'Who else could have done it?' asked Steve.

I realised that I had barely thought about that one and I was shocked. It was a measure of how much I doubted Mona's innocence.

'I suppose there are the other governors,' I ventured. 'Bridget, Brian, Cynthia, Rajesh. There's Maggie, the school administrator – but I would bet money she didn't do it. One of them could have stayed behind after the meeting and jumped on Thornley as he came out of the school. Though how they would have got the knife is anyone's guess. Or it could have been someone who knew Thornley was at the governors' meeting – a teacher, maybe, a pupil, or Thornley's wife or son.'

'That narrows it down a little,' said Steve, smiling. 'Cuts out the milkman.'

'I don't know who killed him, and I almost don't want to know,' I said peevishly. 'It's terrible going to see her. If it weren't for Robin and Clancy pushing me into the role of good Samaritan – '

'You don't normally need a push,' said Steve drily.

'This time I do,' I countered. 'There could have been a queue of people waiting to stick a knife in Thornley. Any one of them probably had some reason to hate him. He was that sort of person.'

'I wonder if he ever thought of becoming a theatre director?' mused Steve.

He asked why Robin and Clancy were so keen to get involved and I told him about Robin's crush on Mona and how he wanted to help her because he felt the system would be stacked against her and she wouldn't be in any state to fight it. Clancy's motives were easy to explain – she was an activist in the true sense of the word and always took up the cause of the underdog fighting against the system. I admired her for it, but I didn't always have the heart to join in. I reached for my mug of tea.

'I want to help, but it's hard. It all feels a bit hopeless.'

Steve smiled at me, and the smile reached the crinkles at the side of his eyes.

'Who appointed you saviour of the world, Sara?'

An image of Mona inched its way into my consciousness – Mona, unsmiling, her shoulders hunched; Mona crushed by the belief that the world had abandoned her. I shook my head. 'If you could only see her, Steve. Holloway's a dreadful place. To have worked so hard to escape a childhood like that and then to end up . . . ' I couldn't find a way to finish the sentence. 'At the very least, she deserves a proper police investigation and a fair trial.'

Steve took a slug of beer and smacked his lips. 'It can't harm to go and see some of these people – the wife, if she'll see you, the other governors. Knowing you, they'll probably tell you their life histories before you've had your first cup of tea.'

It's true, I do tend to attract the confidences of strangers, but that's my job. It's only a disadvantage when you nip into a caff for a sneaky coffee and the woman beside you is on about her miscarriages before you've even stirred it.

'If you find something useful,' continued Steve, 'all to the good. But don't beat yourself up over it. Let Robin be Mona's knight in shining armour.'

I smiled at the thought. It was a good image – I could just see Robin in a suit of armour.

'Now tell me,' said Steve, piercing me with a look. 'Who's the new man?'

As usual – right between the eyes. I flopped back on the settee and sighed.

'It's going nowhere,' I said brusquely, 'end of subject.'

'As good as that?' murmured Steve, his eyes twinkling.

I turned over onto my stomach and muzzled my chin into my arm. 'He's a twenty-three-year-old security guard and I remind him of his mother.'

Steve's explosive laugh hurtled through the room.

'We bumped into my cousin in a restaurant, and she phoned my mother and told her I had a toy boy,' I added glumly.

Steve threw back his head and laughed all the more, his belly vibrating with effort.

'Sara,' my mother had said on the phone the next day, 'tell me this isn't true. You know my state of health – are you trying to kill me?'

I managed to stay poker-faced for a minute or two, but Steve's laugh was so infectious, I allowed myself a tiny smile.

'Some help you are,' I complained.

'Twenty-three!' he chortled. 'You cradle-snatcher.'

'Steve . . . ' I warned.

'I'm only jealous.'

He continued to laugh irritatingly for several minutes. But I was glad I had finally told him. The secret was out and my friend had not rejected me. And my mother, four days after hearing about Pete, was, mercifully, still alive.

* * *

Cynthia Marsh's house was between Acton and Ealing, just over that invisible border where knife-edge inner city becomes shopping-mall suburbia. The cultural contrast is remarkable, like crossing over into a different country. The lush horse chestnut trees of Ealing Common mark the border. Suddenly, the homeless winos are gone, replaced by women in Marks and Spencer's separates and sensible shoes; the betting shops give way to 'quality' chain stores, computer shops staffed by eager young men and tasteful cafés where staff don't turn a hair if you ask for it 'on ciabatta'.

By the time you reach Ealing, the littered mean streets have become leafy avenues, with an air of sedate respectability. It's DIY and garden-centre land – and it makes me nervous. As if, one of these days, I might be tempted to think I could fit in and then get trapped before I'd had time to realise my mistake.

I contacted Cynthia Marsh because I wanted to come at the Thornley story from a different angle. According to Clancy, who had been doing some digging on her for me, Cynthia Marsh did know Tony Thornley well in another context – the Conservative Party local government network. He was a leading light on the circuit – successful businessman, treasurer, councillor in a ward in North Ealing and would-be MP. Cynthia was an LEA governor, appointed by the local party, and she too had ambitions to be a local councillor. Clancy had found out that Cynthia did a lot of fund-raising for the local Conservative Party, and that she had been married to the chairman before last but was now a single woman. She ran her own business, buying good-quality 'seconds' from children's clothing manufacturers and selling them through schools and playgroups. I recalled seeing her posters, at Hannah's school, but I had never been to any of the sales because they were always during the day. Clancy said she had a reputation for social climbing, and was supposed to be more interested in the status aspects of politics than having a desire to change the world. She had one child – a daughter – who was in her early teens and attended a private girls' school in Kensington. So much for the Arkwright governors supporting the state sector.

Cynthia had agreed to see me, albeit grudgingly, first thing in the morning, so I went straight there after dropping off Hannah and Jake. Jake would be leaving nursery in the autumn and going to school with Hannah. In some ways, I dreaded it – my baby, hurled out of the cosy world of nursery into the strictures of the classroom – but I had to admit it would make the mornings easier, having to go to just one place instead of two.

I pulled up outside Cynthia's bang on nine fifteen, took a deep breath and checked my face and hair in the rear-view mirror. I saw my usual morning look – rag doll crossed with Bride of Dracula. I had made an attempt at mascara, but it was already smeared, so I wiped the lot off with a tissue. My nose seemed even more prominent than usual, but that always happened when I ventured into territory where people cut their lawns regularly and clip their hedges into the shape of birds. I sighed and hoped the Indian silk dress and ankle boots would buy me a little credibility in Cynthia's eyes. If I remembered rightly, she was a woman who cared about those things. I wasn't looking forward to the meeting. Some instinct told me that we were not destined to be soulmates.

Cynthia lived in a compact, 1930s semi-detached, in a street tucked well away from the main shopping centre. The front garden was adorned by a grey stone cupid, surrounded by hyacinths and daffodils. It looked like it should be in the middle of a formal lawn of some mansion in Kent, instead of a suburban semi in Ealing. As I listened to the doorbell chime, I pondered one of the fundamental mysteries of the British mind – how normal people can be seduced into putting up a varnished mahogany sign dubbing their house 'Merrilees' and then write it as part of their address without blushing. Why do they do it? I just had time to come up with 'Brick Shit House' for my own humble abode, when I heard footsteps and saw, through the frosted glass, a blurred figure approaching.

When Cynthia opened the door, my first thought was that she was prettier than I remembered her, but perhaps she looked better with less make-up and dressed more casually in an expensive jogging suit. At the governors' meeting she had come power-dressed in high heels and a suit with a short skirt. Now she had designer trainers on her feet and her hair was bunched up on top of her head in a gold ruche, with a pony-tail flopping to one side. I guessed she must be in her early thirties. She was tall and slim, with a well-toned body and flawless skin. Her mouth was full-lipped and curved down-wards into a pout, which might have been attractive except for a faint line from the corner of her mouth to her nose which made the pout into a sneer. Her carefully moulded eyebrows arched gracefully from a well-shaped nose. I wondered how many hours were spent plucking out the hairs to get the line just so.

'You found it all right?' she asked.

'Yes thanks.'

'Do come in.' Her accent was a little too precise, like an elocution teacher keeping a careful watch on her vowel sounds.

I stepped into the hall.

'Excuse the boxes. I've just had a big order in and I haven't had time to sort it out yet.'

We stood for a moment contemplating a row of cardboard cartons, each about three feet high, which took up most of her hall. Just for something to say, I asked her if business was good.

'I can't complain,' she said. 'It's been a difficult year, but it's the same for everyone, isn't it?'

I murmured agreement. 'Have you got a partner, or is it just you?'

She shot me a puzzled look. 'Just me. Shall we go through?'

I wondered if I had said the wrong thing. Small talk with business people never was my forte. Unable to come up with a suitable reply, I followed her into the kitchen.

'Coffee?'

'Please.'

We sat at the breakfast bar on high, uncomfortable stools, which suggested to me that, despite the offer of a drink, I was not expected to stay long. The coffee was already made. Cynthia poured the milk, offered me sugar and made a great play of searching through the cupboards until she found some, implying that she herself was far too self-disciplined to take it. She watched closely as I took two spoonfuls.

Anxious to get to the point as quickly as possible, I told her why I had come, keeping the explanation brisk and casual. I said that Robin and I were shocked by the murder and Mona's arrest. I said that although the police were confident they had arrested the right person, Robin and I wanted to make sure they were not just taking the easiest route.

'I'm sure I can't tell you anything you don't already know,' she said quickly.

'You spoke to the police about Tony Thornley's death – '

93

'At length,' she interrupted. 'I gave them all the help I could.'

'I'm sure you did. But I wondered whether you could shed any light on why Mona might have been driven to do such a thing.'

'I have no idea.'

'You knew Tony Thornley,' I began.

'I've known *of* him for years,' she said, waving her hand dismissively, 'but I wouldn't say I *knew* him. I saw him at selection committees and socials. My ex-husband was chairman of the local branch, so we met, of course.'

'What was Tony like with friends?' I prompted. 'He seemed a very forceful sort of person . . .'

She laughed – a short, brittle laugh – and reached for a packet of cigarettes from the counter behind her. She made a token gesture to offer one.

'You don't, I suppose?'

I shook my head.

'Some kind of therapist, aren't you?'

'A counsellor. I work mainly at a centre in Acton.'

She nodded, snapped her lighter and lit the cigarette with one smooth action. She blew the smoke out of the side of her mouth and it wafted towards a pine spice rack.

'Forceful . . . that's about right. What do you want to know? If he wanted something, he usually got it. So I'm told.' Then she added, 'Mind you, he had a soft side to him as well.'

'Really?'

I looked at her, wide-eyed, encouraging. Tony had a soft side? I had a sudden image of Tony Thornley, grinning like a gargoyle and clutching a teddy bear. It was too awful to contemplate.

Cynthia pinched the end of her pony-tail between her finger and thumb and twisted it round her finger. 'I'm a bit of a people watcher. I can always see through people. My daughter says I'm like a laser.'

'I'm sure you are.'

Cynthia dabbed a finger at the corner of her glossy lips. 'There's a picture of her there.'

She pointed to the fridge, on which there was a gallery of photos, fixed grotesquely with 'My Little Pony' fridge magnets. They were all of a girl with powder-blue eyes, long blonde hair and an expression that was hard to read. I slipped off my stool to look at them. She was uncannily like her mother, tall and leggy. She would be quite beautiful when she was fully grown. The pictures were mostly holiday snaps: the girl, long-limbed and gawky by a swimming pool; reading under a beach umbrella; standing beside Mickey Mouse at Disney World; then, looking older, on a horse, all kitted out in riding gear. Only in this one was she smiling.

'Fay,' crooned Cynthia. 'My pride and joy.'

'She's lovely,' I said, nodding.

I resumed my seat and Cynthia picked up her coffee cup, keeping her little finger clear.

'As far as I'm concerned, local government is all about good housekeeping. You spend your money wisely, make sure you're getting the best value for money and the rest takes care of itself.' Good, solid, market philosophy. 'But Tony was ambitious. Local politics was like a game to him – a stepping stone to bigger and better things. He used people. He'd set his sights on Westminster and didn't care how he got there. He'd have made it too – if he'd lived.' She paused for a moment, as if observing a minute's silence for the dead. Then she added, 'He made a lot of enemies in the local party, making promises and going back on them.' She took a small sip of coffee. 'Biscuit?'

I indicated no, despite the fact that there were custard creams – I had learned my lesson over the sugar. Perversely, Cynthia picked out a custard cream, holding it carefully between a finger and thumb. Her nails were painted pale strawberry, to match her jogging suit. She nibbled the biscuit and licked away the crumbs.

'I didn't have much respect for him, to be honest. He had it all too easy. The business came to him from his father, so he never had to work for anything, it just fell into his lap.'

Of course. It made sense now. Cynthia would describe herself as a self-made woman, whereas Thornley –

'I'm a self-made woman.' She patted her collarbone to emphasise the point. 'I started from nothing, went to night school, picked myself up and got on with it.' She took another drag on her cigarette, alternating it horribly with her biscuit.

'And Tony's soft side?' I prompted, wanting to steer clear of Cynthia's life history, which I could see looming ominously ahead. 'I've heard he was a bit of a ladies' man . . . '

'Really?' she said coldly. 'I'm not surprised. From what I've heard, his wife is so wrapped up in the son and her charities, she'd hardly notice.'

I answered noncommittally. Interesting that she took Tony's side on that one. Me, I sympathised with the wife – I'd rather crochet pullovers for Peruvian yaks than spend cosy evenings with Tony Thornley.

'Did Mona have any sort of grudge against Tony Thornley?'

Cynthia crossed her legs. 'You've been to a meeting – you know what it's like. Tony wanted to make Arkwright a decent school with decent standards. Mona's got all these liberal ideas. She panders to the lowest common denominator. That's what's wrong with the whole state system, if you ask me.'

I tried to keep her to the point, hoping to avoid a right-wing diatribe. 'Could there have been anything between them – Mona and Tony?'

'Tony and a coloured woman?' The crease between Cynthia's nose and mouth deepened with distaste. 'He'd turn in his grave at the thought.'

I managed to hold back the sharp words that were on my tongue to ask smoothly, 'Was there tension between them at the meeting before Tony died?'

'Not particularly. If anyone had it in for Tony that night, it was Bridget.' She smiled through eyes half closed by the smoke. 'Tony used to say, "What that woman needs is a man."'

A man like Tony Thornley, I suppose.

'Bridget was in quite a state, very annoyed with Tony. Do you know what she said when the decision on special needs funding went against her? She said, "You'll regret this," I don't know if she was talking to Tony or Mona or the whole lot of us, but anyway she stormed out.'

'She stormed out of the meeting?'

No one had mentioned that before. Certainly not Bridget.

'It had just about finished. Mona wrapped it up and went off to find Bridget, but she'd already gone.'

'Do the police know that she left the meeting early?'

'Of course.' Cynthia took a final drag on her cigarette and stubbed it out on a cut-glass ashtray. 'But it wasn't Bridget caught holding the knife, was it? It was Mona.' She leaned forward conspiratorially and I felt her agitation – even Cynthia was not untouched by the horror of the murder. 'She didn't just stab him once, you know. Fifteen stab wounds, they said. All over his chest and stomach.'

The idea of it seemed all the more sinister in Cynthia's oppressively respectable kitchen. Mona confronting Tony, consumed with hate. Mona plunging the cold steel into his flesh not once, not twice, but again and again and again.

Cynthia shifted back on her stool and reached for another biscuit to cover her anxiety. 'It just shows you, doesn't it? It's always the quiet types. Lucky they caught her.'

Her certainty goaded me into countering, 'If she did it.'

'What do you mean?' Her eyebrows spoiled their perfect line by frowning.

'You said yourself it's out of character. Mona can't remember anything about it probably because of shock. Maybe someone else killed Tony and Mona was just in the wrong place at the wrong time.'

Even as I said it, I realised that it strained credibility. Cynthia's expression told me she was not convinced.

'She may not have seemed the type, but people can do all sorts of things in the heat of the moment. I know there were

97

times with my ex-husband – ' She stopped and asked suddenly, 'Are you married?'

'Divorced.'

'There you are then. You know what I'm talking about. Men can make you act out of character. Mona was a dark horse.' Her nervous laughter filled the kitchen. 'Excuse the pun.'

I stared at her, stony-faced, and wondered how she could be so indifferent to Mona's plight.

'Mona was wrong for that school and Tony knew it. Arkwright needed someone with a bit of get up and go, who knew how to manage a budget; someone who could get funds in from local businesses, so that the school would attract a higher calibre of pupil. Their exam results are appalling – fifth bottom of the league table, if I recall.'

'They have a high proportion of children who can't speak English,' I said, through gritted teeth, wondering how we'd got on to this.

'Exactly!' she exclaimed triumphantly. 'Which is precisely why Tony and I were trying to phase down this Section 11 funding, so the school didn't have to cope with so many foreigners. Mona couldn't take it, so all of a sudden – ' Cynthia clicked her fingers – 'she snapped.'

I paused for just one beat and then asked, 'Did you have any joint business interests with Tony Thornley?'

I had caught her off guard, as I meant to do. I wanted to see if I could get her to shed any light on what Maggie had overheard, though I knew it was a shot in the dark.

'Why do you ask?' Moving carefully, like a cat, Cynthia reached for another cigarette and took her time lighting it. Her studied nonchalance told me I was on dangerous ground.

'Just a thought.'

Her eyes locked on mine – azure blue and hard as diamonds. 'I'm in kids' clothing. Why would I do business with a company that makes veneer panelling?'

'I just wondered whether you thought Tony was a good

businessman,' I hedged. 'Did you have much to do with him in the local party?'

'Very little.'

'But you're in charge of fund-raising and he was treasurer . . . '

'That was last year. We met once a quarter.'

'Oh.' I would have to sack my researcher. 'Was he good with money?' I persisted lamely.

Cynthia exhaled smoke and then fanned the air with her hand. 'He was a competent treasurer if that's what you mean.' Her eyes flicked pointedly to the clock on the wall. 'I hate to rush you, but if you've finished . . . '

'Of course.'

I gathered up my bag and, moving backwards, tripped over the stool. As I struggled to get my balance, I remembered something else I'd meant to ask her. 'I'd like to speak to Frances Thornley and Rajesh Patel,' I said. 'Do you think they'd see me?' I was hoping she might be on good enough terms with them to ring them up and ask.

'Frances probably wouldn't talk to you,' she said, putting the emphasis on the 'you'. 'She's a snob at the best of times. Rajesh will see you if you pay him, or if he thinks he'll benefit financially.' There was that laconic smile again. 'He's an accountant,' she said, shrugging.

I thanked Cynthia for her time, and edged my way past the boxes again.

'I wouldn't worry about Mona,' she cooed as she followed me down the hall to show me out. 'If she gets a good defence together, she should be out in five years.'

She held the front door open and I shot out to my car, so appalled by the remark that I barely managed to say goodbye.

The air outside was sweet with the promise of spring. The breeze carried the aroma of hyacinth and new leaves, and the cherry trees were almost ready to burst into frivolous bloom. I drove with the windows open, despite the chill in the air, to try and dispel the sting of Cynthia's words. Five years! I had seen a report recently on conditions in Holloway – the women banged up for twenty-three hours a day, the rats and cockroaches that gathered to gorge on leftover food, the mounting anger of the women deprived of any activity because of staff shortages and the new emphasis on security. A nightmare to live through – a double nightmare if you were innocent. I wondered if Cynthia ever thought of that, tucked away in her cosy kitchen. It was all too depressing. I chugged through the slow-moving traffic on the Uxbridge Road and headed for work. To take my mind off things, I switched the dial to a jazz station and sang along to a howling blues, one of the few to which I happen to know some of the words.

Chapter Six

We spent Passover in the bosom of my family. When the traditional question comes up at the beginning of the Seder, 'Why is this night different from all other nights?' I am always tempted to answer, 'Because tonight we pretend to be a happy family on account of the presence of my mother's two sisters, but on every other night of the year, we argue.' That is not the right answer. The answer is that this night is different from all other nights because we celebrate the liberation of our people from slavery in Egypt. 'Our people.' It's taken me some time to come to terms with that phrase but, I have to admit, Pesach brings out the traditionalist in me. I love the ritual, the food, the singing – I love the way my father intones the prayers in a strong voice, for once openly proud of his traditions. Jake, being the youngest, gets his moment of glory in asking the four questions, and Hannah somehow always manages to find the afikoman (the piece of unleavened bread that is hidden away and for which there is a small prize). Sometimes she cheats by getting my father to give her a clue as to its whereabouts; sometimes one of her cousins locates it simultaneously, a scuffle breaks out and my mother has to intervene.

There were twenty-five of us squeezed round trestle tables in my parents' living room. My sister and her husband were there, with their two non-communicative children who always remind me of robots; my mother's two sisters; my father's brother; and numerous assorted cousins. My mother's sisters are all that is left of a huge family, which was largely wiped out by the Holocaust; my father's family was smaller, and it lost more members to drink than to pogroms. Yet it is my father who insists on a Seder which veers more towards the political than the religious. Strangely for a man who has spent most of his life trying not to stand out as a Jew, he exhorts us each year to remember, as we celebrate the deliverance of the Jews from slavery, that there are many people who are still held in captivity, whose silent weeping goes unheeded. He asks us to think of people for whom liberation is still a longed-for dream, who are oppressed and discriminated against, and of prisoners of conscience.

Mona didn't come into the category of prisoners of conscience, but it was she who came into my mind as my father said his piece. If what she told me about her childhood was true, she had overcome many hurdles to make something of her life. I felt she didn't deserve to end up in prison. Yet if she did kill Thornley, she shouldn't get away with it. If only someone had helped her face up to her background and make her peace with it. Thornley was the catalyst – but it could have been anyone, confronting her with her past and dredging up painful memories, long buried.

After my father had finished, there was the usual heated 'discussion' about the Hebrew text – irrelevant quibbles over certain words. As the argument bounced back and forth across the table, I fingered the maror – the bitter herbs – supposed to signify the hardship of slavery in Egypt, and thought of Mona locked up with her pain and bitterness. I reminded myself that although the evidence was stacked against Mona, it didn't mean she did it – but in my heart, I didn't believe it. When we finally drank the last cups of wine and Uncle Leon started up the singing, Jake launched himself onto my lap and I pushed thoughts of Mona aside; but it strengthened my resolve to uncover the truth about Thornley's death, so that at least Mona would not be cheated by the system as she had so clearly been cheated by life.

On the second day of Passover, the children slipped the confines of their heritage of oppression and went to their father and Angie's to celebrate Easter with their Christian grandparents. I beat back the demons of misery which always threaten to engulf me when the children leave for any length of time and took the plunge – invited Pete to stay on the Friday night.

I tried not to think about my motives. Since our dinner the week before, I had hardly given the subject of Pete a thought – questions surfaced, but I pushed them down. Just for once, I promised myself, I wouldn't try to plan or control things, I would be spontaneous. I wanted to see Pete. I wanted to touch him, badly – sex with him was like a drug – but I didn't want to go to his bedsit. The children were away, so the only sensible thing to do was to ask him to my place.

I refused to think about the implications of it, whether I was giving the wrong message about wanting to let him into my life. Agonising about it was a waste of time, I told myself. Pete would fall out of love with me long before I got tired making love with him. Despite his apparent acceptance of my age and responsibilities, he would soon get bored and want to move on to someone younger with fewer ties. That was what I was relying on – and what I most feared.

When he arrived in the early evening, we went straight to bed. It was a delicious luxury to explore his body in the warm confines of my own bed. We made love, slowly and carefully; his tongue travelled so surely over my body, I felt as if he were following a map. Unlike my other lovers, Pete seemed not to have any set pattern of lovemaking. He sprang surprises constantly. Perhaps all the other men I had been to bed with were simply boring – or perhaps they were too experienced to divert from the path they knew to be effective. Pete said nothing as we made love, but he managed to communicate a good deal by what he did. And I responded in kind, resisting the temptation to translate it into words.

When it was over, I felt energised rather than lethargic. I sprang out of bed and went downstairs to make dinner. I had planned a pasta dish – penne with freshly made pesto sauce and Parmesan. Pete followed me down and wandered around the kitchen, peering into cupboards, asking questions about Hannah and Jake. I gave the briefest of answers, feeling uneasy and wishing he wouldn't ask. He insisted on chopping the garlic and basil. I tolerated his presence up until the time when he commented that his mother made pesto sauce in a slightly different way, then I shooed him out of the kitchen and told him to go and watch the snooker.

We ate in front of the television, guzzling penne steeped in the pungent sauce which – even if it wasn't quite like his mother's – Pete agreed was delicious. We talked little, allowing ourselves to be lulled into a trance by the tap and click of balls on the green baize. I started out tense, but relaxed more and more as the evening wore on. By the time we turned the light off and snuggled together naked under the duvet, Pete's presence seemed as natural as the drunken singing of the Friday night stragglers, coming home from the pub at closing time.

He left early on the Saturday morning to go to work. I was glad not to have to give our fledgeling relationship the further test of a face-to-face breakfast – often a stumbling block with me, feeling as I do in the mornings. When I don't have the children to deal with, any human interaction beyond the monosyllabic is more than I can tolerate. After he had gone, I threw together a combination of muesli, Coco Pops and Weetabix in the kind of ideal proportions which I can achieve only when I breakfast alone and give it my full concentration, then I sat at the kitchen table and pondered Pete's temperament. He seemed so uncomplicated, it made me suspicious. I was waiting to discover some difficult complexity in him – possessiveness, or a propensity for manipulation or deceit – but nothing turned up. I consoled myself with the fact that I had found out he couldn't cook (though he wanted to learn), he cleaned his teeth noisily and he farted in his sleep. It wasn't much, but it was still early days.

Just as I had swallowed the last mouthful of my cereal combination, the telephone rang. It was Robin.

'Sorry to disturb your Saturday morning, Sara.'

'No problem.'

'I've found out something. I think it could be important.'

I tucked the phone under my chin and poured my second cup of coffee of the morning.

'I'm all ears.'

Since Robin had announced his intention of helping Mona's cause, he had become more like himself again – calm and purposeful. There was that confidence in his voice again which made you feel that whatever was about to come out of his mouth would be worth listening to.

Robin told me that the previous evening he had met up with a contact of Clancy's – a Labour councillor who had been on the local government finance committee with Thornley. The guy disliked Thornley intensely and was only too delighted to have a good gossip about him over a pint. They talked mainly about Thornley's political ambitions, but then the conversation moved on to his propensity for sexual harassment which, according to the contact, was common knowledge in the council chamber.

'Thornley *was* having an affair,' declared Robin finally.

'I never doubted it.'

'He ended it because his wife threatened to leave him if he didn't. His mistress was, apparently, none too pleased and was making life as difficult for him as possible.'

'Interesting. Did you get a name?' I asked Robin. 'Do we know her?'

'We do indeed.' He paused just long enough for me to guess.

'Cynthia Marsh!' we said in unison.

It all made sense now. Her bitterness, her constant sniping at Thornley in the governors' meeting, even her answer when I suggested Thornley was a womaniser – denigrating the wife and excusing the husband. Her dismissive response when I suggested that Thornley might have been involved with Mona – not just blind racism, but maybe also a touch of jealousy.

Robin and I agreed that it did put a slightly different complexion on things, although it didn't change Mona's position directly. Cynthia had lied to me that she didn't know Thornley that well – had she lied to the police as well? I wondered aloud if Gould had investigated Cynthia's alibi and whether the forensic results were back. Being rejected by your lover is as good a reason as any for murder. I told Robin what I had planned for the day and promised to call him if I turned up anything interesting.

The clock in the bedroom said eleven thirty as I donned a tan corduroy skirt and a slim-fitting black top and knotted a silk animal-print scarf round my neck. I brushed back my crisp bush of hair and pulled it into a twist at the nape of my neck, holding it fast with a leather grip. I finally found the amber earrings I was looking for in Hannah's treasure box – I told myself I would give her hell for appropriating them, but knew I wouldn't. I slipped them through my ears and added a small stud in the second hole of my right ear.

I looked in the mirror and judged the effect to be rather elegant and uncharacteristically feminine. It wasn't quite the Jaeger country woman that I wanted for a craft fair in an Ealing church hall, but near enough to make do. In a fit of subversion, I stared at my nose and wondered whether I could bear to break a lifetime's self-consciousness about its shape and length and put a stud in my right nostril.

I decided I would mention it to Clancy, whose recent interest in body piercing was causing some problems with her girlfriend. If she suggested, tactfully, that my navel or some other hidden part might be better, I would abandon the idea altogether.

As I dressed, I pictured Cynthia Marsh and wondered what she saw in Tony Thornley. She was independent, pretty and sexy, while he had been a bullying puffball. It must have been his ruthless and ambitious aura. They say that power is a strong aphrodisiac – one has only to think of the slobbish, forty-something male MPs who have affairs with nubile young women to see there must be something in it.

One of Clancy's friends had mentioned a sale of works taking place at twelve o'clock in a church hall in South Ealing. It was Frances Thornley's church and, since she was one of their chief parish organisers, the word was that she was sure to be there. Clancy was determined to come with me, though she promised to let me do the talking.

Before the craft fair, I had arranged to meet Barry for a sandwich at a pub in Chiswick. He hadn't exactly been keen, but he knew he owed it to me. I guessed that he was sensitive about discussing a case that was not being handled by his Division, and reluctant to have to defend Gould, whose list of pet hates included homosexual as well as black people. I was one of the few people who knew of Barry's sexual preference and the secret bonded us in a way that would otherwise have been highly unlikely. Barry had integrity and he trusted me, but the last thing he wanted to do was to get in the way of a pernicious homophobe like Gould.

Barry stood up when I walked up to his table and gave me a light peck on the cheek.

'You look smart.'

'Thanks. Don't I always?'

'Last time I saw you, you were hardly wearing anything.'

I looked blank for a moment and then remembered – we'd last met at John's Christmas party. A pang of regret shot through me, but was gone in a moment.

'So many men, so little time,' I commented.

'Too true,' agreed Barry.

We smiled conspiratorially.

'Let's order lunch.'

We strolled over to the bar.

'John and I are not together any more,' I said, as we perused the menu.

Barry looked surprised. 'That's a shame.'

I shrugged and said that the relationship had been going downhill for some time. There was a pause while we discussed the merits of the various sandwich combinations with the barmaid.

'Are you seeing anyone?' I asked Barry, when she moved off. Barry's relationships are a tricky subject, which we rarely mention, but I ask occasionally, in case he feels like opening up.

He smiled self-consciously. 'As a matter of fact, yes.' He looked pleased.

'That's good.'

I returned his smile, but he didn't say any more. It sounded like a proper relationship. Usually, he just answers 'no one special' and I know he is seeing people on a casual basis in areas where he isn't known.

I ordered an orange juice, not wanting to arrive at a respectable venue with alcohol on my breath. We took the drinks and went back to our seats. When we were settled, I told Barry, as tactfully as I could, that Robin had misgivings about Gould's objectivity in the case. I told him what Robin and I had found out so far, adding what he probably already knew – that Mona claimed not to be able to remember whether she killed Thornley or not.

'Robin is convinced that Mona is innocent,' I concluded. 'He's determined to publicise her case.'

Barry was heavily sceptical. 'The caretaker found Pearson

holding the knife, staring at the body. Her footprints in blood coming away from the body, then back again, her hairs on his jacket . . . What more do you want?'

'A confession. Or hard evidence that she actually killed him. She says he made a pass at her in the office. She remembers going out after him, but she swears she didn't have a knife.'

'So why was she holding it?'

'She pulled it out.'

Barry made a face. 'I've been in the job fifteen years, seen countless stabbings. Never heard of anyone pulling out a knife.'

'There's always a first time. She was traumatised.'

'So was he! He was stabbed fifteen times, in the chest and stomach. Why didn't she call for help? Come on, Sara.' Barry took a pull on his pint. 'The guy was stabbed from the front with a five-inch sheath knife. Whoever did it hated the guy's guts and meant to kill him. The attack was from the front, which suggests that Thornley knew his attacker and didn't try to run, even when he saw the knife. All right, I know what you're going to say – what about the wife and the woman he was having a affair with, Cynthia what's-her-name.' So the police did know about Cynthia. 'I'd say, good point, except that their alibis check out. Cynthia says she went straight home after the meeting and the daughter and a neighbour confirm it. Besides, there's nothing to put her at the scene. The wife has three witnesses willing to swear she was playing bridge all evening. One of them drove her home, at ten fifteen – the approximate time of the attack.'

Barry had certainly done his homework.

'And the son?'

'Hanging out with friends at a pub in Ealing Broadway. The bar staff aren't keen to remember him because he's under age, but two of his friends will vouch for him being there at least up to nine o'clock, and he was home by the time his mother got in.'

'What about Bridget Scudder? She stormed out of the meeting, pissed off at Thornley.'

'She doesn't deny it. But there's no forensic that I know of to put her with Thornley.'

'You seem to know a lot.'

'I had a word with Gould. Looked at the case file.'

An idea gnawed at the edges of my consciousness. Yet it was so obvious, I hardly dared mention it lest I invite Barry's derision. I decided to risk it.

'Barry?'

'Yes . . .'

'When someone stabs someone from the front, they get covered in blood, right?'

He was cautious. 'They can do.'

'Was Mona covered in blood?'

'I believe she had some blood on her.'

'From holding the knife, but what about on her clothes, her shoes?'

Barry thought for a moment. 'The knife went in deep. He bled a lot internally.'

'Isn't it a bit too easy, Barry? Mona standing there, holding the knife, waiting to be caught bang to rights?'

Barry sighed. 'You want to make it complicated?'

'I'm saying that you're taking everything at face value, yet if the roles had been reversed – if a white man was caught holding a knife and a black woman lay dead in front of him – the police would ask a lot more questions to make absolutely sure the guy did it.'

Barry shook his head. 'You're wrong.'

The sandwiches arrived and we both took a bite and swallowed before continuing.

'All we want is for the police to ask a few more questions. What about checking the autopsy to see if Thornley did have a bruise on the side of his hip where Mona says he knocked himself against her desk?'

Barry made a note, but he didn't agree to do it.

'And the knife . . . neither Maggie nor Mona locked the drawer after they took out the petty cash. Mona swears she didn't have the knife when she went after Thornley. Could someone have taken it? Was anyone seen lingering outside Mona's office that afternoon?'

Again, Barry made a note, still munching on his sandwich. I searched my brain for other suspects.

'Where was Thornley's brother?'

'Out of the country, on a business trip.'

'Brian Farrell?'

'Didn't go to the meeting. His wife was having a baby.'

'Rajesh Patel?'

'Patel, Cynthia, the school secretary – everyone left the building at about the same time.'

'How do we know they didn't stay around and wait for Thornley?'

'We don't. But equally we don't have any evidence that they did.'

'Has anyone asked them?'

Barry was getting irritated. 'What do you think?'

'I think everyone is only too pleased to have this one neatly wrapped up.' Then I added slyly, 'I also think that when you see the psychiatric report on Mona you won't be such happy bunnies.'

Barry stopped chewing for a moment. 'Why?'

'Because in my view – though she's not my client and I'm not a psychiatrist – she could well get off on a defence which relies on her state of mind at the time.'

That would get him. I chewed my sandwich and watched Barry weigh up whether or not I was bluffing. Nothing gets to a detective more than a solid case being dismantled in court by a shrink. I told myself that although it wasn't strictly true, it did have a basis in fact. Mel's barrister friend had said that they had got three women off in the last year on that defence. The psychiatric report was crucial. If it could be shown that because Thornley attacked and threatened to blackmail her, Mona had temporarily lost control over her behaviour, she stood a reasonable chance of an acquittal.

'Sane automatism or temporary amnesia is a definite possibility,' I added, trying to inject a note of authority.

Barry grunted. 'I'll mention it to Gould. Chances are he's thought of it already.'

'I doubt it.' Which told him that I knew something Gould didn't and I wasn't telling. They would find out about Mona's past soon enough – in court, probably; I certainly wasn't going to tell them.

'Don't look at me like that, Barry. I don't know whether she did it or not, but I'm convinced that the truth isn't as simple as it seems.'

'It never is,' said Barry gloomily.

Time was getting on and I didn't want to be late for the craft fair. I finished my sandwich and told Barry I had to go.

'If you know anything pertaining to the crime – ' Barry began.

'I don't,' I interrupted him. 'All I have is a gut feeling about Mona's psychological state, based on what she has told me.'

'So we wait for the report,' said Barry.

'Exactly.'

I said goodbye and headed back to my car, which was squeezed into a tiny space near the library. I wasn't sure if I had gained anything from seeing Barry, but at least I had sown a few seeds of doubt in his mind, without using Gould's racial bias as the reason.

Frances Thornley turned out to be a small woman with unhappiness written very large on her face. It was not just that she didn't smile – she was, after all, newly widowed – it was the lines of misery in the middle of her forehead and around her eyes. Her mouth was set in a grim line, giving her a sad, stoical look. Her grey-green eyes seemed to be constantly searching for something or someone, and never settling on the person to whom she was speaking.

I watched her for almost an hour before speaking to her. The fair was well attended and her stall drew a lot of interest, but one suspected that it wasn't just the hand-sewn oven gloves that were attracting the punters. There was subtle nudging as Frances took the money and gave change; some glanced at her uncomfortably as she chatted to the woman who was behind the table with her. I noticed how few people offered their condolences directly; those who did got a brisk set-piece from Frances. She thanked them for their sentiments in a way that cut short the conversation and put paid to any thought of pursuing the subject. Such is the way with English people. Grief is an embarrassment which is endured alone and which goes away eventually if everyone agrees to ignore it.

I got my chance when I overheard Frances' friend declaring that her feet were killing her and that she simply must sit down with a cup of tea. Frances said that she could manage quite well alone, but the friend was pleased, if a little surprised, at my offer to step in and hold the fort with Frances until she got back. I squeezed in behind the table and introduced myself, and saw Clancy shoot an admiring glance in my direction from her vantage point at the second-hand book table. Close to, the lines of suffering on Frances Thornley's face were even more pronounced, etched into dry tissue skin. Her thin brown hair was lightly permed and fading into grey at the temples. Her clothes were good, but drab and unimaginative: a mud-coloured skirt, a cherry blouse and a brown cardigan which might or might not have been cashmere – the sort of clothes one finds in jumble sales in church halls everywhere, donated by women like Frances Thornley, who buy the same 'classic' styles year after year. She had no earrings or jewellery of any kind, except a wedding ring – which got me thinking how off-the-wall my idea of a nose ring had been, and how it might seriously affect my credibility in encounters such as this. (Clancy had confirmed it by recommending nipple rings.) I settled in behind the stall, sold a tray cloth and moved a few things around unnecessarily just to look busy. We chatted in a desultory fashion for fifteen minutes or so. No, I didn't live in the parish, I just came to see the crafts. It certainly was cold for the time of year, but the forecast said it would get warmer later in the week. Yes, two pounds fifty was far too cheap for such a lovely rag doll; we should definitely make it three pounds fifty and see if anyone bought it.

My luck continued in that the subject of Tony Thornley came up quite naturally, initiated by someone else. A loud, bossy woman approached the stall and, without buying a thing, trumpeted at the top of her voice how sorry she was about the 'passing on' of Frances' husband. Frances' body went rigid, she thanked her coldly then half turned away, but this particular woman was determined to press home her sympathy. She asked about the funeral; commiserated with the plight of Tony's son and finally launched into a reminiscence of her own experience of widowhood.

'Of course, it wasn't quite the same,' she admitted. 'My husband died of natural causes, whereas yours – '

'Would you mind moving out of the way?' I interjected. Frances looked pale, as if she were about to faint. 'You're making it impossible for other people to get to the stall.'

'Well!' the woman exclaimed, but she moved to one side.

A gaggle of ten-year-olds pushed through to look at the embroidered pendants.

'If there's anything I can do, just give me a ring, dear,' she offered finally.

Frances made an icy reply. A few minutes passed while she regained her composure and then, in a low voice, Frances thanked me for getting rid of her.

'If you don't mind my saying so, you seem to be managing very well,' I offered quietly.

'Really?' she asked, surprised at my candour. Underneath the mask, she was hungry for feedback. 'One doesn't want to appear too cheerful, or people think one is callous. On the other hand, no one likes a moaner, do they?'

'I think most people understand,' I assured her. 'With one or two notable exceptions.' We shared a conspiratorial smile.

★

When the other stall-holder returned, refreshed by tea and sponge cake, she insisted on sending us both off for a break, even though I had been on duty for less than half an hour. There was a quiet room in the rectory, she said, where the helpers could get a pot of tea and delicious cake provided by the vicar's wife. We made our way through the throng, making polite noises as we shoved people out of the way. I understand that's the way they do things at church fayres, and who am I to question it?

I managed to keep the subject of Tony Thornley open through all the business of pouring tea and cutting cake and sitting on a sunken sofa. We were the only people in an icy sitting room, apart from the vicar and a young man who were huddled together on two chairs at the far end of the room. The vicar offered a vague smile and a greeting, then carried on talking to his companion who was all hunched up – hands clasped between bony knees – and seemed to be going through an intense crisis of faith.

Frances, meanwhile, was being surprisingly forthcoming. She seemed glad of the opportunity to unburden herself to a stranger. 'My husband was not an easy man, but one misses him all the same,' she sighed.

'Of course.' I tried not to shiver – whether from the cold or the thought of missing Tony Thornley, I wasn't sure.

'The next thing is the trial. They say that will be harrowing.'

'It may not be for some time, surely?'

'Perhaps not.'

I stirred my tea and remembered not to lick the spoon. 'Why would a woman like Mona Pearson do such an awful thing?'

'You know her?' Her tone was edgy, suspicious.

'Slightly,' I hedged. 'I know that she and your husband disagreed about school policy, but why on earth would she kill him?'

Frances' eyes darted back and forth and the muscles round her mouth tightened.

'I believe they're fairly excitable.'

'Black women, you mean?' I tried to keep the hostility out of my voice.

'Tony could be quite – ' Frances interrupted herself and switched tracks. 'The woman was deranged,' she said firmly. 'It's the only explanation.'

I let that hang in the air for a decent length of time, before saying, 'Is there anyone else who might have wanted to kill your husband?'

Frances' whole body jerked at the question. 'No one! Why do you ask?'

'I'm just surprised at Mona, that's all,' I soothed. 'She seems such a gentle person.'

'They've all got it in them, however nice they seem.' Frances spoke quietly, almost wearily, as if that were the only lesson life had taught her – you can't trust people, because everyone has within them that vicious kernel of violence which reveals itself given the right circumstances.

I realised that, despite the tight lines on her forehead and around her mouth, she must have been pretty in her youth. Her face was well proportioned – a small, straight nose, with eyes set wide apart and she had a delicate bone structure with well-defined cheekbones. I imagined her in 1950s styles, her slim figure perfectly suited to pencil skirts and cashmere twin sets. I wondered if she had had a job at that time, one that she cared about. She must have been quite a catch for Tony Thornley – a real lady.

'It's funny, but it's only now that he's gone that I see how similar he was to my father.' She said it almost as though she was talking to herself. 'Fine men, of course. But nothing was ever good enough for them. They always wanted something better. One tried so hard to please them, but it was all useless – one would always get the blame in the end.' She became aware of me again. 'Listen to me! What must you think?'

'I think we are often pressurised to sanctify the dead,' I said quickly. 'It's good to remember things as they really were – the bad as well as the good.'

'I agree,' she breathed, relieved not to be censured.

For a woman who had all the trappings of middle-class status, Frances was remarkably lacking in self-confidence. Instantly, I thought of Mona. It was ironic that both their lives should be so blighted by violent men. Scratch the surface of their cool exterior and they were like two little girls, cringing in readiness for the next blow. It made me think of the Thornleys' son, Richard. I wondered how he fitted into all this.

'How is Richard taking it?' I asked.

At the mention of her son, she became agitated, her hands squeezing the material of her skirt. 'He's quite upset.'

I searched her face to find out more. It was such a pallid understatement of how a son might feel about the death of a father — nothing about shock, or disbelief or confused feelings.

'Were they close?'

'Oh, yes.' There was no conviction in the way she said it. She frowned and shook her head. 'Why did I say that?' Her eyes on mine were apologetic, almost pleading. 'There is no need to keep up appearances now, is there? No, Miss Kingsley, Richard was not close to his father, but he is very close to me. We had to stick together, as it were. My husband could be quite . . . irascible. I often had to take Richard's side, and he mine.'

My heart sank. Poor boy. His mother's companion and protector — no wonder he was making such a concerted effort to rebel.

'It must have been difficult for both of you.'

'It was. But Richard sees this as a fresh start, and so do I. Tony wanted him to go into the business, but he's a sensitive boy and he's more interested in the arts. He draws extremely well. He also talks about being an actor.' She sipped her tea and gave a weak smile. 'You met my husband — you can imagine how he felt about his son doing something like that.'

Too right I could. I nodded. We shared another smile and paused to take a sip of tea and a small bite of cake.

I wondered how she would cope alone. She seemed frail and incomplete, as if her husband had stolen the biggest part of her and taken it with him to the grave. I had seen women professionally who, like Frances Thornley, stayed in an abusive marriage because they could not imagine doing anything else. The husband often insisted on them giving up work early in the marriage and did his best to isolate them and keep them dependent on him. As they got older, it became harder and harder to escape.

'Then there are all Tony's affairs to sort out.'

My heart skipped a beat until I realised she was talking finance rather than sleaze.

'It's quite a responsibility, but the bank manager says he'll help me.' She allowed herself a ghost of a smile. 'Apparently, Tony has left us very comfortable, especially as a result of a sale he made a few weeks before he died.'

No mention of Tony's brother, Geoff. I wondered if they were on good terms.

'Will you stay in the area, do you suppose?'

'I expect so. We have a cottage in the country, but I shall probably sell it. Tony liked it, but I hardly ever go.'

A handy little love nest, I dare say.

On the spur of the moment, I decided to tackle Frances again on the subject of Mona. She had been remarkably open about her marriage – if she could just suspend her prejudice about Mona's colour, maybe she could even feel some sort of kinship with her.

'Mrs Thornley,' I began, 'Mona Pearson told me that your husband was very abusive to her that night of the meeting. He threatened her.'

Frances looked at me and started blinking rapidly. I continued, as gently as I could, 'Mona was very angry with Tony. She was also frightened of him – of what he might do to her. When Tony left, she went after him but she can't actually remember – '

Frances' reaction prevented me from finishing the sentence.

A strange sound came from her throat, somewhere between a squeal and a cough. She tightened her grip on her skirt and started to breathe in shallow gasps. Two livid points of red appeared on her cheeks.

Alarmed, I put my hand on her arm. 'Mrs Thornley?'

She pulled away her arm as if I had stung her. When she spoke, it was in a hoarse whisper. 'That – black – woman was f–found with the – knife that killed Tony!' she stuttered. 'Don't – try to tell me – it could have been anyone else because it c–couldn't!'

She was on the verge of hysteria. Part of me understood why she was upset – she was probably still in shock – but part of me thought it was strange that she had such a strong investment in Mona being the perpetrator. If Frances simply needed to see someone caught and punished, Mona was the perfect candidate – an apparently strong, independent, black woman onto whom she could project all her murderous feelings towards her husband. But her reaction could signal something quite different – perhaps her own alibi was not as watertight as she would like it to be.

In an effort to calm her down, I began, 'Mrs Thornley, I only meant – '

Frances leapt up and the crash made even the vicar jump. The teacup smashed into pieces, the saucer split in two and tea spattered the upholstery.

'Oh dear!' she cried, grabbing a handful of tissues and starting to mop ineffectually at the tea.

The vicar loped over and assured us that no harm was done; he would go and fetch a cloth. When he had gone, I got down beside Frances and started picking up the pieces of shattered china, but she shooed me away.

'Just go!' she said between clenched teeth. 'Haven't you said enough?' She was crying, the tears spilling down her cheeks and making shiny rivulets through her face powder.

I apologised for upsetting her.

'I thought you meant well,' she hiccuped, 'but I see you're

just another of those vultures who appears when someone dies. I suppose you're a journalist or something.'

I opened my mouth to deny it, but she cut me short.

'Just go!' she shrieked.

There was nothing I could do. I left the room, feeling guilty and miserable.

On the way home with Clancy, I tried to work out why Frances had suddenly erupted. 'She couldn't bear to even hear me out,' I told Clancy. 'I don't know whether she's upset because she can't stand another uncertainty or because she knows for certain Mona is guilty – '

'If she knew that, she'd have told the police,' reasoned Clancy.

' – or because she knows something the police don't and she doesn't want to rock the boat.'

Clancy looked thoughtful and fiddled with her eyebrow ring, newly installed that week. 'So she thinks black women are excitable,' she said grimly. 'She ain't seen nothing yet.'

Chapter Seven

'Gutted. Totally gutted. It's just – what a fucking bastard!'

I was sitting opposite Pete in a pub in Shepherd's Bush where the smoke was so dense, you wondered if they kept respirators behind the bar for the regulars. Pete was slumped at a table in the corner, cradling his chin with one hand and gripping a pint of lager with the other. He wasn't exactly drunk, but his eyes were dewy and his speech was thick. It was Monday night and I was playing Mother Teresa.

Pete had rung me from the pub to say he was desperate to see me and could I come to the Dog and Duck just off the Green? I was reluctant, but he sounded genuinely upset, and, with the children still away, I couldn't think of a good enough reason not to. All the way down to the Bush, I gave myself a grumpy lecture about how stupid I was to have agreed to meet him. What if he turned out to be a moaning, erratic adolescent who wanted me to bale him out of every crisis? It was unfair – he had never asked for help before – but I knew that the most natural thing in the world was for me to fall into a pattern of mothering him. That would throttle the relationship prematurely, before it died its natural death. So much for my good resolutions. As soon as I set eyes on his angelic face, upturned to greet me but drooping with despondency, my heart contracted and I felt an irresistible urge to clasp him to my bosom. I compromised with a hug and a kiss on the cheek and settled into the chair opposite to listen to his tale of woe.

'Start at the beginning. Why are they making you redundant?'

'They're not – yet. But they will. I wouldn't care, only this is the best job I've had, good bosses, good people and everything. Mandy in accounts reckons – '

'Pete! Just tell me what's happened!'

'Tony fucking Thornley sold the company.'

'He what?'

'Sold it before he died. Sold his bit, anyway. Behind his brother's back.'

'He couldn't do that – could he?'

'Well, he's done it. Sold his half to Bowker-Tindall.'

'Never heard of them.'

'No one's heard of them. But they're the new bosses and they're going to want to change things. Geoff's gutted.'

'I bet he is.'

I tried to get my mind round this new information. Did Frances know about the sale? Was that what she meant by Tony leaving them comfortably off? It certainly explained why Geoff Thornley wasn't rallying round helping the harassed widow. If the sale was legal, Tony had completely disenfranchised his brother, and he wasn't even around to take the consequences.

'So I can kiss me budget goodbye,' moaned Pete. 'Be just like any other job if Geoff's not in charge.' He sighed and gulped down an inch of his pint. 'Probably get laid off anyway.'

'Oh, shut up and let me think!'

His eyebrows curled up in the middle with a such a childish expression of hurt self-pity, I laughed out loud.

'I thought I might get a bit of sympathy.'

'What for?' I scoffed. 'I thought you had a terminal illness, the way you sounded on the phone. Nothing's happened yet. What are you worried about? The new owners may be fine.'

'Is this the way you talk to the patients? No wonder they want to top themselves.'

'They're not patients, they're clients, and, yes, that's the way I talk to them if they're just wallowing in self-pity. If Thornley's is as successful as you say it is, they're hardly likely to want to make radical changes – not immediately, anyway.'

'You know all about it, then?'

I carried on over his complaints, the Kingsley sympathy express. 'You're young and strong and good at your job. If they get rid of you, so what? You'll find something better.'

'Yeah? Well, listen, smart-arse. I was getting on okay before Tony Thornley buggers it up for me. The boss told me I could go on day release come September and I'm due for a pay rise.'

I couldn't resist teasing him. I said in a therapist monotone, 'I can see you're upset, Peter.'

Pete took the bait. 'Upset?' he bawled. 'Too right I'm fucking upset! What sort of comment is that?' He glared at me, nose to nose.

The smokers at the bar looked in our direction and nudged each other.

'It's what I say to clients.'

'What?'

'I can see you're upset.'

'Oh.' He rolled his eyes. 'Great.'

I grinned and tapped his arm. 'Listen, buy me a drink, will you? Gin and tonic. Doesn't it seem odd to you that Thornley sells these shares and then suddenly gets stabbed?'

I saw a light of curiosity switch on beneath his furrowed eyebrows. He really does have wonderful eyes.

'You think it's connected?'

'What do you think?'

He didn't answer. Punching his hands into his pockets of his jacket, he waded through the fog to the bar. When he came back with a gin and tonic and another half-pint for himself, he looked thoughtful, and there was no trace of the hangdog expression.

'Geoff didn't kill his brother, if that's what you're thinking. He was – '

' – on a business trip, I know. Maybe he got someone else to do it.'

'Nah, not Geoffrey. He's not the type.' He sounded certain.

I thanked him for the drink and lifted my lips skywards to receive his kiss. When I managed to extract myself, I asked him, 'Pete – if Tony sells his shares, who benefits?'

Pete sat down and smoothed back his hair. It was more greasy than usual, which made it blue-black, like raven's feathers. 'Tony does – or his wife. It's a lot of money. They say the company's worth a million at least, so Mrs Tony will inherit a cool 500k.'

'Anyone else?'

'The son, eventually.'

'What about Cynthia?'

'Who?'

'The mistress. Cynthia Marsh.'

'Not unless he promised her some of it.'

I took a mouthful of my icy drink and thought about it. I was willing to bet she was involved somewhere. Cynthia fancied herself as the astute businesswoman. I could just imagine her encouraging Tony to sell his brother down the river for the sake of some ready cash. Perhaps he had promised to leave Frances and marry her. Yet the sequence of events was hazy. Did their relationship founder before or after he sold the shares?

'Why did Tony want to sell?'

'The word is that he wanted out so he could concentrate on politics. Geoff can't afford to buy him out, so he asks Tony to wait a year or two. But Tony can't wait. He gets this offer from Bowker-Tindall and takes it.'

'I still don't see how he did it without Geoff's agreement.'

'One of the guys said that things weren't properly sorted out after the old man died, that it was all taken on trust.' Pete shook his head. 'They were brothers – they shouldn't need to get it in writing.'

My mind was racing. I wondered if Robin knew about the shares yet and whether I should call him from the pub to let him know. He might know someone he could call to find out more about how Tony Thornley managed to pull it off without his brother knowing.

'You're getting a buzz out of all this, aren't you? It's not just about getting your friend out of prison.' Pete was leaning back in his chair, observing me through half-closed eyes.

I started to deny it in a roundabout way and then stopped. When you work in the caring professions, especially counselling or psychotherapy, there's a great temptation to use complicated psychological justifications for everything you do. Pete was so direct, so lacking in any game-playing, that I felt obliged to give him a straight answer. I thought for a moment and decided he was right. I was beginning to find Thornley's life of intrigue and subterfuge fascinating. He cheated on his wife, bullied his son, betrayed his brother, sexually harassed his staff and rejected his mistress. On top of all that, he threatened to blackmail Mona if she wouldn't sleep with him. I wondered if his mother was still alive – his parents had a lot to answer for. Was he weaned too early, or what?

I told Pete he was right – I was curious about the murdered man. But I wouldn't feel the need to get involved if it weren't for Mona. Suddenly, I found myself telling him about Frances Thornley, about Clancy and Passover and being Jewish and Mona in prison with rats and cockroaches and the frustration I felt coming up against police officers like DS Gould. It came out all in a jumbled rush, a torrent of disconnected thoughts and unformed feelings. I had no idea why I was telling him – perhaps because I thought he was pissed and wouldn't remember in the morning.

Pete said nothing at all – he just listened and nodded. It

struck me as ironic that he was acting just like a practised therapist – but without the jargon, the fee or the fuss. Once I started, I couldn't stop. I had come to help him, but ended up being the supplicant, confiding in him all my pent-up feelings about Mona and the injustices of the system. For some reason, I felt he understood it. He lifted his hand gently to my face, stroked my cheek with his fingertips and murmured something comforting but meaningless. It was just what I wanted. He seemed to be able to lock straight into the emotion, without using the distorting prism of words.

When I stopped to draw breath, I realised suddenly what it was I found relaxing about him – apart from the fact that he let me chunter on without interrupting. He reacted to everything purely intuitively, without thinking, without analysis. I was used to men who rationalised their emotions, who hid behind words, ducked and weaved their way through arguments, so they lost you in a maelstrom of justifications.

'Have you got your car?' he asked suddenly.

'Yes, why?'

'Drink up, I want to take you somewhere.'

'Where?'

'Surprise.'

'But, Pete it's – ' I glanced at my watch. It was ten thirty, time for an old biddy like me to be in bed. I had to be at the clinic at seven thirty the next morning to see an early client.

'Come on,' said Pete. 'It won't take long.'

I told myself to loosen up, chill out and all those other phrases that make me want to murder people when they use them. I was the one with the car, after all. If it got too late and I wanted to go home, I could just drop him off where he wanted to go and come back.

Pete drained his drink and stood up, steadying himself slightly on the table. I finished my gin and tonic and sucked the lemon briefly before following him to the door. Several people smiled and said goodbye and one man added, somewhat unaccountably, in a voice cracking with emotion,

'Look after her, sonny, she means the world to me,' and Pete answered solemnly, 'I will.'

We got in the car, still laughing, and I followed his directions, winding through side streets in the direction of Hammersmith.

'Where are we going?'

'You'll see.' He tried to nestle close and kiss my neck as I drove, but I pushed him off.

'Settle down. Is it left or right at the lights?'

'Left – no – the other one!'

After several more turns, we finally drew up outside a terraced house in a quiet residential street. The drive seemed to have sobered Pete a little. I was beginning to get slightly nervous about what he was up to.

'What's the big secret? Who are we going to see?'

'I want you to meet someone.'

I followed him reluctantly to the front door. He rang the bell and the door was opened by a stocky, balding man of about thirty-five, wearing jeans and a check shirt. The greeting was less than warm.

'You're late,' he said. 'What happened?'

'I'm sorry. Something came up.' Pete was hangdog again and contrite.

'You were supposed to come for dinner. We were worried about you.'

'I'm really sorry, Joe.'

The man looked significantly at me and gave me a thorough scrutiny. Pete put his arm round me.

'This is Sara. I told you about her.'

We shook hands solemnly. 'And you are – ?'

'Joe Corelli,' he said, slightly puzzled that I didn't know already. 'His brother.'

Shit. Pete must be mad. What a way to meet the family! I turned to Pete with a why-didn't-you-tell-me look; he met my gaze, but simply gave a silly grin in response. I mentally rejected everything I had thought half an hour before about how sensitive he was; in fact, he was a jerk.

Joe suddenly seemed to register that we were still standing on the doorstep. 'What am I thinking of? Come in.'

We stepped into the house, which was larger than it looked from the outside. The hall had a rough wooden floor and was only half decorated, in the way of houses that people have bought as wrecks and haven't quite finished doing up. A child's tricycle was parked by the stairs, alongside two small pairs of shoes. There was a familiar aroma in the air. I tried to identify it as something specific, until I realised that it was simply the smell of a family house in which people cooked with garlic and other proper ingredients.

We followed Joe through into a large kitchen where a dark-haired woman sat at the table. She stood up when we came in and I saw that she was heavily pregnant. She was in her mid-thirties. Her face looked tired and slightly puffy from the pregnancy, but her expression was soft and resigned. 'You're here, then.'

Pete kissed her. 'Sorry, Kate. I got sidetracked.'

'So I see.' She smiled at me, friendly but noncommittal. She put out her hand. 'You must be Sara.'

I was suddenly self-conscious. I may have stopped thinking of Pete as a one-night stand, but I certainly didn't think of us as a couple. I took her hand awkwardly and tried to smile, silently rehearsing the roasting I would give him when we left. What had Pete said about me? All my insecurities about being divorced, being a single mother, having a relationship with a younger man came crowding in. Kate was about my age, sitting in a kitchen similar to mine, calm and round-bellied. Here was I, turning up unannounced with her young brother-in-law, reeking of drink and no doubt looking like I had been dragged through a hedge backwards. My hair was wild and uncombed; I was wearing jeans and a baggy sweater, with my weather-beaten leather bomber jacket – hardly the outfit I would have chosen for the occasion.

I half considered making my excuses and bolting, but Joe

waved us to seats around the table and told us to sit down. The couple offered us drinks and food and, despite my protests, insisted that they would microwave the remains of dinner and throw together a salad.

Suddenly there was lots of bustle and talk. Pete launched into his sob story about Thornley's as the excuse for being late; Joe listened, chipping in with a question every now and again. I asked Kate when her baby was due and commiserated on the boredom of the last month of pregnancy. We chatted about babies and discovered we had both given birth in the same hospital in Hammersmith. I started to feel slightly less self-conscious.

In a matter of minutes, there was a steaming bowl of chicken in a rich tomato sauce on the table, crusty white bread and lettuce tossed in a thick garlic dressing. I had eaten something earlier, but the smell was so delicious, I couldn't resist tasting it. I refused a glass of wine reluctantly, on the grounds that I was driving, so Kate fetched orange juice. Pete wanted a beer, but after some sharp words in Italian from his brother, he accepted a Coke.

There was little resemblance between the two brothers. Pete was tall and slim; Joe short and slightly overweight. He had a round face, with a wide expanse of shining forehead, and was rapidly losing his hair. Only his colouring was the same as Pete's — olive skin, heavy stubble and dark, intelligent eyes. His glasses had thick lenses which magnified his eyes out of proportion to his face. I wondered what he did for a living. They must have a reasonable income; the house was on the borders of Fulham and probably cost quite a bit.

Joe had listened to Pete's story without commenting. Now he lit up a cigarette and blew smoke with a pensive air. 'So the older brother sold the shares,' he mused. 'That's tough on the one that built up the business.' Joe had more of an accent than Pete, as if he felt slightly more at home in Italian.

'Yeah, and I'm looking for another job.'

Joe waved the comment aside. 'Why do you always think the worst? Wait and see.'

Pete grinned and jabbed his thumb in my direction. 'That's what she said.'

Joe gave me a half-smile; Kate shot me a quick scrutinising glance and my paranoia returned. I wondered if they were comparing me with Pete's previous girlfriend – probably a skinny twenty-one-year-old with legs up to her armpits. Did Pete go for that type, I wondered, before his mother complex kicked in?

'He thinks the world owes him a living,' said Joe, smiling.

'What do you do, Sara?' Kate's question was pleasant, not intrusive.

'I'm a counsellor. I listen to people's problems.'

'Doesn't it get you down?'

'No. It's interesting.'

'Have you heard all Pete's problems?' said Joe. 'He could keep you busy all day.'

I caught Pete's eye and smiled. 'What sort of problems?'

'He's a hypochondriac. Surely you've noticed that?'

It was clearly a well-worn theme with Kate and Joe. Pete made a half-hearted protest.

'Headaches . . . ' said Kate.

'Bad back . . . ' said Joe.

'Leg ache . . . '

'Earache . . . '

'Now you mention it . . . ' I said, nodding.

They laughed. Pete took it good-naturedly, but still felt the need to say, 'So I play a lot of sport, whereas you – '

Joe ignored him. 'It's his mother's fault. When he was a kid – '

'Oh no . . . ' Pete rolled his eyes.

' – he just had to sneeze and she would have him tucked up in bed. Never went to school – '

'He's the baby son,' added Kate.

'They're the worst,' I agreed, still smiling.

Pete cut short the banter by saying, 'Joe – can Geoff Thornley get the shares back?' Then he added to me, with more than a hint of pride in his voice, 'Joe teaches business studies at college.'

So that was why we were here.

Joe sipped his wine meditatively. 'I don't know – it all depends on what it says in their memorandum and articles. If nothing was written into them about giving the other brother first refusal, that's pretty bad news for Geoff. But I suppose if Geoff gets a good solicitor onto it they may find a loophole somewhere.'

'Will Geoff stay in charge, do you think?' I asked.

'If you buy 50 per cent of a company like that, the chances are you want the lot. I guess they'll try and persuade Geoff Thornley to sell up.'

'What a shame,' I said.

'What a bastard,' said Pete.

We left just after midnight. When we got in the car, I rounded on Pete.

'What did you do that for?'

He gaped. 'Do what? What did I do?'

'Take me to your brother's without even warning me.'

He frowned, puzzled. 'You liked him, didn't you? It was okay.'

'That's not the point! I hadn't agreed to be introduced to your family – '

'They liked you – '

'Pete! That's not – '

'They liked you, you liked them. And Joe answered your questions about Tony Thornley. What's the problem?'

What's the problem? It was his favourite phrase. I started to explain, to argue, but I got no response, so after a while I gave up, started the engine and headed back the way we had come. Either he was a great actor or he didn't have a clue what I was on about. Being with Pete was like rafting down the Amazon without a map.

Halfway back to Hammersmith, I asked, acidly, 'So – did I pass the test?' I pretended not to care about the answer.

'What test?' Pete rubbed his hands over his face and yawned.

They liked me, I reminded myself. He said they liked me – but anyway, what did I care? I'll probably never see them again.

When I stopped for a red light, just before the multilane maze of Hammersmith Broadway, I stole a look at him. He was asleep, his head leaning uncomfortably against the window. The dim light and shadows inside the car made his face look older and more knowing; behind his head, a red neon sign proclaiming 'Open all nite' lit the sleek ribbed surface of his hair. I reached across and touched his face, running my fingers down from cheek to chin, to feel his smooth skin become rough stubble. He didn't move. His lips were slightly parted, pouting gently with each exhalation. I decided not to wake him. I drove straight to my house and woke him up there, mercilessly, with a sharp dig in the ribs, to which he strongly protested.

I fell asleep with Pete naked beside me, my hand cupping the smooth dome of his shoulder, vaguely unsettled by the idea that Thornley had died leaving his wife substantially richer than she might have been if he had lived.

★ ★ ★

My seven-thirty client was a forty-something man with a mid-life crisis. He was under pressure at work, trying to adapt to massive restructuring, trying to do the jobs of two other people who had left and not been replaced. Every day, he half expected to be called into the bosses' office to be told that he had been made redundant. It was the same story everywhere, of course. Greg and I were looking into the idea of starting a stress management group, meeting in the evenings or early mornings, specifically geared to help people cope with change and insecurity at work.

At half past nine the phone rang and our receptionist Doreen said that DS Gould had arrived. He had called just before Easter and rudely demanded an immediate appointment. Doreen told him I couldn't see him until the Tuesday, so he grudgingly agreed to wait until then. My stomach churned in anticipation of the interview. I always dreaded interviews when I knew there was a danger of losing my temper. Gould had come to badger me about Mona and find out why I had told Barry I thought her defence could be made by a good psychiatric report. I gritted my teeth and asked Doreen to send him up.

Gould sat heavily in the chair and grinned unpleasantly. 'We know all about Pearson being a tart,' he said nastily.

My stomach flipped over. How did he know? The police, I was almost sure, would not be allowed to reinterview a suspect once charged. Someone else knew and had told the police.

'Not impressed, I'm afraid. You really think a jury will fall for that? Just because the victim airs Pearson's dirty linen, she goes mental, knifes him and then claims she can't remember a thing about it. I don't think so.'

He wanted me to rise to the bait, but I said nothing. Either he had questions for me or he didn't. I was not going to get drawn into a pointless discussion of what would or would not hold up in court.

He gave up waiting for a reply and cast a dismissive look around the room. 'So this is where it all happens, eh?' He got up and lay on the couch and clasped his hands up behind his head. 'It was all my mum's fault, Miss . . . '

He laughed at his own humour and looked over to gauge my reaction. I watched him, chin resting on hand, mentally decoding his body language. It struck me how much less threatening he looked when he was supine, suggesting that most of his confidence came from the fact that he was big and muscular and could overpower most people physically if he wanted. His square jaw and jutting chin, set in that macho 'Don't-mess-with-me' expression, looked ridiculous when viewed at a lower angle.

Uncomfortable with my scrutiny, he got up and sat in the

chair again. He fiddled with his nails, hoping to intimidate me by the silence. Little did he know that he was behaving exactly like a first-time client. I could sit quite comfortably in silence for as long as he chose to stay. Finally, he looked up and said, 'Was Mona Pearson one of your patients?'

'No. And we call them clients.'

'Clients.' The tone was sneering. His blue eyes stared out of his face like minerals glinting from a rock.

I locked my eyes on his and tried to stare him down, glad we were on my turf.

'How did you get to know her?'

'The Arkwright governors couldn't make a decision without World War Three breaking out. We were called in to mediate – like the UN.'

'What sort of head calls in a pair of shrinks to sort out the board of governors?'

'What sort of inspector calls in a pair of shrinks to sort out his police officers?'

'A stupid one.'

'I'll tell him you said so. We're running a course on rape counselling on your Division in June.'

Gould blinked. His short-cropped ginger hair bristled, like the fur of a bad-tempered terrier.

'We've done quite a few courses for the police,' I added. '"Tackling Racism" is an interesting one.'

Gould pretended not to have heard. 'Pearson was cracking up even then, wasn't she? She was the one who needed the psychiatrist, not the governors. She wanted Thornley out and she brought you in to help her.'

The adrenalin surged, but I reined it in and decided to try and play him. Why shouldn't I get information from the interview as well as give it? I sat quietly for a moment, and then said, 'I've heard Mona's version of what happened the night Thornley died. Why don't you tell me your version?'

He was slightly taken aback by the question. I saw him weighing it up, examining all the angles and then deciding that he couldn't lose anything by answering. It might even wind me up and get me to tell him something useful. He crossed his legs and scratched fastidiously at a tiny speck that marred the pristine state of his uniform. I couldn't help thinking, as he did so, of how unattractive I've always found red-haired men. I'm not a fussy person in terms of looks, but I am definitely repelled by men with see-through eyelashes.

'You want to know what I think.' It was a statement rather than a question, an introduction to the big man's theory. 'I think it all happened just as Pearson said. But it's funny, isn't it, that she's only just remembered that Thornley threatened to blow the whistle on her? She's got a real problem with her memory, hasn't she?'

'Not as much of a problem as Thornley had with his willy,' I said. Then added, sweetly, 'I hope I'm not being too technical for you. That's speculation, not a professional diagnosis. Do carry on.'

Gould stared at me as if I were an alien – Is it real? Will it bite? Then, clearly deciding I was mad but harmless, he continued, 'Thornley thought it was his duty to tell the other governors about Pearson's conduct. He was concerned, naturally, about the young people of Ealing having an ex-prostitute as a role model.'

'Naturally.'

Gould narrowed his eyes, just about managing to catch my sarcasm. 'So he warns her he's going to tell the other governors. Pearson reacts, yells a bit, pushes him backwards, he bumps up against her desk – '

'So the pathologist's report did show a bruise?'

'Nothing strange about that,' countered Gould. 'She was in a corner. She reacted.' He pressed on, cold and nonchalant. 'Pearson knew Thornley was serious, but she also knew he's a bit of a ladies' man. So she offers to be co-operative in that department if he'll keep quiet.'

I laughed, incredulous. 'You really believe that?'

Gould's eyes were expressionless. 'It isn't what I believe, Miss

Kingsley, it's what the jury will believe. An ex-prostitute? What could be more natural?'

My heart sank. The idea that the credibility of Mona's story would be shot to pieces as soon as the jury heard about her brief career as a prostitute had not even occurred to me. I wondered how I could have been so naïve. Perhaps they could be convinced.

Gould was continuing with the story. 'But Thornley doesn't like coloured girls – '

'Black women – '

' – so he politely declines. Tells her to think about what he's said and get back to him when she's decided whether to resign before he has her kicked out.'

'What then?'

'Pearson grabs the knife – '

'From where?'

'From the drawer.'

'How do you know it was in the drawer?'

'Where else would it be?'

'The drawer was unlocked – anyone could have taken it.' Gould folded his arms, unconvinced.

'All right,' I conceded. 'She takes the knife – '

' – follows Thornley outside and – '

' – stabs him.'

'Not immediately. He was attacked from the front. She talks to him again – makes another offer – and whatever he says in reply, she goes crazy.' Gould slipped into lecture mode. 'This murder, Miss Kingsley, was a frenzied attack. It was committed by a strong, right-handed person who was very, very angry.'

'Right-handed,' I repeated. 'Does that eliminate any of the suspects?'

'The brother,' said Gould, 'and the school secretary.'

That was no help. I had already eliminated both in my mind.

'Pearson had been found out. Killing Thornley was her only option. Dead men can't talk.'

'But someone else already knew about her past!'

The policeman's gaze held steady. 'She wasn't to know that, was she?'

I desperately wanted to know who told Gould about Mona. I doubted that he would tell me if I asked him directly, but there was no harm pretending that I already knew.

'I wonder why she waited until now to tell you about Mona,' I mused, looking off into the middle distance. I didn't know it was a woman, but I had a fifty-fifty chance of being right.

'The deputy head?' Bingo! Gould was stupider than I thought. And Bridget Scudder was more vindictive than I thought. 'She said Thornley told her about it, and she thought it was worth mentioning. We just put two and two together.'

And made six, I added silently.

'So there's no way your friend will get off,' concluded Gould. 'Murder is what we're looking at. No two ways about it. She'll get life.' His smile was broad and smug, and I fantasised about wiping it off his face with a shovel.

'Why did you want to see me?' I demanded. 'Didn't you want to ask any questions?'

Gould kept it casual, as if he didn't much care whether I answered or not. 'DI Evans tells me you've got some idea about getting an expert witness to say she didn't know what she was doing. How does that work then?'

I sighed impatiently. 'I was speculating. Mona doesn't remember anything after Thornley threatened to expose her past life. Given the kind of childhood she had, it's quite possible for a shock like that to jolt her into a mental state in which she had literally no idea what she was doing.'

Gould's smile slid into a sneer. 'Who's this expert witness – you?'

I glanced at my watch. 'Any other questions?'

Gould leaned back in his chair, to prove he would leave only when he was ready.

'What's it called, this state of mind? Legally.'

'Automatism.'

He noted it down. 'Is that like sleep walking?'

'Sort of.'

He grunted and snapped the notebook shut. There was a moment's pause and then he slipped in slyly, 'DI Evans some kind of friend of yours, is he?'

'I know him,' I allowed, keeping my voice even. I was determined not to let him rile me.

'Are you his girlfriend?'

'That's none of your business.'

Gould laughed. 'I was beginning to wonder if he had any. Or if he might be – you know – ' He flipped his hand over, indicating a limp wrist.

I fixed him with a penetrating stare. 'Do you have a problem you wish to discuss? Impotence with women? Worrying feelings about other men?'

Gould's face flushed with a mixture of embarrassment and annoyance. It's a curious thing about homophobes – they're such easy targets. He stood up and straightened his jacket. Thin-lipped, he spat, 'My only problem is people like you, who go round nobbling witnesses so that members of ethnic minorities can, literally, get away with murder.'

I stood up to face him and said quietly, 'One of your problems, Sergeant, is that you think being a member of an ethnic minority is a crime in itself.'

'Isn't it?' he said, lifting his eyebrows. Then, as he made for the door, he raised his hand, flat and placatory, 'A joke, Miss Kingsley. A joke.'

As I opened the door to let him through, I murmured, close to his ear, 'If you ever want to talk about it, Gary . . . '

I've never seen a police officer move away so fast without actually sprinting.

Chapter Eight

Clancy was in high dudgeon, pacing up and down Robin's office.

'It's about *racism*!' she cried, 'Institutionalised, systematised racism! From the wife who thinks black women are excitable to the policeman who sees an innocent black woman as a castrating whore with a knife – '

Robin was on his feet too, his back to the room, hands clutching the radiator, staring out of the window.

'It's about *Mona*,' he added hotly. 'A woman damaged in childhood, with underlying low self-esteem, who is so used to injustice she doesn't believe that she deserves any better.'

I was leaning back on the swivel chair, feet on the coffee table, wishing they would cut the speeches and sit down. They had been ranting for the last ten minutes, venting their wrath, neither listening to the other.

'You're both wrong,' I announced, slapping the arm of the chair so hard that they both jumped. But Robin did not turn round and Clancy continued to pace. 'It's about evidence,' I said. 'Rhetoric won't help Mona. A man died and somebody

139

killed him. Maybe it was Mona, maybe it wasn't.'

Robin bit his nail and looked pensive. Clancy frowned and nodded.

'Look, I know you're both upset,' I said with uncharacteristic reasonableness. 'I'm upset too. But we won't get anywhere berating the system. Sit down and let's think about what we've got.'

They both sat down. It was a short-lived triumph.

'She needs a good psychiatrist,' persisted Robin, chopping the air with his hand, 'articulate and experienced – someone who'll come across well in court.' He looked at Clancy and adjusted his glasses.

'If you're thinking about Kershaw, forget it!' snapped Clancy. 'He may have been to Eton, but he has the IQ of Conan the Barbarian and about as much sensitivity.'

Robin sighed. 'Clancy, you are so – '

'Robin!' I interjected. I knew that if we got on to the relative merits of London psychiatrists, we could be sitting here until Mona's trial.

' – narrow minded,' finished Robin. I swear he jutted out his chin as he said it. 'Kershaw is a fine doctor. You only object to him because you think he's too Freudian.'

Clancy appealed to me. 'Can I be the only one who thinks he's too Freudian? The only shrink left in the world who still believes in *penis envy*?'

'You are taking his remarks out of context. The paper you are referring to said that – '

'Have you two finished?' I interrupted.

' – said that we were all too willing to throw out the concept of penis envy on the grounds of political correctness.'

One of Robin's less endearing traits is that on just one or two subjects, he is as stubborn as a stalled car on a frosty morning. Psychoanalytic theories are one of them.

'Evidence!' I repeated. 'Did someone take the knife from Mona's office? The drawer was unlocked between four o'clock and eleven o'clock that evening. Was anyone seen going into

Mona's office? Maybe we should ask again at the school.'

It was like tossing stones into a pond. A gentle plop, one ripple and it was gone.

'Maybe someone set Mona up,' mused Clancy, unable to stick to the point for even five seconds.

'Because they hate Mona,' insisted Robin.

'Because they hate black women,' countered Clancy.

'What about Cynthia Marsh?' I persisted. 'I'd like to know when her relationship with Thornley ended, and when the shares were sold. See if there's a connection between the two.'

'You don't seem to understand the effect that Mona's childhood has had on her,' said Robin to Clancy, 'on her self-esteem, her sense of her own worth – '

'And you don't understand how much of that is part of the experience of all black women!'

I gave up – I know when I'm beaten. I flung my feet off the coffee table and stood up. 'When you two have finished deconstructing Mona, let me know.'

I left the room, shutting the door behind me. They would probably carry on until Doreen rang upstairs to say that a waiting client was threatening mass murder in reception.

Back in my office, I found it hard to concentrate. My conversation with Gould the day before was still fresh in my mind. Robin and Clancy were definitely missing the point. Never mind the vagaries of the system, or the psychological implications of Mona's childhood – her chances of getting a fair trial were slipping away with every piece of information that came to light. Her memory lapse was a typical example of truth being stranger than fiction. We believed her, because we knew it could happen, but would anyone else? In my experience, psychologists are given credence only when they confirm the common-sense view of events. Standing over a dead body with a knife, unable to remember what happened five minutes before, does not come into that category. Her background made the idea of amnesia through trauma even less credible. An ex-prostitute traumatised by a man making a pass at her? Tell us another one. Then there was the teacher factor. A teacher, especially a head teacher, was supposed to be a moral guide, a role model for the whole community. There would be little sympathy for a teacher who did not have a 'blameless' past. However much one might argue that Mona's life experience made her even more suited to the position she held, the conservative factions would disagree. Mona Pearson hoodwinked the respectable Arkwright governors in order to further her own career, so she was dishonest as well as immoral. The more I thought about it, the more I felt that nothing could save Mona now except incontrovertible evidence which not only exonerated her but also exposed the true murderer. It was depressing. All we could do was to continue to make a noise, to show publicly that we at least were prepared to keep an open mind. The only thing I could hold on to was the belief that Mona was telling the truth in one respect – she herself had no idea whether she was innocent or guilty.

Robin and I had arranged to meet Rajesh Patel for lunch at a pasta place in Ealing, not far from the Town Hall. We wanted the accountant to tell us exactly what happened at the meeting the night Thornley was killed. His forte was watching and observing – he didn't miss a thing. Robin had set up the appointment because I felt that he, as a man, stood more chance of getting Rajesh to see us. We had both noticed that at the governors' meeting he had addressed his remarks, such as they were, to Robin. Although his office was just behind the Broadway, the accountant said he preferred to meet at a restaurant. Robin reported that he was polite but guarded, and that he had made it clear he could spend no more than an hour with us.

He arrived bang on twelve thirty, meticulously dressed in a charcoal suit, a dazzlingly white shirt and an olive-green tie. Rajesh Patel was a measured, careful man whose every gesture seemed to be planned in advance. He shook both our hands, sat in the empty chair nearest the door and took immediate control of the small talk. It was appalling about Thornley's murder; sad for the widow and the son; scandalous that Mona Pearson had been arrested. Little did we know, when we all met not two months ago, that one of the group would be in prison and another one dead.

The patter was definite, unhurried and seemed almost rehearsed. He spoke precisely and without emotion, articulating each word, with the quiet confidence of a person who was used to not being interrupted. It was hard to guess how old he was. He had a long face with high cheekbones and eyes like currants, dominated by eyebrows which formed a single straight line across his forehead. His skin was pale brown and smooth, quite young-looking. Only his hands gave his age away, prominent veins criss-crossing the wrinkled skin. He was probably in his late forties.

At his suggestion, we got the business of ordering the food out of the way before getting on to what he described as 'the matter in hand'. Robin and I went for the maximum stodge option – pasta with a rich creamy sauce. Patel ordered a chicken salad, with hardly a glance at the menu, as if the whole idea of food was slightly contemptible.

'I was not Tony's accountant,' Rajesh was saying, in answer to Robin's question, 'though I advised him occasionally on financial matters. I knew him socially and through being a governor of Arkwright.' He paused and cocked his head to one side. 'Small businessmen have much in common.'

I wondered how Rajesh felt about Tony's racism and whether it had extended to affluent Asian businessmen.

'Did you know that Tony sold his share of Thornley's before he died?' asked Robin.

'Tony made no secret of the fact that he wanted to withdraw from Thornley Veneers,' said Patel. 'He asked his brother to buy him out, but Geoff was not able to raise the finance. Is it the sale of the shares that interests you? I thought you said on the telephone that you were working for Mona Pearson.'

'Not working for her exactly,' explained Robin. 'We believe the police may have been over-hasty in charging her with Thornley's murder. Do you mind if we ask you a few questions?'

'Not at all.'

Patel's body language did not quite match his cool co-operation. His eyes flicking back and forth from Robin's face to mine told me that he did not trust us one iota. He pressed his hands together, resting his elbows on the table, and drew his fingers to his lips. 'Ask away,' said the gesture, 'but don't expect a direct answer.' Did he have something specific to hide or was this the natural reticence of a man well practised in the art of the deal?

Robin's interrogation technique was gentle and respectful. He started with general questions about being a governor – how much time it took, whether the staff understood, and were responsive to, the financial imperatives of local management. Rajesh spoke dispassionately but approvingly of Mona's competence as a manager of funds, but he would not commit himself on any of the policy issues.

'I see my role as a purely financial one,' he said. 'I leave educational issues to the experts.'

If I had been asking the questions, I would not have been able to resist asking if Rajesh considered Tony Thornley an educational expert, but Robin let it go. He was trying to get Rajesh talking freely, building up a rapport so that he could ask him about Thornley.

The food arrived and we all tucked in. I was able to give full attention to the pasta, since Robin was doing most of the talking and Rajesh was acting as if I wasn't there. Rajesh picked at his food and addressed all his remarks to Robin and Robin alone; I marvelled at the man's restraint – and at his rudeness.

When Robin finally moved the conversation on to Thornley, Patel's assessment was short and to the point. 'Tony Thornley was not a popular man,' he announced, matter of factly.

This was a slight understatement – Tony Thornley was almost public enemy number one in Ealing.

'Did you trust him?' asked Robin. Rajesh inclined his head and looked amused. 'I'm a businessman, Mr Howard. I trust no one.' He picked a sliver of chicken from his salad, placed it carefully on a corner of bread and lifted it delicately to his mouth.

'Selling the shares was not a very honourable thing to do, was it?' Robin's tone was casual, but I could see he was sharpening up, preparing to show his mettle.

'Honourable? Perhaps you are not very used to the ways of business, Mr Howard. These days, it is the survival of the fittest.'

'Mrs Thornley must be delighted about the shares.'

Heavy eyelids now hooded the flicking eyes. He was wondering what Robin was getting at. I had to admit, so was I. 'Mrs Thornley is a very lucky woman,' confirmed Patel. There was an awkward silence. Rajesh Patel picked at another piece of chicken and glanced at his watch.

Robin caught the gesture and knew he had to move on. 'Perhaps we could ask you about the night Tony Thornley died. We are quite confused about what happened at the governors' meeting.'

'It was quite a short meeting,' said Rajesh.

'What time did it start?'

'I arrived at seven thirty.'

'And the others?'

'They came at about the same time – perhaps Mrs Marsh – Cynthia – was a little earlier. Bridget Scudder and Mona, of course, were already there. And the school secretary.'

'Where was the meeting?'

'It's always in staff room – just as it was the night you attended. Mona chaired it. Wait – ' Rajesh reached under the table for his briefcase and drew out a sheet of paper. 'I thought you might be interested in this, so I brought the minutes.' How efficient. How helpful. He scanned them. 'That's right. Apologies from Brian – his wife had gone into labour – and a parent–governor who never turns up. We started with some business about the homework policy – Mona gave out copies for us to take away – but the main topic of discussion was the two children Mona had admitted into the school. Problem children.'

'That's a particular interest of Bridget's, isn't it?' I prompted.

He answered to Robin, 'It is very expensive for the school.'

Robin said shortly, 'We are interested primarily in the way people spoke to each other rather than the issues. Who was the argument between?'

'There was no argument. It was a discussion.'

'A heated discussion.'

Rajesh shrugged. 'Bridget wanted to increase Section 11 support, but Tony pointed out that the budget could not accommodate such a decision without something else being cut.'

'Can you remember what was said?'

'It became personal.' Rajesh said it like a sardonic robot, as if he were above such things. 'Bridget said that she could not understand Tony's position on this, in view of the fact that his own son was a problem child.'

Robin and I made eye contact briefly.

'She said that?' Robin asked Rajesh.

'Something like that. His son is quite difficult, I believe.'

Robin caught my eye again. However Bridget phrased it, that was a hell of an incendiary remark to make to a man like Tony Thornley.

'Does Richard have a statement of special need?' I asked.

'No,' replied Rajesh, to Robin.

I was beginning to feel like a talking ghost.

Robin asked, 'How did Tony respond?'

'He said that his son did not cost the school a single extra penny. He told Bridget that he did not like her attitude. He made other remarks which were probably misjudged.'

'Personal remarks?' prompted Robin.

Rajesh did not answer at once; he believed in making

people wait. He took a sip of water and then said, 'Tony said that Bridget's narrow focus and her inability to manage a budget were the main reasons why she did not get the headship of Arkwright High. And why she would never get a headship.'

'Good God!' I was beginning to feel a deep sense of gratitude that we had not been at the meeting.

'Bridget made some more comments about Tony's son – some nonsense about Tony ruining his life by wanting him to go into the business with his uncle, and said that the boy had an inferiority complex.'

'What did Tony say?'

'He laughed. Asked her how she could possibly claim to understand children when she had none herself. Then Mona put a stop to it and said that we should vote. The decision went against Bridget and she walked out.'

'Did she say anything else before she went?'

'Only to Tony, I think. A parting shot – that he would regret it, or some such thing.'

'Quite a meeting!'

'Most unpleasant. And unnecessary. Anyone could see that savings had to be made in other areas if extra Section 11 staff were brought in.'

I was tempted to point out that there seemed to be rather more to the dispute than balancing the books, but I held my tongue.

Robin moved on to ask about Cynthia. 'Did she agree with Tony?'

'Of course.'

'Of course?'

'They agreed on most things.'

'We know she was his lover,' I put in.

Rajesh raised his single wall of eyebrow, just enough to remove the shadow off his eyes. 'Ex-lover,' he corrected, unsmilingly. He still did not look at me.

'Have you any idea why they split up?' asked Robin.

Rajesh turned away, searching for the waitress. 'Tony and I did not discuss those things. We talked only about financial matters.'

'Was it something to do with the shares?' I asked.

Rajesh bristled at the question, but probably only because it came from me rather than Robin. He signalled to the waitress to bring the bill. 'I must be getting back to the office now.'

'It could be important.' Robin's tone suddenly became authoritative. 'Do you happen to know?'

Rajesh paused and frowned. 'I believe Tony Thornley considered many investment opportunities for his capital, including Mrs Marsh's children's clothing business. In the end, he decided not to give Mrs Marsh the money. This could have been a factor in ending their relationship. I have no idea.'

I smothered a smile. 'It's a reasonable assumption. Did you advise Tony not to invest?'

'I did.'

'Why?'

He looked at me for the first time, eyebrows raised, as if the question hardly needed asking. 'Because the profit margins were not there,' he replied.

I recalled Cynthia's pride as she talked, about her business – it obviously meant a lot to her. Clearly, this had been Thornley's way of showing her it was over. What a cruel way to end a relationship.

The bill arrived and we paid it – Robin and I had agreed beforehand to split the cost of the lunch. Patel made only token protestations. He thanked Robin for the meal, wished us luck, shook both our hands and left. Only after he had disappeared into the lunchtime throng did I realise that we had hardly mentioned Mona, and that Rajesh had shown very little curiosity about what we were doing. Perhaps he already knew; perhaps he didn't want to know. It was a strangely unsatisfactory interview. I felt we had been manipulated, but I wasn't sure in what way. Rajesh had told us exactly what he wanted us to know, but he had betrayed no feelings on the matter of

Thornley's murder – no speculation, no emotion. A friend and business associate had been violently killed. Why was he not more perturbed? Why didn't he have questions about Mona's reasons for turning violent?

We lingered over our coffee for a little while longer.

'I went to see Mona yesterday.' There was a catch in Robin's voice as he said it.

'She agreed to see you?'

'She's desperate for visitors.'

I felt a stab of guilt that almost two weeks had passed since my last visit. 'How was she?'

Robin grimaced and shook his head. I thought I detected his brown eyes darkening with tears. I put my hand on his, in sympathy. It must be hard for him. It was obvious that he had a very deep regard for Mona. I just hoped he was being realistic about it and not mythologising a relationship because it was doomed. He squeezed my hand in return and then withdrew, assuming his professional persona again.

'She's depressed. Part of her probably believed that it was all a bad dream and that she would be released. Now it's dawning on her that she could be in prison for a long time – for years rather than days or weeks.'

'She has to try and take a day at a time.'

'That's what I said to her.' Then a little too casually, he added, 'I'm putting up the bail – if we can get it. I spoke to her solicitor on the phone and she seems to think there's a chance.'

My heart sank. He was getting into this far too deeply. 'It'll be a huge amount of money.'

'I know.'

Robin's family were wealthy, but I couldn't believe they would be delighted to put up bail for a woman charged with murder.

'It's all right, Sara. I know what I'm doing.'

'I hope so,' I said. But the voice of doubt came knocking again on a door at the back of my mind. What if Mona had killed Tony Thornley? How would Robin feel then? I pushed

the thought back as quickly as it had come. The only
important thing was to get at the truth, whether it meant
disillusionment for Robin or not.

Chapter Nine

Bridget Scudder was giving me a hard time in her office at the school.

'Ms Kingsley, we are using the Easter holidays as an opportunity to get the school back to normal. I do not want my staff upset by more probing and questioning.'

I was trying not to imagine myself in front of the headmistress at my old school, but sitting in front of Bridget's desk on a school chair brought out the rebel in me. I could feel myself slouching down in the chair and I had an overwhelming desire to chew gum noisily and hum under my breath – a simple technique which could, over time, incite my old head teacher to a quivering rage.

Already Mona's office was changed beyond recognition. The African batik was gone and in its place was a set of posters depicting smiling children with learning difficulties, with two lines of poetry underneath each one. There was something manipulative and chastising about the pictures: 'I'm on the moral high ground, where does that leave you?' The rest of the room was a mess, with files stacked up on the floor and columns of books against the walls.

'I am acting head,' continued Bridget, as if to underline her right to be behind Mona's desk. 'It is my job to steer the school back on course and to put this terrible thing behind us as quickly as possible. I do not think it will help to have you opening old wounds.'

How could the wounds be old? It was only three weeks since the murder.

I drew up one leg and hugged my knee, resting my trainer-clad foot on the crossbar of the chair. Bridget's eyes flicked over me, distracted and annoyed by the gesture. We both noticed, at exactly the same time, a gaping hole in the knee of my jeans.

Not wanting to incense her, I slid my leg down again and said, 'I'm afraid people are speculating, even if they don't do it in front of you.'

'What do you mean?'

'Mona was a popular head – '

'It's not a question of – '

I raised my hand, asking her to let me finish. 'The staff, the parents, the pupils all looked up to her. They must be feeling let down, confused. People think they know someone and then that person is accused of something as terrible as taking another person's life. Staff, students, parents – they're all wondering whether or not Mona did it, and, if she did it, *why* she did it.'

Bridget stared blankly, as if it had simply not occurred to her to look at it this way.

'People need to go over things, talk about them, air their feelings. I'm not here to suggest group counselling – though I think that would be a good idea – I'm just saying that what I'm asking is unlikely to do any harm. Quite the reverse.'

Bridget pursed her lips. I felt her thawing slightly, though she was not yet convinced. 'I think,' she said loftily, 'you have an over-romanticised view of our former head. She had many more flaws than people realised.'

I saw my chance and took it. 'Like being an ex-prostitute,' I suggested flatly.

The remark registered on Bridget's face like an electric shock. She opened her mouth to speak and then closed it again. Whatever she was expecting from our conversation, it wasn't this.

'I had no idea the police were so loose-tongued,' she gasped.

'Did you think they'd keep it to themselves?'

Shock turned to outrage. She began to bluster. 'It was a vital piece of information – a murder had been committed – I had to tell them!'

'Just like you had to tell Tony Thornley?' I retorted.

Her anger was quick and formidable. 'I was simply doing my duty!' she spluttered, leaning forward. Her face flushed red. 'What was I supposed to do?'

'Why did you have to do anything?'

Her colour went one shade deeper. 'The head of a school like this has to be exemplary in her behaviour.'

'Mona was.'

'She was not! She lied about her past life in order to advance her career. She acted as if butter wouldn't melt in her mouth. When I think about her assemblies!' Bridget mimicked Mona's voice. "You have to respect yourself, girls and boys." "Self-respect", "truth", "honesty". Such hypocrisy!'

For some reason, I had the urge to quote the New Testament at her – 'Let he who is without sin among you cast the first stone.' Happily for my Jewish credibility, I resisted. Instead, I demanded, 'What were you hoping to achieve by telling Thornley? To have Mona fired so that you could take her place? Or did you know that Thornley would use it to try and blackmail her?'

It hit the mark and I instantly regretted it. Bridget sat back, breathing deeply, her mighty chest heaving up and down. Her skin was mottled with plum-coloured patches.

'I'm sorry. I shouldn't have said that.'

She continued to breathe deeply.

'Bridget – are you okay?'

She pressed her lips together as if trying to hold herself in, but the emotion overtook her and suddenly her face crumpled. She buried her face in her hands and started to sob. I pulled my chair forward and reached across the desk.

'Bridget?'

She looked up. There was thin line of blue down her left cheek where her eyeshadow had run. I was distracted by it, because I had not noticed that she had any make-up on. She sniffed and hiccuped, trying to get herself under control. I spotted a box of tissues and passed it over to her. She nodded mutely, extracted one and firmly wiped away the smudges.

Finally, she blurted out, 'Fourteen years I've been in this job. Fourteen years supporting children who have been rejected by everyone else. I − I don't ask for thanks − the job is thanks in itself. But then to have a man like Tony Thornley throw it all away − it's too much!'

She blew her nose loudly. Then she took a deep breath and exhaled slowly. Her cheeks were returning to their normal colour. 'You know what he really wanted to do, don't you? He wanted to make Arkwright selective. To make us turn away every child who wasn't English-speaking, well behaved and academic. And Mona was just sitting by and letting it happen.' She shook her head. 'But I was wrong to tell Tony − to tell anyone − about Mona.'

She looked up at me and her eyes were almost pleading. 'I didn't realise . . . She seemed so . . . strong, yet she wouldn't stand up to Tony. I thought if he got tougher with her, she'd get tougher with him.'

I nodded. She fell silent and stared at the floor beside her chair. I asked again, more gently this time, 'Bridget, what did you hope to achieve?'

She sighed. 'Can't you guess? Tony got to me too, but he didn't have enough mud to make it stick. It was a few months ago, when I was kicking up a stink about the referendum for opting out. Tony hinted that if I didn't go along with it, he would start a few rumours. You can imagine the kind of thing. He said: 'You're not married, are you? I believe you have a friend in Herefordshire you go on holiday with. I could make things very difficult for you.' I thought Mona had been complaining about me, so in the heat of the moment I said, "Well, what about Mona? Her past isn't exactly blameless, is it?"' Bridget shrugged. 'That's how it happened.'

It all made a horrible kind of sense. Tony attacks, so Bridget counter-attacks, using Mona as ammunition.

'I felt dreadful about it. I knew I should confess to Mona, but when Tony seemed to keep it to himself I thought, "No harm done, I'll keep it to myself."'

Presumably, Tony had been saving the information until he could decide what he most wanted in return. Which turned out to be a few sexual favours from Mona. I looked at Bridget's puffy, unlovely face and felt a stab of sympathy for her.

Bridget frowned, misinterpreting my silent pity as an accusation. She stuck out her chin. 'What's done is done. It can't bring back Tony and it can't get Mona out of prison.'

She was right about Tony but I wasn't so sure about Mona.

Just out of curiosity, I asked, 'How did you find out about Mona?'

'Purely by chance. I met someone at a party who knew a Mona Pearson years ago in Notting Hill – a real tearaway. She said she often wondered what had happened to her. I was sure we were talking about two different people. But then I got to thinking how strange it was that Mona never mentioned her family and hardly talked about her past at all.' Bridget's eyes disengaged from mine and slid away. 'This Mona Pearson had been in care at a children's home in Southwark, so I got a friend of mine who works in residential care to look up her name in the records. Sure enough, it was Mona – my friend saw her photo. There were two sisters, twins, who were adopted. Mona's father wasn't a lecturer, he worked on the buses.'

The story was doubly sad – sad that Mona felt the need to hide her past and sad that Bridget felt compelled to uncover it.

I didn't see any mileage in continuing the conversation. All I wanted was to get Bridget to let me talk to the staff, to see if anyone knew who had been in and out of Mona's office the afternoon Thornley died. I had just one more question.

'Bridget, did Mona give any indication during the governors' meeting that she was reaching the end of her tether with Thornley?'

Bridget seemed deflated now. 'It was hard to tell,' she replied, shaking her head. 'She was a very hidden person. You never knew what she was thinking.'

I noticed that Bridget spoke of Mona in the past tense.

'I don't think she seemed any more annoyed with him than usual.'

The telephone rang and Bridget answered it.

'Tell him I'll be two minutes,' she said, giving me a meaningful glance.

Taking the hint, I stood up. 'Please may I have a few minutes with the staff?' I pleaded. 'I just want to try and jog their memories, to make sure the police haven't missed something that might be important.'

Bridget sighed. 'I suppose so. But please keep it factual. I don't want to stir up any more anxiety than is already there.'

Relieved, I thanked her and promised to be circumspect.

As she saw me out she said, 'I do feel sorry for Mona, you know. But she brought it upon herself.'

I shook my head. That was a matter of opinion.

Maggie was waiting for me in the corridor. She drew me to one side and said in a low voice, 'I went to see Mona on Monday.'

'Great!' Mona was having a good week for visitors.

'She looks awful!' whispered Maggie.

I nodded, knowing what she meant. Mona's appearance was a shock when you were used to seeing her so confident and well groomed.

'She's lost weight and she looks, I don't know, *smaller*. I tried

156

not to mention IT – you know, anything that might upset her – but she seemed keen to talk about it. She says now that she thinks she must have done it. She says she must have had a brainstorm or something and killed him without realising it.'

Poor Mona. She had every second of every hour to analyse and reanalyse what happened, and to try and retrieve those crucial memories.

'Has she remembered anything else?'

Maggie shook her head. 'Neither of us locked that drawer, though. We're sure about that.'

We started walking slowly towards the staff room.

'She kept on about Mr Thornley leaving her office and how she went after him. She went over and over it. To be honest, she was a bit strange. I wondered if she was – you know – cracking up.'

'She's under a huge amount of stress and she probably has very few people to talk to. I'm sure she appreciated your visit.'

Maggie smiled and said simply, 'She did seem pleased to see me.' She quickened her step but then, after a few moments, her pace slowed again. 'She seems to be trying to remember exactly what she did. She kept saying "I went out of my office, down the corridor, past the library, turned right . . . "'

That seemed to ring a bell. 'The library? I thought Thornley was found outside the back entrance – '

'He was, but she didn't know which door he was heading for, so she went the wrong way at first. When she didn't find him, she came back to her office and went the other way. That's the sort of thing she's worrying about – going over and over it.'

I wondered how long Mona waited before going after Thornley. However long it was, that detour added several seconds to it.

'I must go and see her again,' I murmured more to myself than to Maggie. I dreaded the prospect of facing the prison again, with its smell of neglect and the sight of so many despairing women. 'All the more reason for doing it!' shrieked my Jewish conscience.

'I was glad I went – it felt like the right thing to do,' finished Maggie, hammering the final nail into my coffin of guilt.

Considering it was still Easter holidays, there were quite a few people around. Maggie came with me and introduced me to some of the staff. Everyone I spoke to was still in shock about Thornley's death and Mona's arrest.

'I still can't believe it.'

'She seemed such a gentle person.'

'Whatever she's done, we'll miss her.'

Tony's son came in for a lot of sympathy too.

'Poor kid. He always looks so lost.'

I spread the word around that some of us at the clinic were in contact with Mona and that we wanted to make sure the police had looked at the facts from every possible angle. Most people wanted to help, although they said so in hushed voices, with half a glance over their shoulder to make sure they were not being overheard. Bridget had clearly put the fear of God into them. I asked everyone the same thing. Had they seen anything unusual that afternoon – someone hanging around Mona's office who shouldn't have been there, for example? Had they seen any of the governors arriving for the meeting? I emphasised that the slightest detail could be important. No one came up with anything, but they all promised to think about it. Most sent their good wishes to Mona and hoped that she would be proved innocent. But not even the most optimistic mentioned her coming back.

Before I left, I sought out the caretaker, Mr Breeley. He was a tall man with a marked stoop and a large beer gut. I remembered him from my very first visit, at the governors' meeting, when he had given me a surly lecture about obstructing a fire exit with my car. He was leaning on the doorjamb of the science building, staring into space. His lank hair was combed across his head to hide his receding hairline and his face was an archetype of petty officialdom – gloomy and doom-ridden, but with a quick eye that misses nothing. You knew, somehow, that he would notice every breach of every petty rule, but if you needed a shelf putting up he would be nowhere to be found. I went up to him and introduced myself. I told him that I had just come from the staff room, where I had been asking the teachers about what they remembered of the day the chair of governors was killed, and I wondered if I could ask him a few questions too. Rather than brush me off with a monosyllabic reply, as I had feared he might, he seemed pleased to be asked. Maybe everyone else had heard his story so many times, he had no one left to tell.

'Here? Or in my office?'

'Here is fine.'

We moved outside and sat on a wooden bench, side by side. It was a typical spring day, warm when the sun struggled through but cooled by a sharp, gusty breeze. Breeley had a very didactic delivery – he was one of those people who check continuously that you are listening by saying 'Yes?' interrogatively, meaning, 'Got that?' It's a habit I find excessively irritating. Perhaps it came from being around so many teachers.

'It was getting late. Ten past ten, because I was watching the news and they were just getting on to the sport. Yes?'

'Yes.'

'I come out of me house, to see if they've finished the meeting so I can lock up. The wife was already in bed – she goes early – and I come in the front entrance thinking to go to the staff room and see if they're still at it. All right?'

'Clear so far.'

'Staff-room door is open – there's no one there. So I come back round to see if Miss Pearson is in her office. She always checks with me before she goes – says something like, "They've all gone, Mick you can lock up." Has a quick word and thanks me. Always thanks me, right?'

I nodded, wondering if I'd made a mistake initiating this conversation. It could take some time and I had to be back at the clinic by noon.

'But on the way, I spot her at the end of the corridor going towards the north entrance. That's G2 – yes?'

'Sorry?'

'G2 – the corridor. G2.'

'Ah, right.'

'So I cut across to F3, thinking, "That's funny, that's not like her going off without telling me they're all off the premises and thanking me for working late." And I start thinking about whether she's got it in for me over something – not that she's the sort, but there was a bit of unpleasantness a few weeks ago when I went down the pub on a Friday lunchtime – '

'Mr Breeley?'

'What?'

'I'm losing the thread. You saw Mona going towards the back entrance, so you cut across the middle of the school to catch her before she left.'

He was dogged, determined not to be rushed. 'As I said, I go through F3 and come out near the door, and that's when I hear the groans. All right?'

'Groans?'

'It must've been loud, because I could hear it inside the door.' He thought for a moment and then threw back his head. 'Ooooooaghhh! Aaaaarggggg! That sort of thing. See?'

'Yes.' I wished I hadn't asked. The moaning demonstration had undone two buttons on his shirt, revealing a hummock of white flab. 'What happened next?'

'I rush out. The sound's coming from the refuse area, to the left of the door. D'you want to see it?' He made as if to get up, but I put out a restraining hand.

'Not just yet. Maybe afterwards. What then?'

He leaned forward, gesturing with his hands. 'I go over, wondering what the blip! I'm going to find, and the first thing I see is him, Mr Thornley, propped up against a dustbin clutching his middle. It's a bit on the dark side out there – I keep meaning to fix the lights, but I've got a list of jobs as long as my arm. But there he was – see? – sitting there, moaning. Then

I look up, and who should be standing right outside the door but Miss Pearson. Such a strange look in her eyes too, all glassy. She's standing there with a knife in her hands, blood all over it. I go, 'What the hell – !' Can't take it in at first. It's not a sight I'd like to see again, I can tell you.'

He had enjoyed telling the story at the outset, but I could see that he was beginning to relive the shock. A double shock, of seeing a man badly injured and a woman, his boss, as the murderer.

'There must have been a lot of blood.'

'I'll say! It was like on the telly, one of those cop shows – '

'Were Mona's clothes soaked through?'

'Not that I could see. But her hands – '

'Her clothes were not soaked with blood?'

'Like I said, it was just on her hands – '

'And on the knife.'

'That's right. Bloody great thing – pardon my French – and she was just standing there, holding it.'

'Were you scared?'

'Of her? Nah. She was out of it. You know how people get when they're in shock? Like a zombie. If you went like that – ' he gave my shoulder a light shove with his finger – 'she would have gone over backwards.'

I conjured up the scene in my mind's eye. Mona and the caretaker staring at each other, paralysed for a moment – and between them a man dying noisily.

'What did you do?' I asked.

'I could see he was in a bad way – his clothes were wet through with the blood and it was spurting, like, out of him. I reckoned he was a goner, even then. I shouted at Miss Pearson to go and get help, but she didn't move – she didn't seem to hear me – so I put my jacket over him and belted back to the office to ring for an ambulance. Never run so fast in me life.'

'How long did it take for the police to arrive?'

'Five minutes, I suppose. I didn't know whether to wait for them or go back to Mr Thornley. I go back just to check on him, but by then he's a goner. Miss Pearson is kneeling beside him, holding his head. She's crying by now, she knows what she's done.'

'You must have felt very distressed.'

He shook his head and blew the air out of his cheeks – momentarily lost for words.

'What did Mona say to you?'

Breeley looked shifty, as if this was uncomfortable ground. 'You couldn't make out much.'

I wondered what he had told the police.

'Did she actually admit to stabbing him?'

'Oh, yeah.' He didn't sound very convincing.

'I know it's hard to remember . . .'

He rose to the challenge, as I hoped he would.

'Let's see. "Don't die, don't die, don't die" – she said that a few times. Yes? She must have regretted offing him as soon as she done it. Then she kept on about how she *shouldn't* have done it – '

'What exactly – '

'You want the exact words? Gor, you are a stickler. All right. "I knew it was wrong. I shouldn't of done it." I told her, "You should have thought of that before you stabbed him, Miss Pearson. He's dead now."'

Good old Mr Breeley. A real rock in a crisis. 'What did she say?'

'It didn't seem to register. She was hysterical by then.'

She said she shouldn't have done it. But did she mean she shouldn't have killed Tony Thornley or something else – like lying about her childhood?

A gust of wind picked up a crisp packet and dumped it at our feet. Mr Breeley didn't move, so I reached out automatically, picked it up and dumped it in the bin beside the bench.

'Litter louts,' said Breeley absently.

The action prompted me to remember something in his account that had bothered me, something I had made a mental note to return to when he had finished telling the story. 'Mr Breeley?'

'Mmm?'

'You said you caught a glimpse of Mona going towards the north entrance on corridor G . . . ?'

'G2. That's right.'

'Is that the corridor that goes from her office straight to the back door?'

'It goes from her office, past rooms G201, G202, G203 . . .'

I felt a stirring of excitement, as if I was in sight of something important at last. I interrupted just as we were getting into the higher Gs.

'The library is the other way, isn't it? In the corridor facing her office.'

'That's right. Corridor H1.'

Arkwright High seemed to be a real geographical challenge.

'Mr Breeley, try to think back to that moment when you saw her. Are you sure it was her? Did you see her clearly?'

'Of course it was her. All the lights was on, she was clear as day.'

'How long did you see her for – a second, two seconds?'

'More. She crossed in front of me, but she was so busy looking where she was going, she didn't see me.'

'Walking from left to right.'

'Yes.'

'Did you call out to her?'

'No I didn't like to yell. I knew I could head her off at the back door.'

I paused, almost afraid to ask the next question. 'Mr Breeley?'

'What?'

I tried to keep my voice neutral. 'Was Mona carrying a large sheath knife in her right hand?'

'No. She wasn't carrying anything.'

It was a spontaneous reply, without a trace of hesitation. Breeley opened his eyes wide and then relaxed them and made a few contortions with his lips to indicate that he was giving it some thought. Then he said firmly, 'No, she wasn't carrying it then. She must have gone back and picked it up.' He frowned. 'No, that's not right. She would have taken longer to get to Mr Thornley.' He thought again. 'Perhaps she hid it in her pocket.'

I thought, 'A *five-inch* sheath knife?' But I said nothing.

The discrepancy did not seem to trouble him. 'Would you like to see the dustbins now? Scene of the crime?'

I thanked him but said I had to go and that I was already running late.

I drove back to the clinic with a sense of expectancy, as if something were about to happen. The discrepancy in his account did not bother Mr Breeley. But it would certainly interest Mona's solicitor, and it sure as hell was going to bother DS Gould.

Chapter Ten

Pete propped up two pillows behind his back and lay there with his arms up, hands clasped behind his head. The pose demanded that I plant kisses on his chest, muzzle the soft, burgeoning hair around his nipples, moving up until I was high enough to kiss him several times on the mouth.

'Time to talk,' he said cheerily.

I groaned and slipped back down under the duvet. It had become a standing joke that I wanted sex and he wanted to talk, though in reality he wasn't much of a talker, and my physical appetite for him had lessened in direct proportion to how much I was enjoying his company. I wasn't too worried about it. I had started out insatiable, so there was still a long way to fall.

Pete yanked the duvet, which I had wrapped around me for protection.

'Sara! Tell me what you did today.'

'Piss off.'

It was warm under the covers and I was enjoying the satiated feeling of making love on a Friday night with the whole weekend ahead. The next day had the added advantage of the children coming back from David's. I had missed them terribly and couldn't wait to see them.

Pete stopped pulling and put his arms back behind his head. 'Frances Thornley came to see Geoff today.'

'Really?' I released the covers and looked up at him.

'Thought that would get you interested.'

The telephone rang downstairs, but we ignored it; the answering machine would pick it up. I had already spoken to the children earlier in the evening, so it couldn't be anything important. I sat up and snuggled close to him, my head nestling perfectly into the hollow of his collarbone. I breathed in through my nose, taking expectant pleasure in the scent of his body – a child waiting for a story.

'She was well upset. I couldn't believe she'd show her face, to be honest, but Geoff was expecting her – told me to send her up. When she came out, you could see she'd been crying. I let her off signing the book. I signed out for her.'

'You're so sensitive.'

He was so serious about his responsibilities, I couldn't resist teasing him.

'Yeah, go on, laugh. You're just the type who can't be bothered signing in and out of a place, but you're the first to complain when things get nicked.'

He was right of course.

'I wonder what she wanted,' I mused.

'I know what she wanted,' continued Pete, obviously pleased to have some news that hooked my interest.

'What?'

Pete tapped my nose; I snatched a bite at his finger, but missed.

'Lucky for your nosiness, the walls in that company have ears – especially the wall between Geoff Thornley and his secretary. The word is that Tony's wife wants the sale to be called off. What d'you call it when the Pope says you're not married because you haven't bonked yet?'

166

I looked at him blankly. He was asking *me* about the *Pope*?

'Annulled?'

'That's it. She says the sale can't be legal if Geoff didn't agree to it.'

'Why would she want the sale called off? She must have made a fortune out of it.'

'Maybe she feels bad about what that bastard husband of hers did to Geoff.'

Call me cynical, but that didn't quite tally with what I knew of human nature.

'Does she know something which makes the sale illegal? Does she have a way out?'

'Don't ask me. I'm just telling you what Gwen said — Geoff's secretary. She knows everything that goes on in that office. She took in the coffee and forgot to shut the door.'

'So what's Frances gone crying to Geoff for? If he knew how to get the sale annulled, he'd have done it.'

Pete lifted one shoulder, indicating that he didn't know. 'Gwen thinks there's something funny about the sale — a middleman, who hasn't been paid, who is hassling Mrs Thornley for his money.'

That sounded like Tony's sort of deal. Make as much mess as you can and then leave it to everyone else to clear up. I wondered if he was up there now — or down, in hell or whatever — having a good laugh about the trouble he had caused. I puzzled over what could have prompted Frances to go to Geoff. When I had seen her on Saturday, she seemed quite complacent that Tony had left them so well off. It's true she didn't mention the shares directly, but she did say that a sale Tony had made in the last few weeks of his life had made them especially well off. I thought back to our lunch with Patel and tried to recall what he had said about Frances' reaction to the sale. He said he believed she was delighted. I remembered his exact words — 'Mrs Thornley is a very lucky woman.'

'Gwen said Mrs Thornley was crying, asking Geoff to forgive Tony for doing the deal behind his back. She says she doesn't want to sell out to Bowker–Tindall. She wants Geoff to buy her out in his own good time.'

'I still don't know why she went to Geoff.'

'You're hard.' He stroked my hair and twisted a lock round his finger playfully. 'Maybe she isn't independent like you. I bet Tony did everything for her. She doesn't want to deal with this crap – she wants Geoff to sort it.'

'Hmmm.'

That was probably true. Even when I was with David, I always did things for myself. It was a huge advantage when we separated – at least I knew how to open a bank account and change a light bulb. But even so, I still found Frances' timing hard to understand. If she felt bad about the sale, why did she wait until now to say so?

'D'you want a beer?' I asked, feeling suddenly parched.

'Love one. Shall I get it?'

'You don't know where they are.'

'Okay.'

He smiled and settled back into bed. A lock of his hair had flopped over his face, just reaching his chin and he tried to blow it out of the way. His lips were a deep, healthy red, smooth and supple, a lovely contrast to his stubble, which was, by now, as rough as a nutmeg grater. He watched me get out of bed with a smile in his eyes and, if it hadn't been for the ice-cold Czech brew I knew was waiting downstairs, I would have leapt back into bed and made love to him all over again.

I padded downstairs on the carpet made rough by the grime of children's feet and thought, happily, that this time tomorrow I would be yelling at them, as usual, for trailing muddy shoes up the stairs. I would also have introduced them to Pete. I pulled the beer out of the fridge and took the glasses into the sitting room, so I could listen to the answerphone as I poured it.

John's voice startled me so much, I missed the lip of the glass and got froth all over the table. He sounded subdued, even depressed. He asked how I was and hoped I was fine. He missed me. He was moving to Manchester in a fortnight and wondered whether we could get together to say goodbye before he left. 'For one last analysis session,' I thought sadly. The longing I felt momentarily at the sound of his voice was quickly replaced by resignation, mixed with relief. How had my relationship with John been brought to such a swift conclusion, when I had been struggling for the previous three months to decide what to do about it? I knew that the answer was to be found in a gorgeous young man, currently fiddling with the radio in my bedroom in search of his favourite station. I mopped up the beer froth with a tissue which I then tossed into the waste basket.

As my finger traced a line down the condensation on the glass, I thought about my dismal record with men. My problem, I decided, was that I always went into a relationship with an unrealistic view of what I wanted. I thought I wanted couple-dom, togetherness, a soulmate. But time and again I proved to myself that I couldn't handle total commitment. I couldn't handle possessiveness, analysis – deep, intense and intellectual. I needed a relationship that was emotional rather than intellectual – spontaneous rather than planned. John had considered himself a new man – liberal and politically correct – but all that meant, as far as I could see, was him being around me all the time wanting attention. Pete expected life to be unpredictable, he expected it to be unfair, even though he complained about it long and loud. He wanted attention and to be looked after – but he also demanded that I let him look after me in return. I liked that. Astonishing as it may seem, this continuous role switching was something I had never encountered before. The men I had been with either expected me to look after them or to engulf me with a smothering blanket. Pete took it for granted that he should take care of me. He might be unknowingly sexist, but he was also sensitive and intuitive. More than all that, he was fun. He wasn't a towering intellectual and he didn't have the benefit of my education, but I knew, if I could conquer my snobbery about that, I could learn a lot from him. Did I really need to be with a man, like John, who could solve all the mental arithmetic problems on *Countdown* before the clock stopped? A man who knew the names of every Cabinet minister? My parents thought John was wonderful. An accountant! How perfect for Sara, who can't even manage the children's pocket money! The only fly in the ointment was him not being Jewish. I knew they would be deeply unimpressed by Pete. He came from an immigrant family — not our sort at all, we were totally assimilated. He didn't plan or worry about the future; he just reacted to things as they came along. I felt relaxed with him, as if there was no pressure on me to be something I wasn't. He cheered me up. I felt I had reached a stage of life where I should not feel the need to justify my choices to my parents, or anyone else. I didn't store John's message; I deleted it. I would ring him tomorrow and wish him luck, but politely decline the chance to rake over the embers of a fire which had been extinguished almost as soon as it was kindled.

I picked up the tray to take our beers upstairs, but on my way through the hall, I suddenly noticed a letter on the floor. It had come by post, but I hadn't seen it when Pete and I came in. I picked it up and looked at the postmark — it was from Holloway, from Mona. Surprised, I slit it open with my finger and pulled out a single sheet of paper. It was just a few lines. written in biro in a scrawled hand.

Dear Sara

I saw Robin today and he told me about the trouble you have gone to on my behalf. This is a note to thank you, but also to tell you not to continue. I have decided to plead guilty. It is no use trying to remember the details. I have to face up to what I have done. I am to see a psychiatrist this week. I didn't think I was mad, or evil, but I've decided that we know less about ourselves than we think.

With good wishes,

Mona

My heart sank. My self-indulgent musings about parents and boyfriends seemed shallow by comparison. Such a strange, sad letter. 'I didn't think I was mad, or evil . . . ' Poor Mona. I wondered whether her decision to plead guilty was based on a real belief that she killed Thornley, or whether she simply wanted an end to the uncertainty.

Feeling miserable and deflated, I started up the stairs with our beers, but as I reached the second step the telephone rang again. This time, I answered it; it was for Pete. Suppressing my irritation that he had given anyone my home number – we would have words about that later – I called upstairs for him to pick up the phone in the bedroom, and started up the stairs again. Mona's letter had completely destroyed my sanguine Friday night mood. I felt powerless. I had spoken to Mona's solicitor that afternoon – a brisk, efficient woman at a firm in Islington – and she had seemed cautiously optimistic about Breeley's information about the knife. I'd told her too about my conversations with Bridget and Cynthia; she took notes as we spoke, and said it was all useful background. She seemed particularly interested in the shares and a possible business connection between Cynthia Marsh and Tony Thornley. I had asked her how things looked for Mona, but she wouldn't be drawn and said that she hoped to have a better picture when Mona had seen the psychiatrist.

I put the drinks on the bedside table just as Pete was putting down the phone. He reached out for his beer immediately. 'Shit! I have to go into work. The alarm's gone off.'

I felt a stab of disappointment. What had started as a relaxing romantic evening was degenerating rapidly into a stress-filled depression-fest. I made a face and folded my arms, but the lip-pout had barely completed before I had the germ of an idea which was not, as my mother would say, worthy of me. Pete was not going to like it, but then Pete, I decided quickly, need not know a thing about it.

'Can I come with you?'

Pete glowered suspiciously. 'What for?'

'I'm curious. I'd like to see the place.'

'If you've got some kinky idea of getting up to something in reception, you can forget it.'

'Pete! I'm shocked.' The idea hadn't occurred to me, although now he mentioned it, it did have a certain grubby appeal. 'I just want to have a look round, get a feel for where Tony Thornley worked.'

'Tony Thornley didn't work, he just fucked around.'

'Okay, to see where he fucked around. Go on, it can't do any harm.'

'All right. But we're only staying for as long as it takes to check the building and reset the alarm.'

I knew he was agreeing against his better judgement; and he was right, especially in view of what I had in mind.

Park Royal at this time of night was a spooky wasteland. The few streetlamps that were actually working cast a limpid yellow glow for a few miserable yards, leaving gaping holes of darkness in between. The area is completely industrial, apart from a cemetery which sprawls incongruously between two warehouses. The factories crouch side by side in shadows, like giants watching over the dead. The industrial estate stretches for about two miles, starting at the A40 motorway, which runs from the west into central London. It's mainly light engineering here – nuts, bolts and grommets – with the odd food or furniture company thrown in. At night, even the main roads are deserted. Once the rumble of the motorway receded, the ragged engine of my Vauxhall Chevette was the only sound and the rough tarmac, pitted by the wheels of lorries, made every rattle count. I was glad Pete was with me – it was the type of area where, if you are a woman alone and your car breaks down, you wish you had been wise enough to carry a mobile phone.

We turned left just beyond the biscuit factory into a street which was lit only by the white glare of security lights on the unit nearest the road. On a road running parallel to ours, a car passed, its headlights on full beam. It turned out into the main road and disappeared. The only other sign of life we passed was a floodlit lorry bay where two men were unloading crates. They appeared as silhouettes, staggering down the ramp, bent low by their heavy loads, the smoke from their cigarettes curling upwards in silver streams. The scene was like a tableau from a *film noir*, except for the sign on the lorry saying 'North Acton Freight Company', which didn't have quite the right ring to it.

Following Pete's directions, I negotiated a series of right and left turns on small service roads, weaving a path through the darkened warehouses and factories. A number of signs boasted that the buildings were protected by guard dogs, but there was no visible sign of life, either human or canine. Thornley's, Pete said, was on the west side of the estate, a real pain to get to; it was quicker if you were walking, because you could cut through the alleys which ran round the perimeters of many of the buildings. I repressed a shudder at the thought of those deserted pathways. I wondered whether the police patrolled the streets and whether you stood a chance in hell of being heard if someone attacked you.

I picked out Thornley's without Pete's help, because it was the only place emitting an ear-splitting ringing tone. Pete said it was usually Geoff Thornley or one of the senior managers who was called out when the alarm went off, but they were all away this weekend, so they'd asked him to leave a number where he could be contacted. I realised it was a measure of how much they trusted him; and again I felt guilty about the prying I wanted to do. We pulled up outside the entrance and I turned off the engine. There was no police car in sight; Pete said they often left before the key holder arrived if they couldn't see anything amiss.

From what I could see behind the glare of the security spotlights, Thornley Veneers was a two-storey factory made of brick, with square metal-framed windows – probably state of the art in the mid-1950s. From the outside, it was squat and functional, a building with no pretensions to be anything other than what it was. Pete said the building was bigger than it looked – the workshops and production area were at the back, with the supplies area and the lorry bays. There were lights on outside the building, and two lights on inside – security lights on a timer, according to Pete.

My heart was beating fast as Pete unlocked the door – not from fear, but because the alarm was deafening and the high pitch seemed specially designed to get the adrenalin pumping. Pete let us in using a bewildering array of keys, flipped on a light and moved swiftly to a cupboard behind the high counter to turn off the alarm. Once the piercing bell had stopped it was easier to think, although the noise seemed to linger in the air for several minutes. The front door led straight into a small reception and waiting area. The decor was plain but pleasing – cream-coloured walls and a speckled oatmeal carpet, a couple of black director's chairs, a black ash coffee table. There was even a token plant.

'What do you think?' said Pete, looking around.

'It's nice.'

'This is where I sit. He motioned me to come behind the counter. 'Telephones – internal, external. Books to sign in and out. Security camera – ' He fiddled with some buttons on a control panel which controlled the screen, calling up views of different parts of the factory. 'Look, that's one of the workshops . . . upstairs offices . . . supplies . . . ' He flipped a few more pictures. 'Seems okay. We better check round the workshops though.'

'Can we go through the offices first?'

Pete gave me an enigmatic look. 'If you like.'

He was proud and proprietorial as he showed me round.

'This is Mandy's desk – accounts. Good laugh, old Mandy.'

It was strange looking at people's workspace when they weren't there – almost more personal than prowling round their home. Everyone had their own patch, marked out by

174

fetishes and small possessions. We went quickly through the offices on the ground floor. Pete led the way, stalking and alert, his eyes peeled for any sign of anything amiss. He moved through the rooms like a panther, swinging his hips round obstacles as he checked all the windows and doors.

'We'll do upstairs now,' he said, when we had checked the final office.

Geoff Thornley's office showed none of the trappings of a paternalistic managing director running a family business – no dark oil paintings of the founder, no oversized polished oak desk. It was an office about the size of my living room which clearly doubled as a meeting room. It was square-shaped and, like the rest of the building, it still had the original small-paned windows, starting quite high up the wall. There was a board table with several chairs and a more informal space with a couple of easy chairs. The shelves that covered one wall were mostly full of trade magazines stored in labelled boxes. Geoff Thornley didn't really have a desk; it was more an L-shaped surface, made up of several units, to accommodate a variety of computer equipment, as well as leaving a space to write. There was a telephone and intercom, and a box with samples of veneers of different thicknesses and finishes. I picked up a photo of a smiling woman, with a boy and a girl, aged perhaps nine and eleven. It was obviously a posed family shot, but the woman's smile seemed genuine and the kids looked happy to be sitting close to her.

'Geoff's wife, Mary, and the kids.'

One had to wonder about Geoff and Tony's parents – what had they done to end up with such different sons?

Pete walked to a window, cupped his hand against one of the panes and peered out.

'You can't see much in the dark, but you get a good view from here down into the workshops and the yard,' he said. 'It all looks okay, but we'd better just have a quick wander.'

'Can I stay here?'

He swivelled to face me. 'I knew it.'

'What?' Wide-eyed, me. The picture of innocence.

'You want to have a poke about, don't you? See if you can find out about the shares?'

There was no point denying it – I didn't want to lie to him. 'Do you mind?'

'Course I mind.' The glint in his eye beneath the frown told me he was going to let me do it all the same.

'Just ten minutes, okay?'

'Make it five. The police could be back any time.' He waggled a finger at me in warning. 'And don't mess anything up. My boss is the type to notice if something's out of place.'

I splayed out my hands. 'He won't know a thing. Promise!'

Still frowning, he went off to check the rest of the building, leaving me alone in Thornley's office.

I stood, looking around me, wondering where to start. Frances Thornley had come to see Geoff earlier that day and, since the shares must be the most pressing thing on his mind, it stood to reason that he would have all the papers to hand. They would have searched Tony's office and computer files to get all the documentation. I started by looking through the papers on the desk. There was surprisingly little there – a few letters from suppliers, an employee reference that had to be written and several application forms from people looking for jobs. There was a photocopy of an article from a technical journal, full of diagrams and completely incomprehensible. There were no other papers lying around – another sign of a highly organised manager.

With a tentative glance at the door, I switched on the PC nearest to Geoff's chair. My computer skills had improved enormously since I'd been on a week's course the previous autumn. It was something for which I would be eternally grateful to John – conquering my fear of computers. He'd encouraged me to borrow one of his for a few weeks and play around on it – press buttons and enjoy the feeling of controlling something electronic rather than it controlling me. I was no expert, but I knew how to construct a simple database and use a spreadsheet, and, more to the point, I wasn't afraid of using them any more. The program manager on Geoff's computer looked surprisingly simple. I double-clicked on his word processing package and scrolled through the files to see if anything looked likely. Lo and behold, good old Geoff had constructed a whole directory called 'Tony'. It contained fifty or so documents. From their titles, it looked as though Geoff had gathered together all the stuff relating to Tony's unfinished business in the company. I opened one or two to have a look. There was a letter to their rep in Northern Region; a sales report for March; an internal e-mail, dated the week Tony died, informing Geoff that he, Tony, was giving a final warning to one Jim Ferguson and that if he still failed to meet his targets, he would have no option but to fire him. None of the documents had names suggesting that they might be to do with the sale of shares.

All of a sudden, the sound of a bell ripped open the silence. I jumped to my feet and then realised it was the telephone. After three rings it stopped – Pete answering it somewhere in the building. With my heart still beating too fast for comfort, I turned back to the computer screen. I noticed that at the top of the directory there was a whole series of files that were numbered rather than named. Probably invoices. Expecting nothing, I opened the first one. Bingo! It was a confidential memo from Tony, reiterating the outcome of a meeting. His style was stiff and pompous.

> In short, as I outlined in our meeting last Thursday, I have considerable interest in selling my share of the TV equity, provided that a buyer can be found which matches my financial expectations in this regard. I await with anticipation the result of your meeting on 22 January with Bowker-Tindall management. I enclose with this memo the figures you requested for April/May/June of last year. They are supplied, of course, in the strictest confidence.

I looked at the header of the memo – To RP from TT. No copies.

Pete's noisy arrival broke into my thoughts. 'That was one of the managers. They called him out as well – stupid bastards – and he's on his way. Doesn't trust me, I suppose. You'd better turn this off.' He reached for the mouse, but I snatched it back.

'Pete – wait! I've found the files. Who's RP?'

'What?'

I opened another document and the answer leapt out. It was a letter arranging a meeting between Tony, his middleman and the managing director of Bowker-Tindall. The man arranging the sale of the shares was Rajesh Patel. I scrolled down the letter and tried to fit this piece of information into the muddle of Tony Thornley's relationships. Rajesh had not exactly lied to us about his relationship with Tony – he had just chosen not to tell us that he played such an active role. I wondered how much Rajesh hoped to make out of the sale – the shares were worth several hundred thousand pounds. If he had been promised a percentage, he would have done extremely well. Pete had said that Frances came to Geoff because the middleman was pressurising her for money.

'He'll be here in a minute. Come on, Sara.'

'Tell me when you hear the car – I can turn it off in a moment.'

Pete looked anxious, but he went and stood in the doorway. Eagerly, I started opening the other files to see what I could find out about the deal between Tony and Rajesh. Tony had been quite careful with his letters and memos – they were all written guardedly in a pompous business style, but he had not been at all careful with his e-mail. He seemed to believe that because it was electronic, it didn't leave a trace. This confirmed what I had always suspected about Tony Thornley – he was not only greedy and unpleasant, he was also stupid. In a note to Patel dated 15 February, he said that he was pleased with Patel's report on the negotiations and believed that Bowker-Tindall were 'almost hooked'. He told Patel that he had been thinking over their conversations about how to transfer the money for the shares 'without giving the tax man a huge percentage'. He thought it might be a good idea to split the money in half; they could 'use the offshore company solution again' for one part and only declare the other half as the revenue for shares. He wondered what Patel thought of the idea. If Patel responded via e-mail, Geoff Thornley did not have a copy on his computer. There were several e-mails from Patel confirming meetings, but nothing about money or offshore accounts – Patel was a clearly a more circumspect correspondent. One e-mail did refer to payment terms for a potential deal, and these were confirmed by Tony Thornley in a letter which was written before Patel had found a buyer. If he could sell the equity, Thornley wrote, Patel would get 8 per cent of the net selling price, paid in two chunks – half on signature of the deal and the rest on completion of the transaction. Was this the money Rajesh was complaining to Frances about? And was being cheated out of the money a good enough reason for Rajesh to kill Tony – or have him killed?

'He's coming! Turn it off!'

I had been so absorbed in reading the correspondence, I nearly jumped out of my skin when Pete called out. Hands shaking, I whipped out a disk I had brought with me and copied the e-mail and one of the letters onto it.

'Kingsley!' he hissed.

'All right!' I hissed back.

I took out the disk, closed down the computer and switched it off, the noise of the fan subsiding just as a voice called out from the lobby. A balding head appeared round the door.

'Everything all right?'

'Fine, Mr Carter,' said Pete. He waved vaguely at me. 'My girlfriend, Sara. We was just leaving.'

The manager nodded briefly, his eyes swivelling round the room looking for anything out of place. 'Thanks for coming out,' he said.

*

As we drove away, the streets were just as we had left them, still and empty. I thought uneasily of the unlit passageways between the factories, imagining what it would be like to be walking alone in the gloom.

'You nearly lost me a job there,' complained Pete.

I reached out my hand and stroked his leg; his hand on mine told me he had forgiven me, but he thought it was at least worth mentioning.

I mused aloud, 'If Tony dodged taxes on the sale of the shares, I doubt if anyone will be running to their lawyers. Geoff, Frances and Rajesh will work it out between them.'

'Patel'll stand more chance of getting his money off them than Tony.'

'Exactly.'

The car clattered back into Acton. The bingo hall was just spewing out its customers and a group of women stood on the pavement, laughing and comparing luck. I was glad to be on familiar territory, where streetlights illuminated pavements alive with wind-blown litter and listing drunks making for the Indian takeaway. With a sigh, I recalled Mona's letter and wondered whether the information about Patel would make any difference to her fate.

Chapter Eleven

Mona's cheeks had become hollow and her face seemed to have been stripped back to its bare essentials — prominent cheekbones, nose set high above a wide-lipped mouth, a face which was still serious and lovely despite its pale gauntness. I was shocked to see that she had cut her hair short; all that was left of it were stubby curls, clinging close to the contours of her head. It was cold in the visitors' room. The warders looked on, bored and vacant, as riven families struggled to get beyond the superficial. Misery hung on the stale air like a fog. Mona seemed calmer than when I had seen her last, but after a moment or so talking to her, I began to see what had prompted her to write the letter — she had entered a deep depression and had lost all hope of being released.

'The woman in my cell just talks all the time,' she complained. 'I've stopped answering; I've even stopped telling her to shut up. I can't sleep and the food is like shit.'

I let her talk. She needed to complain and to feel that someone on the outside was listening. I debated whether or not to tell her about my talk with Breeley, but decided against it. There was no point building up her hopes. I told her that Robin and I had been talking to people, asking questions, and that we had come up with a few facts that might be relevant. I told her I had spoken to her solicitor. She thanked me listlessly and repeated what she had said in the letter – that it was all in vain now because she had decided to plead guilty. I didn't ask her why and she didn't volunteer the information. She showed no curiosity about our investigations. She was unable to meet my eyes – hers were bleak and despondent. She didn't want to talk about Thornley, or the school, or what had happened. I asked her if there was anything she needed, but she shook her head and ran her hand back over her hair. She said she had seen a psychiatrist – someone recommended by her solicitor. Yes, the woman seemed competent and nice, but the session had failed to dredge up anything useful. Mona had agreed to see her again, but doubted that any good would come of it. She was consumed with irritation about her cellmate, and with the small and large indignities that made up the daily grind of her confined life.

'This Marian, she tells the same stories over and over again. She worries and frets about her kids. She phones them every night and every night there's some fresh disaster to report – Darren's broken his finger, Terry was caught nicking cigarettes. It's relentless. She doesn't spare you a single detail. Now she's convinced that another woman has moved in with her husband but no one wants to tell her.'

Mona described the stench in the cell, the cold sweats which came upon her at night, with feelings of unbearable claustrophobia. She whispered her distress at having to use the toilet in front of another woman and at having no sanitary towels when her period started in the night. It was sobering to remember that the conditions Mona described were those of a prisoner on remand, who was awarded special privileges for being 'innocent until proven guilty'. How inhuman must be the lives of the convicted prisoners, women who were packed like rats into foetid cells, left for hours every day with no stimulation and no exercise. I let Mona pour out her woes, keeping my part to the odd question and a few sympathetic noises. I stayed with her until visiting time was over and then left, hugely relieved to be back through the security doors and into the outside world. Even the Holloway Road, choked with traffic and bathed in a weak spring sunlight which served only to highlight how filthy the buildings were, seemed like paradise by comparison. I had a terrible sense of walking along a rock edge with nothing between me and the abyss of Mona's situation except a fragile screen of luck and serendipity which could give way at any moment.

I tried to organise my week to spend as much time as possible with the children. They didn't return to school until the following Tuesday, so I intended to take time off so we could go swimming, ride bikes and go to a few museums. They see me so little when I'm not stressed and working, it's a treat for all of us not to have me hurrying them along, hissing, like the white rabbit, between gritted teeth, 'we're late! we're late!'

Monday and Tuesday were fun, but by the end of Wednesday I had started to feel my age and was furtively checking the calendar to see how many days were left before school started. I had squeezed the entire week's appointments into the Thursday, because Steve had offered to take them out for the day on his own. He was happy and expansive because his play had opened in the West End to great reviews, one of which singled him out particularly. He had planned a highly ambitious day with them, which included the Science Museum, a picnic and a puppet show.

Thursday morning dawned bright with sunshine and spring dew. I drove them all to the tube station and watched them go in. My heart contracted at the sight of them. Three adventurers – a tubby, balding man, slightly harassed and sporting a knapsack; an eight-year-old androgyne, in jeans and jumper, sleek pigtails shining in the sun; and a tousle-haired, button-nosed boy in continuous motion, head upturned, body bobbing up and down in time with his unbroken chatter. I waited until they had disappeared into the gaping mouth of the station entrance. Three most precious things. I felt lucky to have them, and glad to be alive and free.

I went to the clinic to see some of the clients I felt could not be put off to the following week. The couple with the baby were finding things slightly easier now, but the young mother still wanted to come in once a week, as a bolt hole from the pressures of new motherhood. We usually managed to time her session to coincide with the baby's nap, so he slept in the corner in a carrycot, blissfully unaware, while his mother offloaded guilty fantasies of smothering him with a pillow. Social services, I knew, were keeping a close eye on them; but I felt the baby was a lot safer with this mother than with the countless others who couldn't even acknowledge the fantasies, let alone seek help for the feelings that gave rise to them.

I also saw a mother whose twelve-year-old son had severe behaviour problems and had attacked her over Easter. She told me what had happened and I made suggestions about where they could go for help, but it didn't take long to see that what she really wanted was for me to persuade a reluctant social worker to have him taken into care. She had a new boyfriend who hated the kid's guts and wanted to get rid of him. I tried to talk to her about how the boy might be feeling, but she wasn't interested. 'I've had enough of the little bastard and I'm kicking him out whatever happens.' When she saw I wasn't going to play it her way, she left in a huff, and I had to chalk it up with all my other failures. I rang the social worker to tell him the mother had been in – he sighed in a knowing way and said he would talk to them again as soon as he could. We discussed a few strategies to try, but we both agreed that the mother was quite determined, so the boy would end up either in care or in custody.

Slightly more successful was my final meeting with the man who was under pressure at work. His counselling had been short-term. He had done a lot of thinking in between our three sessions and was determined to make some changes in his life. He promised to let me know how he was getting on and said he would certainly be interested if Greg and I started our stress management group.

At twelve thirty I left the clinic to drive down to Chiswick to meet Barry. I had been trying all week to get an appointment to see him, but he'd given me the feeling he was avoiding me. Now, all of a sudden, he was keen to talk. I wondered if there had been some developments, or whether he just wanted to catch up on the case before subjecting himself to another diatribe against the police in general, and Grisly Gould in particular. As I passed through reception on my way out, Doreen collared me.

'Someone's trying to get hold of you,' she said.

'Who?'

'Someone who doesn't want to leave his name. The voice is a bit strange and slightly different each time, but I'm sure it's the same person.'

An ex-client? Someone who had been given my name? It could be anyone.

'Young? Old?'

'Hard to tell. It's a bit . . . muffled. He asks if you're there, when will you be in, goes through several days of the week. Then when I ask who is it and does he want an appointment, he rings off.'

'Try and offer him a specific day and time if he rings again,' I suggested. 'He's probably just working up to it. Mind you, I'm pretty full over the next couple of weeks. Could Greg see him? He might prefer a man.'

'I'll try, but it's you he's asking about.'

I shrugged. 'Give it a try.'

Doreen has a gift for dealing with shy and difficult clients. Her manner is perfect – kind, matter of fact and totally non-patronising. If anyone could find out what he really wanted, she could.

*

I met Barry in the Café Noir – one of those places with Toulouse-Lautrec posters and artificially smoke-stained walls that are springing up all over London to try and convince you that you are really in Paris. (It doesn't work – the coffee is too weak, the food is dire and the waiters aren't rude enough.) He looked crisp and dapper as usual, sitting squarely in his chair, with his muscular arms and large hands resting loosely on the table and making the china teacup and saucer look incongruously small. Periodically I notice, with surprise, how handsome he is, in a classic, boy-next-door way. His blond hair, always kept meticulously short, is smooth and silky and shows no sign of thinning. His eyes, nose and mouth are perfectly placed above a square jaw and his mouth is pleasantly upturned. But it is the azure blue of his eyes which makes his looks so stunning and probably sets more than a few hearts beating among his colleagues. The fact that he is so good-looking makes his sexuality even more of an issue, particularly for envious male officers.

After a few minutes' small talk, Barry dropped his bombshell. 'I've been seconded to the squad for a few days.' He was trying to keep it matter of fact, without much success.

'Really?' I said, trying not to sound too gloating. 'Why is that?'

'It's just for a few days,' he repeated. 'Local knowledge. The Super thought I might be able to help.'

So Gould's incompetence had finally been noticed. They were worried they didn't have a good enough case.

'I thought DS Gould had the thing all sewn up.'

'So did I. But one or two stitches have come undone.'

'Glad to hear it.'

'You shouldn't be.'

I wondered if Barry meant that they had found more evidence against Mona, but his next comment reassured me. Setting his jaw sternly, he said, 'DS Gould is not happy about you and Robin chatting up witnesses.'

I tried not to laugh. 'What shall I do – faint? Do I exist only in order to make DS Gould happy?'

Barry was not amused. 'Haven't you heard of conspiracy to

pervert the course of justice? It's not going to help Mona Pearson if you two go around – '

'Oh, leave it out, Barry.'

I waved my hand dismissively. We knew each other too well for that sort of crap. He was very well aware that we would share everything we found out with the defence. Gould couldn't stop us talking to witnesses and he knew it.

'We're working with Mona's blessing and we're passing on everything to her solicitor. The only reason Robin and I are taking any interest in this is because your DS Gould has tunnel vision. He's only seeing what he wants to see.'

Barry sipped his tea impassively. 'You want to give me an example?'

I shook my head. 'I'm not falling for that one.'

'I'm giving you a chance to put your side of this, Sara.'

'You're giving me a chance to help you build a case against Mona, because you're beginning to see that yours is full of holes.'

Barry decided that a different approach was needed. 'All right, I'll be honest with you. One or two things that have come to light since Mona's arrest are worrying me.'

'Such as?'

Barry turned his hands face up to emphasise his openness. 'Thornley selling out. We didn't know about that when we arrested Mona. And Rajesh Patel was the middleman.'

'I know.'

'He says he didn't think it was relevant. But he must have made a packet.'

'Yet says he didn't.'

'Really?' Barry pounced.

Damn! This was news to him. A tactical error on my part. Why do I always give people information without meaning to? The last thing I wanted was for Barry to ask how I found out about Patel.

'Did Patel say he hadn't made money on the deal?' asked Barry eagerly.

'Not exactly,' I hedged, then added vaguely, 'maybe what he meant was that he didn't make enough.'

Barry looked thoughtful and made a brief note on the pad he always seems to keep in front of him. I had a fleeting image of him in a pub with his new man, surreptitiously making notes as they chatted each other up. It was unfair – Barry did unwind occasionally, but I found it irksome the way he took every comment literally and insisted on recording it. It was his job, of course, but it was still an irritating way of conducting a conversation.

'What exactly did he say?' asked Barry, still writing. 'Can you remember?'

I pretended to think for a minute and then smiled apologetically. 'I'm not sure. He only spoke to Robin. Mr Patel doesn't acknowledge the existence of women.'

Barry sucked in his lower lip. He didn't believe that I couldn't remember, but that was okay. I wanted him to know I had no intention of making this easy for him.

'Any idea what's frightening the widow?' asked Barry, keeping his eyes down on his notes. 'She's gone all nervy, according to the officer who spoke to her yesterday. He wondered if she was cracking up.'

'She's probably still in shock.'

He looked up and our eyes met. Neither of us wanted to give away our hands.

Barry said, 'She's certainly less co-operative than she was a week or so ago. Any ideas?'

'Gould's charm working its magic?'

'Aren't we getting a bit obsessive?'

His patronising tone annoyed me. 'Why are you working on this case, Barry? Has the Super finally decided that Gould has gone too far?'

'I told you why – '

'Has he?'

'A man was brutally murdered. All we want to do is to find the killer.'

188

'To nail Mona, you mean.'

'Only if she's guilty.'

The silence prickled with bad feeling.

Barry carried on doggedly, trying to draw me out. 'DC Drake said Mrs Thornley's getting more and more racist in the way she talks about Mona Pearson. She's whipping herself up into a right old state.'

'She's recently bereaved.'

'I know, but she'll have to be bit more objective than that to go on the witness stand.'

'That's all you're worried about, isn't it? The police looking stupid in court and not getting a conviction.' I sighed, exasperated. 'Don't you care that the bigotry of one of your officers may be inhibiting a murder investigation?'

Barry was riled. 'Of course I care!' he protested. 'Please, Sara, let's calm down and talk this through rationally.'

I sipped my coffee and waited. It was Barry who needed to calm down, not me.

'I'm coming to this fresh and I'm trying to look at the options,' said Barry. He made a steeple with his hands and tapped them against his lips. 'There were six people at that meeting — Pearson, Scudder, Thornley, Patel, Marsh and the school secretary. Pearson, Scudder and Marsh were all closely associated with Thornley in one way or another, and you could say that they all had something against him. We now know there was also a fair amount of money washing around. Patel arranged the sale. The ex-mistress was promised a loan when the deal came through, but Thornley went back on it and told her she wasn't getting it.'

I still said nothing.

'But then — you could also look at it as the perfect scenario for a domestic,' continued Barry. 'Battered wife — '

I raised my eyebrows interrogatively; Barry nodded in response.

'Yes, he belted her from time to time. The son implied it and the neighbours suspected but didn't want to interfere.'

I felt a wave of revulsion. Another jewel in Thornley's priceless personality.

'He saw other women . . . I've seen husbands murdered for less. But her alibi is good. The friend brought her right to the door and watched her go in and a neighbour was passing at the time and said goodnight to her. At 22.15. The kid's a mess too – bullied by his dad and in with a bad crowd, but he's got an alibi too, and the fact is, Mona Pearson was the last person to see Thornley alive. Mona Pearson was the one who was found with the body. Everyone else either has an alibi or can't be put at the scene.'

I kept quiet, letting him think it through. Barry had switched into police mode – serious and official, with timings by the twenty-four-hour clock.

'The caretaker says that all the cars were gone from the car park by 21.30 – except Pearson's and Thornley's. They were the only people in the building.' Barry drained his tea and sighed. 'Marsh arrived at the meeting first – at about 19.15. Thornley and Patel got there at 19.30 – both came by car. The meeting was acrimonious – nothing unusual there. Scudder storms out at around 21.00. No one can confirm her story that she left immediately and went straight home, but, there again, we have no evidence that she didn't. Her car was definitely gone when Marsh and Patel left at 21.30.'

It obviously made sense to Barry, but I was several yards behind him, counting on my fingers to work out the twenty-four-hour clock.

'Forensic confirms that Thornley had a bruise on his left hip, so Pearson was probably telling the truth when she said that he made a pass at her and she shoved him back. The next thing we know after that is the caretaker, Mr Breeley, finding the body and turning round to see Pearson holding the knife.'

I knew a little more than that, but Barry could find it out for himself, in court if necessary.

'You might have expected a bit more blood on her clothes. But that depends on the injury. The wounds were deep.'

I broke into his musing. 'Breeley said the blood was spurting out of him, yet Mona only had blood on her hands when he got there.'

Barry made a noncommittal response and scribbled a few words. I knew he was making a note that I had spoken to Breeley and that he should do so too. He carried on. He was in a talkative mood – I don't think I'd ever heard him make such a long speech in the whole history of our acquaintance.

'We talked to Scudder's friend – the one who told her about Mona being in care – and got hold of the records from the children's home. Pearson's background was a tough one – not what you'd think from her accent. Mother dies, father belts the kids, so they get taken into care. She ran away from the children's home when she was sixteen and they didn't try too hard to find her. That was when she went on the game. No criminal record, though she was cautioned once for soliciting.'

Barry sat for a moment tapping his lips with his pen. He wasn't telling me anything I didn't know already. I wondered where all this was going. He leaned forward. 'So your theory is that when Thornley told her he knew about her past, she went into some kind of trance.'

It was a fairly shallow way of putting it, but I gave him the benefit of the doubt and bit back a sarcastic reply. Instead, I said, 'My theory – in so far as I have one – is that Thornley's threats, together with his physical attack, may have replayed the trauma of her father's abuse.'

'So she follows him out, murders him and then wakes up. Is that it?'

'Don't be crass, Barry!'

His jaw dropped slightly, as if I had slapped him. I had a moment's regret, but I didn't think he was trying very hard. I went into teacher mode.

'It's possible that a shock like that could be enough to prevent her from remembering what happened immediately after Thornley threatened her. Think about it. A large man threatens physical violence and then rakes up her past to beat her into sexual compliance. All this in a dark, deserted school late at night, with no warning at all of what was going to happen.'

I let that sink in. Barry looked chastened. He wanted to understand, but a good imagination is not one of the requirements of police work. In fact, they screen it out on recruitment.

'I don't know whether she killed Thornley or not,' I went on, sticking my neck out. 'But if someone else did it, the only person who might have seen something is Mona and she can't remember a thing about it.'

'We've asked for a psychiatric report,' said Barry lamely.

'Look at it this way for a minute, Barry. Let's just say for the sake of argument that Mona is innocent. It's unlikely, I grant you, but it's possible. Have you done everything you can to explore that scenario? Could there have been any evidence at the scene that was overlooked because Mona seemed to have been caught bang to rights? Fibres? Bloody footprints?'

Barry looked distinctly uncomfortable. 'It was drizzling. And windy.'

I pictured the playground again, seeing it this time as dark and wet, with rivulets of blood trickling down the cracks in the tarmac.

Barry coughed. 'Let's just say the first officers at the scene did not do the best possible job.'

I sighed. 'It was wet and they trampled all over it.'

'Correct.'

I rubbed my forehead in frustration. Someone up there had it in for Mona. I had hoped that if I could get Barry to at least admit the possibility of Mona's innocence, he would reappraise the evidence more closely and be more critical of what Gould was doing – or not doing.

'There was a fair bit of rubbish lying around where Thornley was found. On one piece of paper we found a partial footprint that doesn't seem to be Mona's, or Thornley's, the caretaker's or the police officers'. But it's not good enough to use as evidence.'

'No others?'

Barry shook his head. We both knew the partial was useless. Barry tapped the tips of his fingers together. 'Look, I've only just come on the case. I'll be going through everything in the next few days.'

I refused to be hopeful. He laid one finger on my wrist. 'I'll call you if I find anything.'

'Okay.'

But I knew he wouldn't call, for all sorts of reasons, not least because he knew he had to tread carefully with his homophobic colleague. Whatever Barry said, we were on opposite sides of the fence on this one.

I got back to the clinic at two o'clock, just in time to spend half an hour with Robin before my afternoon appointments. I brought him up to date on what I had found out and, though he tut-tutted about my foray into Thornley's computer files, he was riveted by what I had learned. He was particularly interested in Thornley's arrangements for payment.

'I've heard of this sort of thing before,' he said. 'I wonder . . . '

'What sort of thing?'

In my experience, when Robin wonders something, it's usually a bull's-eye. But he takes so long to get to the point, you lose the thread.

'It was in a novel I read once – one of these city scandals. I think I got it at the airport. A man had been promised a certain percentage of a deal, but once the deal had gone through, the other man would only pay him a percentage on the money that was legally invested. There was nothing he could do about it because the deal itself was illegal.'

I tried to twist my mind round that one. 'You mean, Patel believed he was getting a percentage of the total figure, but once the sale went through Thornley wouldn't include the money in the offshore account?'

'Yes.'

'And Patel is now harassing Frances to pay it. I suppose it's possible.' I frowned, trying to imagine it. 'Does that help Mona's case at all?'

Robin took off his glasses and began to clean them with a handkerchief. He was an endangered species in that respect – he still used cotton hankies, all beautifully washed and ironed.

'I suppose it gives Rajesh Patel a motive,' he said.

'Everyone has a motive. The guy pissed on half of Ealing.'

Robin eyebrows twitched at the expression. He put back his glasses and adjusted them, blinking as he did so.

'Why don't I go and see Frances Thornley?' he suggested.

'With what excuse?'

'Ask her if I can help.'

I shook my head. I thought he was being naïve, but didn't say so. 'She won't see you.'

'She might. It's worth a try.'

'I suppose you could bullshit – tell her you've been talking to Rajesh.'

'I'm not going to lie to her.'

'Would I suggest such a thing?'

'Yes.'

'I'm hurt.'

Robin smiled.

I knew we didn't have much time to talk, but I was curious about something and I wanted to get his opinion.

'Robin – Mona's seen a psychiatrist, but she seems to feel worse rather than better.' I wondered aloud how the psychiatrist would have approached her, and whether one could expect a diagnostic session to have any therapeutic benefit.

Robin was optimistic. 'Mona's ambivalent about unlocking the lost memories – it's obvious if you think about it. At the moment, she has no recollection whatsoever of the event. From a legal point of view, that might be a better state of affairs, because it makes her defence of automatism more convincing. On some level, she knows that. But she's also desperate to know whether or not she actually murdered him.

She's frightened, in the way a child is frightened by the power of their thoughts and wishes. She wished Thornley dead and the next thing she knew, he was lying murdered at her feet. Imagine it — how would you feel?'

I tried to imagine it. 'I think, in her place, I'd want to know what happened.'

'So would I.'

'So what will the psychiatrist do?'

'My guess is that she will come at it obliquely — focus on Mona's childhood and how it made her feel. Getting her to replay the meeting with Thornley over and over again would probably have the opposite effect from the one you want. It would lock the memories in more tightly.'

The sessions would be painful and the process could take a long time. It struck me forcefully that, even if Mona were to be released tomorrow, her life could never be the same again.

After seeing two more clients and checking over some paperwork with Doreen, I rushed out of the clinic hoping to get back home in time to gulp down a cup of tea before the children and Steve returned. I had parked a few streets away — finding a space near the centre was becoming impossible — so I had to go up to the High Street, walk fifty yards or so, and then turn down another side street to get to where the car was parked.

It was near McDonald's that I first had the feeling I was being followed. Nothing definite — just a feeling. I turned round once or twice, half expecting to see a shadowy figure leap into a doorway, but the street was full of shadowy figures all looking bombed out on drugs and shifty — your average Acton High Street on a weekday. I told myself I was just being paranoid. I'm much more nervous since I was attacked the previous summer, even though I've made a conscious effort not to let it affect where I go or what I do. You can't live your life like a victim.

I stopped outside a chemist's shop and glanced back, trying

to work out why I felt uneasy. Then I remembered. That morning, as I'd opened the front door to leave, the gate banged as if someone had been scared away by my exit. As I hustled the children into the car, I looked down the street to see if I could see anyone – milkman, postman or a neighbour – but there was no one in sight. Then again, when I'd arrived at the clinic after taking the children and Steve to the tube station, I was aware that I was being watched by a young man in a dark green leather jacket. I had noticed the jacket because I wanted one just like it and I'd half considered asking him where he bought it. It didn't seem like much at the time, but now it fed my feelings of paranoia which always lurked just beneath the surface.

I moved away from the chemist's window and walked briskly to the top of the road where the car was parked. I turned into the street, strode purposefully for ten yards or so and then turned round. At the top of the road was a young man – no green leather jacket this time, but same build and same general appearance. Whether it was the man I had seen that morning, I couldn't tell, because of a baseball cap pulled low over his face, which was half obscured by a ridiculous pair of wrap-around sunglasses. He was affecting a casual stance against the wall of the pub on the corner, pretending to watch the passers-by in the High Street.

I got in the car, looked in the side mirror and saw that the guy hadn't moved. If he was attempting to stalk me without being noticed, he couldn't have done a worse job. I decided to drive to the top of the road and confront him – ask him why he was following me – but by the time I had done a three-point turn and driven up there, he had gone.

I managed three sips of scalding tea before the doorbell rang, accompanied by squeals and giggles from beyond the front door. Steve's baritone sounded frazzled even from that distance.

'Yes, Jake, but just let me get the door open first!'

I grinned, knowing how Steve was probably feeling after a whole day of Jake's questions. I opened the door to find Steve rummaging in his rucksack to find the key. The children charged through the door and clamoured round me. Jake, as usual, was jumping from foot to foot in his eagerness to be first to speak.

'We saw the dinosaurs!' he shouted. 'We went to see the antipods – '

'Arthropods, you dork,' corrected Hannah.

'Not a dork!' shouted Jake.

'Let Steve get in!' I protested. 'Did you have a nice picnic?'

'Yes,' said Steve, 'we – '

'Yes! And Steve bought us two Mars bars each, Mum, and we ate them all up and he ate a whole mega-bar of chocolate by himself! Isn't he a pig?'

I made a face at Steve. Sweets are one thing we do not see eye to eye on. He whistled and looked skywards.

'I'd better be off.'

'Thanks for taking them, Steve. What do you say – Hannah, Jake?'

'Thank you, Steve,' they chorused, and launched themselves into his arms.

'It was a pleasure.'

The smile in his eyes told me that, despite the hassle, it had been. I gave him a peck on the cheek and saw him out. I wished I could tell him about being followed so that he could dispel my fears and tell me I was being stupid, but I knew he had to get off to the theatre. Anyway, full-scale war was threatening between two tired children in the kitchen. I had plenty to do in the next few hours to stop me dwelling on it.

Later that evening, when I was curled up on the sofa reading a book, the phone rang. It was Robin. I detected a muted excitement in his voice from the moment he said hello.

'Mona just called me. You'll never guess what has happened.'

'What?'

'She's remembered something!'

'Mazeltov!' I held my breath.

'Extraordinary that it should happen so quickly, in view of what we were saying this afternoon,' continued Robin breathlessly. 'I suppose it could have been the session with the doctor. Or it could have been my visit, or your visit – '

'Robin!'

'Yes?'

'What does she remember?'

'She remembers Tony Thornley, half sitting on the ground. She can see it distinctly now – him slumped down by the dustbins. Before, she couldn't remember a thing up to when the caretaker found her holding the knife.'

I could hardly contain my disappointment. 'Just the one image – seeing him sitting on the ground?'

'Just that.'

'Nothing else?'

'It's a good start!'

Shit! How could a mind do that?

'Can't she remember anyone else being there? Did she see anyone running away? Hear any voices?'

'It's a blank.'

I sighed. I don't know why he sounded so chirpy. It hardly seemed anything to get excited about.

'I suppose it's something,' I said doubtfully.

'That's what I told Mona,' said Robin brightly. 'I said to her, "You've opened the door! Now all you need is the courage to go through it."'

Chapter Twelve

I was having one of those awful claustrophobic dreams, where your chest is squeezed and squeezed until you can't breathe any more. I woke up suddenly, drenched in sweat, and lay there in the darkness with my heart pounding. I could still feel the clammy tentacles of the dream clutching at my throat, but the actual images, whatever they were, had faded and I did not dare to try and recall them.

The house was quiet – as quiet as a Victorian house ever can be, just the odd groan and click which I think of as the natural movement of the house as it sleeps. But as I surfaced into the real world, I became convinced that something was wrong. A muffled thud from downstairs jolted me wide awake and I lay in the dark, listening, every sense alert. For thirty seconds or so there was silence. Then the sound of a floorboard creaking on the stairs made my body go rigid. I knew it was the one on the landing just outside Jake's room. When he was a baby, I continually woke him up by stepping on it and I always vowed to have it silenced, but I'd never got around to it. I held my breath and waited. I often fear an intruder when I wake up from a nightmare, but it is usually just the fear making me ultra-suggestible. It was probably one of the children getting up to go to the toilet. I listened. Another creak – there was no padding of small feet, no clicking on of the toilet light.

Then I heard slow footsteps continuing up the stairs. There was no mistaking the heavy tread now. I felt paralysed with fear. I had rehearsed this scenario so many times since David left me. Anyone who has lived alone with small children thinks of it, lying in bed in a darkened house in the early hours. Faced with an intruder in the middle of the night, with responsibility for two young children, do you scream and risk terrifying the children, or do you pretend to be asleep and hope that the burglar finds what he wants and leaves?

I did neither. With my heart banging against my ribs, I coughed loudly. The footsteps stopped. Making as much noise as I could, I sat up in bed and put my feet on the floor, reached out a shaky hand and flipped on the bedside lamp. I grabbed a heavy textbook that was lying on the bedside table – I knew Freud would come in handy one day – stood up and, holding the book out in front of me with both hands, I waited behind the open bedroom door.

Astonishingly, the footsteps started to retreat. I could hardly believe it. The same floorboard creaked again as a foot struck it on the way downstairs. I strained my ears. I heard the bolt on the front door being turned back, and the door being opened and then clicking shut.

It was gone, over, like the nightmare that woke me in the first place. By now I was shaking uncontrollably. I rushed to the window to see if I could see anyone, but whoever it was had run off pretty smartly. I plonked down on the bed and let the book drop into my lap. I sat quaking for another few minutes, trying to calm myself by breathing deeply, then I reached for the phone and dialled 999.

'And there's nothing at all missing?' said the officer, each word dripping incredulity. His exchange of looks with the other officer as I told my story had been equally eloquent. It said, 'Aye, aye, John — we've got a right one 'ere.'

'No, nothing.'

I was beginning to regret calling the police. I was sitting in the living room at four thirty in the morning with two police constables, gulping down a mug of hot tea. Hannah had woken up when they rang the doorbell and was clinging to me, frightened and confused. We had at least established that there had been an intruder. He had got in through a top kitchen window which must have been slightly ajar and left a muddy trainer mark on the kitchen surface.

'And you say you heard him coming up the stairs?'

'That's right.' For Hannah's sake, I tried to sound matter of fact.

'Funny he didn't go for the computer or the video.'

The butterflies in my stomach fluttered with renewed energy. Was he a burglar or was he looking for me? I quelled the thought before it had time to mature. If he had wanted to harm me, he certainly gave up mighty easily.

'Is there anything worth nicking upstairs?' asked the younger, fatter constable.

'Nothing that I can think of.'

'There's your jewellery, Mum,' put in Hannah.

I gave her a squeeze. 'It's not worth much, chick.'

They took a statement, with their radios growling and sizzling in the background. They were thorough, but failed to take any account of how frightening the experience had been. One officer seemed to think it was a novice burglar who didn't know what he was doing; the other thought it was a cool professional who simply didn't find anything worth stealing. That seemed to cover all the options.

'Shall we wake up Jake? He loves policemen,' asked Hannah, her eyes shining with lost sleep and fear.

'No!' I said, aghast.

They asked us not to touch anything until the fingerprint people had been in the morning. They would check to see if there had been any other burglaries in the area and let me know if they found anything. I let them out into a chilly, blue dawn and took Hannah back into my bed to murmur reassurances and snatch a few minutes' rest before the alarm went off.

It was the first day of school. Why couldn't the guy have broken in on the Friday, or during the quiet Bank Holiday weekend, when all we had to do was stroll to the local park and back? I staggered through the breakfast routine in a daze – wiping up milk spilled from the cereal, making a sandwich for Hannah's lunch box, scrabbling under a pile of letters to find her reading book. Jake chattered relentlessly throughout, cross that he had been left out of the excitement, firing questions about why the robber came in the night and whether he wanted to kill us. These are the times when I long for a partner. I knew Jake's talking came from anxiety, and that all he needed was a calm, quiet cuddle and endless repetition of my explanation, but it was all I could do not to scream abuse at him. I tried my best, but my best fell way short of the mark.

'Please try and dress yourself today, Jake. Mummy has to finish clearing up and put the washing on, and take a key to Afsana so she can let the fingerprint men in.'

The talking stopped. His lower lip trembled and a wail reverberated round the kitchen.

'Oh, Jake.' I gritted my teeth, scooped him up in my arms and took him upstairs.

Halfway up the stairs, there was a howl from the kitchen.

'What about me?' wailed Hannah. 'You said I could have more toast!'

I sat down on the stairs with Jake bawling into my neck and tried to gather my strength. Life was not meant to be like this. In the ads, family life meant smiling kids, a big Volvo and a warm, glowing fire. I vowed that if I saw one of those smug, fat Volvos on the way to school I would ram it up the bumper.

*

When I finally reached the clinic at nine fifteen, the shock set in. Clancy, luckily, was free. When I told her what had happened, she gathered me to her ample bosom and ordered me to have a good cry. Naturally, I couldn't, which prompted a lecture about how anal and repressed I was and how I should try rebirthing. But dear Clancy's bullying was exactly what I needed. She left me a hot drink, with instructions to put my feet up on the desk and 'chill out' for the half hour before my first client.

Just as I was starting to feel better, Doreen rang up from reception. 'Cynthia Marsh to see you,' she reported crisply.

'Cynthia Marsh?'

'She doesn't have an appointment. If you'd rather not see her I can tell her — '

'It's okay, Doreen,' I interrupted. 'Send her up.'

A moment later, Cynthia appeared in the doorway. She was dressed in full business regalia — a short navy blue skirt, a silky cream blouse and an expensive, cropped jacket. Her lips were painted deep plum, to match the clip that gathered her hair in a twist on top of her head. I got up to greet her, but she stood in the doorway with her arms folded.

'Is there some good reason why you feel the need to stick your nose into other people's business?' she demanded.

It was quite an opening. I felt myself stiffen, ready to face her aggression.

'Hello, Cynthia. Why don't you come in and sit down?'

'I prefer to stand. It won't take long to say what I've got to say. What did you say to Frances Thornley?'

I did a mental gear shift. 'About what?'

'About me — and her husband.'

'Nothing. Why?'

'Why?' Her blue eyes glittered with anger. 'You've got the cheek to ask me why?'

I didn't need this. 'Sit down, Cynthia,' I said sharply. 'Or I'll have to ask you to leave.'

She pressed her lips together, hardening the lines on her

face. She stepped into the room, appraised it in seconds, then sat down heavily, still with her arms folded. I drew the chair out from behind the desk and sat at an angle to her, trying to defuse the confrontation.

'What's the problem?'

'The problem, as far as I can see, is you. You go around meddling in other people's business, telling lies . . . Mona Pearson stabbed Tony Thornley. Frances knows it. I know it. Why are you telling people different?'

'I don't know what you mean.' I was tempted to ask her how she could be so sure Mona did it, but my counsellor's training told me to ask, instead, 'Why is it so important to you that Mona did it?'

'Don't try that shrink crap on me!' she cried. 'She was caught red-handed! She hated him!'

She glared at me for a second and then, unaccountably, burst into tears. Her weeping was a lady-like boo-hooing – the kind that is designed not to ruin make-up. Maybe I was prejudiced, but the performance failed to move me. Silently, I passed her a box of tissues. She drew one from the box and wiped carefully round her eyes, sniffing pitifully.

'You don't seem to realise – I loved that man.' Her blue eyes peeped up at me, Princess Diana-style. 'You and your friend – dredging everything up. It's upsetting people. Me, Frances . . .'

Since when was she worried about Frances Thornley?

'Who have you been speaking to?' It came out snappier than I meant it to.

She hesitated, but only for a second. 'If you mean who told me about you interfering, it was Rajesh Patel.'

'What did he say?'

Her eyes were like ice, melting with tears at the edges. 'You know, I suppose, that Tony sold his shares in Thornley's?'

I nodded.

'He promised to invest some of that money in my company, but he changed his mind.'

On Patel's advice, as I recalled.

'I'm good at business – better than Tony ever was. I've got plans to expand outside London – get women to sell the clothes at parties, like Tupperware. Patel looked at the books and said that if the deal went through, he would lend me the money.'

The cunning old devil. He advises his client against investing, then takes the opportunity for himself.

'Now Frances wants to go back on the sale – ' Cynthia frowned accusingly. 'Ever since your visit.'

I felt this had gone far enough. I felt tired and raw from my scare the night before. I tried to stay calm, really just wishing she would go.

'All Robin and I have done is to speak to people about Tony's murder and pass on what we find out to Mona's solicitor. I did not mention your name to Frances Thornley. I did not tell her anything about you and her husband – but if you want my opinion, she knew already. I'm not sure what you hoped to achieve by coming here today, but if anything you've made me even more worried that the police haven't looked hard enough to find other suspects.'

Cynthia, tissue poised in mid-air, narrowed her eyes until they were almost slits. 'You're so arrogant. Who do you think you are? A man dies and all you can do is dig up the dirt – '

'Not too hard in Tony's case,' I rejoined. Sensing we were heading for a cat fight, I added, 'I think you'd better go.'

She leapt to her feet. 'I think I had!' She looked round the room once more and gave a nasty laugh. 'You should be struck off – except you're not even a doctor in the first place.' And with that, she went.

I stood up and walked around the room for a few minutes, trying to calm down. Cynthia's attack was extraordinary and I felt vulnerable enough to be upset by it, but I tried to force myself to think about its implications, if any, for Mona. First Frances and now Cynthia were showing a remarkable degree of defensiveness about anyone questioning Mona's guilt. In terms of evidence, nothing had changed – Mona still had to be

205

the prime suspect. Yet so many people had revealed that they had good reason to kill Thornley – Patel because Tony was cheating him out of money; Cynthia, because of the way he treated her as a lover; Bridget, who hated him and all he stood for … And, goodness knows, his wife and son had been abused enough to want to put him out of action permanently.

I saw Thornley's face in my mind's eye – the small eyes nestling in pasty folds of flesh, the protruding lower lip and lascivious smile. I thought of the way he sat, legs apart, his sausage fingers drumming on his pin-striped knee. It was not a pretty sight.

Was it possible that someone had slipped into Mona's office before the meeting and taken the knife? Cynthia, for example, who arrived a full fifteen minutes before anyone else? Then waited outside the school for Thornley and killed him without leaving a single trace? I found myself shaking my head. To get away with that, they would have to be either slick professional killers (unlikely if Barry was right and Tony knew his killer) or so disturbed they were prepared to take mad risks. The memory of Cynthia's eyes, full of contempt, unsettled me. I wondered uneasily if the intruder who disturbed my sleep the night before could have anything to do with my open questioning of Mona's guilt. Before Cynthia's visit, I would have dismissed the idea as ridiculous; now I was not so sure.

A knock on the door jolted me back to the present. I opened the door and Robin strode into the room, with worry written large on his face. I sat down, feeling exhausted and he pulled up a chair beside me and took my hand.

'Are you okay?'

I was touched by his concern. I said I was fine – just a little shocked. I told him the story of the burglar – it seemed less scary every time I told it – and about Cynthia's visit. Robin released my hand, leaned his elbows on his knees and clasped his hands together.

'I suspect that someone is not too happy about us meddling in Mona's case,' he said.

I looked at him expectantly. 'Oh?'

'I've been pestered all weekend with threatening phone calls.'

'Oh, Robin!' I'd been so busy wittering on about my troubles, it hadn't occurred to me he might have come in for some attention too.

'Not threatening exactly,' he corrected himself, 'but certainly anonymous. He asked me if I was alone in my house, said he knew where I lived, that kind of thing.'

It sounded threatening enough to me. 'Have you told the police?'

He nodded. 'There's not much they can do. They told me to call again if they persist.' He seemed to be taking it quite calmly.

'How many times?'

'Ten, fifteen. Once or twice in the middle of the night.'

'Poor Robin. Did you recognise the voice?'

He shook his head. 'Male, no discernible accent. On some of them, he didn't say anything. Just heavy breathing.'

'Scary.'

'More annoying, really.'

Robin was very stiff upper lip – he hated drama. He seemed reluctant to pursue the subject. There was a pause while he scratched at a crusty spot on his trousers. 'My mother got me an hour with Frances Thornley over the weekend.'

'Your mother . . . ?'

How on earth did he swing that one? Robin's lopsided grin said, 'Don't even ask,' then I remembered that his mother was on the national committee of the Townswomen's Guild. That was the most likely connection.

I folded my arms. 'And I suppose your mother was somewhat economical with the truth in order to get you this interview?'

The grin became a full-blown smile. 'She reminds me of you in that respect.'

'Thank you.'

207

Terrific – another person's mother for me to resemble.

'What did you think of Frances?' I wondered whether he had managed to be his usual polite self in the presence of a woman who was determined to put Mona away for as many years as possible.

Robin turned down his mouth and pushed out his lower lip, struggling to be objective. 'I think she's rather sad. Naturally, she didn't know I had anything to do with Mona's case – '

'Naturally. What did you talk about – knitting patterns?'

Robin laughed. 'My mother did most of the talking. I mainly watched and listened.'

The notion of Robin's mother and Frances having a cosy tea together while Robin examined every nuance of the exchange was a diverting one.

'She mostly complained about her husband. That he was disloyal and unfaithful and had left her in a financial mess. She was extraordinarily open about it. My mother offered to give her the name of a good financial adviser. That brought on a torrent of abuse against unscrupulous accountants.'

'Did she say anything specific about the shares?'

'Only that Tony should never have sold his shares without the board's consent and that her brother-in-law, Geoffrey, was going to sort it out. But she did add one interesting comment. Something to the effect that "they all stick together".'

I shrugged – it meant nothing to me.

'I didn't understand it either.' Robin's brow furrowed. 'She seemed to be implying that Patel's demand for money had something to do with Mona – that because they were both "coloured"' – Robin tapped the air with two fingers to indicate the inverted commas – 'Patel was batting for her in some way.'

None of it made sense. Rajesh Patel struck me as the type who was batting for himself, first and foremost. I couldn't see him making any gestures to save the skin of an Afro-Caribbean woman.

We sat in glum silence. I could sense that we were both feeling the same thing – that what had started as an errand of mercy for a friend had become too large and too complex. I got up and walked to the window. It was a beautiful day – bright and sunny. The forsythia in the front garden of the clinic shone bright yellow, beaming its tendrils skywards. Outside one of the houses on the opposite side of the road, two mothers stood chatting, oblivious to their two toddlers leaning over the wall to pick daffodils in a stranger's garden. I turned back to Robin to suggest that the time had come to hand everything over to Mona's solicitor, when I saw to my horror that he was crying. At least, he had his head in his hands and his shoulders were shaking. It seemed to be a morning for tears and tantrums. I went over to him, knelt down and put my arms about him, murmuring soothing noises.

'I'm sorry,' he gulped. 'So stupid.'

'That's right – apologise. Make me feel guilty.' I wondered what it was that had suddenly got to him. 'Is it the phone calls?' I asked tentatively. Robin shook his head and blew his nose on one of his pristine handkerchiefs. Another nail in the coffin of his washing machine.

'I – I haven't been strictly honest with you, Sara.'

I wouldn't bat an eyelid if most people said that, but because it was Robin I felt a flutter of alarm.

'What do you mean?'

He sighed. 'About Mona. It wasn't just infatuation – we were lovers.'

I sat back on my heels and looked at him. I realised with surprise that these last two weeks had aged him. The crow's feet were a little more pronounced, and there were bags under his eyes which I was sure had not been there before. He was pale except for the red tip at the end of his nose.

'I shouldn't have taken on the Arkwright group. But I told myself there had never been anything meaningful between us. Underneath, I was still angry with her really.'

'We all make mistakes, Robin.'

I would have to tell the others, and we would no doubt discuss it *ad nauseam*, but now was not the time to make an issue of it. Robin just wanted to talk and spill the thoughts that had been tormenting him in the weeks since Mona's arrest.

'Mona was the only woman I've ever met who seemed exactly on my wavelength. The only problem was that she insisted on keeping the relationship a secret. She was obsessive about it. We always met in town; she came to my place, never the other way round, and when we finally got round to making love – Do you mind me telling you this, Sara?'

'Not if it helps.'

'I feel disloyal.'

'It's up to you, Robin. You know it won't go any further.'

He nodded and bit his lip. He turned his face away from me slightly, fixing his gaze on my bookcase. 'It was – she was – marvellous, you know, in bed, except that – ' He paused, searching for the words. 'She felt she had to perform all the time. She behaved like a whore. It's the only way I can describe it. She treated every night we spent together as a one-night stand. I couldn't understand it at the time. I tried asking her about it, but she just got angry. I tried to get her to see that I loved her for herself – that, as far as I was concerned, the woman who came to films and plays with me was the same woman who chose to come into my bed, but she refused to even discuss it. If only she'd told me why . . . '

'She'd blotted it out, Robin. She probably hardly knew it herself.'

'So she carried on . . . performing until I couldn't stand it any more. The relationship wasn't moving forward. I started to get jealous, wondering who else she was doing this with. We got so angry with each other! It became destructive – so I ended it.'

I smiled sadly. 'And now you see that you just fell into the trap of replaying the abuse she suffered as a child and fulfilling all her expectations of what men are like. You feel you understand it now, so you want to go back.'

Robin made eye contact again and grinned through his tears. 'And, as a professional counsellor, you have to advise me that we can never go back. That the Mona who comes out of prison – whenever that may be – will be a different Mona from the one who went in; that in all probability, she will have post-traumatic stress disorder and will need specialist help; that I cannot be her therapist and her lover; that interracial relationships – especially for people with widely disparate social backgrounds – have their own problems; that – '

'Excuse me!' I interrupted, 'I'm charging for this, so you may as well let me get a word in edgeways.'

'Sorry.'

'I agree with everything you say. But I do have one small piece of advice.'

'Which is?'

'Wait and see.'

He laughed. 'And for this, you charge?'

'I'm serious.' I took his hand. 'Robin, the chances are that Mona is going down for a long time. I think you will have to face up to that. But in the meantime, see her, talk to her, take it day by day, the way she has to.'

His eyes filled with tears again and he moved towards me awkwardly. I hugged him and patted his lower back – my head only came up as far as his breastbone.

'Thanks, Sara.'

'For nothing.'

The buzzer went – my first client had arrived.

Robin drew back. 'I think it's time we saw Mona's solicitor.'

'I think so too.'

Robin said he would ring her later that morning to make an appointment. In my heart, I was relieved. Turning over the little we knew to the solicitor would be a way of divesting ourselves of responsibility, at least for the time being. I felt that Robin and I had just made an unspoken agreement to let our investigations drop for a while, to let the dust settle, perhaps until we knew whether or not Mona would get out on bail.

As soon as Robin shut the door behind him, I buzzed up the client — a young man referred by his GP for sleep problems. Now all I had to do was get through the day.

★ ★ ★

It was Friday afternoon, after a week packed with work and mothering, with little time to think beyond my own horizons. I was rushing round Acton with two indecisive children, trying to get a birthday present for their father. We always found this yearly ritual a trial, each for our own reasons, and it always got left until the last possible moment. David felt very strongly about birthdays. He always made a fuss of the children's birthdays and he expected them to make a fuss of his. I was exempt from this yearly attention-fest since the divorce, but I was drawn into it through the children. The irony was that, when it came to presents, David was hard to please. It wasn't that a present had to be expensive, but it had to be something with thought behind it, something that was bought with only him in mind. Hence the trek round several shops. Hannah and Jake agonised over what he would like best, competing with each other for the best ideas, while I seethed inwardly about how manipulative it all felt. In most ways, David was a wonderful father, but I did object to him putting such store by material symbols of their regard for him. Birthdays were one thing; measuring Hannah and Jake's love for him by their ability to remember his favourite brand of socks was quite another.

There was a second reason for my irritation. It was obvious that someone was watching us, keeping track of our movements. It was the same guy, in a green jacket, cap and sunglasses, I had noticed outside the clinic the week before. I spotted him as soon as we came out of the house — he was outside the motor spares shop on the corner of our road, pretending to look in the window. But by the time I had shepherded the children out of the house and down the road towards him, he had disappeared, only to appear again behind us when we got down near the High Street. This time, all fear had evaporated and it was just a bloody nuisance. He was totally incompetent as a tail – quite visible, hovering around with an ungainly slouch, almost as if he wanted me to approach him. I was convinced he was the client or ex-client who was ringing the clinic trying to pluck up courage to make an appointment. It's happened before. Mel had a stalker back in the summer who turned out to be the husband of one of her battered women. I wanted to stop and have a word with him, but he was tantalisingly just out of calling range. If I wanted to go over and talk to him, I would either have to leave the children standing alone on the street or drag them with me in some ridiculous counter-stalking exercise.

When Hannah stopped to look at the window display of a computer games shop, I turned round to get a better look at him. He was short and stocky and he had brown curly hair – that was about all I could make out. The collar of his jacket was turned up, his shoulders were hunched and his hands were thrust in his pockets.

'Daddy doesn't like computer games. If he did we could save up and get him something like Sim City or Lemmings,' said Hannah wistfully.

'Sin City?' I was momentarily appalled. What did you have to do – zap the brothels, shoot up the drug dealers?

'Sim City!' she corrected me. 'You pretend you're building a city and you have to build it with all the things people need.'

'Oh.'

Hannah seems to know all about these things since she has become friends with an alarmingly large boy called Terry.

'I'm gonna buy him a computer,' said Jake proudly, his face pressed hard against the glass. 'I'm gonna buy it now,' he added, by way of explanation, as he took his face away from the window and marched into the shop.

'Dork,' muttered Hannah.

We trudged in after him to explain, for the thousandth time, about not buying Daddy things which cost a lot of money.

From inside the shop, I watched the guy in the jacket cross to our side of the road and install himself in a doorway. As Hannah and Jake got absorbed in a computer game, I thought idly about Richard Thornley and the students of Arkwright High. Could it be a prank? Certainly the guy looked fairly young, and there could have been more than one of them. I had only seen them in the distance and had no impression of a particular face or colouring, so all they would have to do would be to pass over the green jacket, hat and shades.

In the end, the present problem was solved by going back to the very first shop we went into – a tatty second-hand shop in Churchfield Road, not far from our house. We walked there in a bizarre procession – a harassed mother dragging one tired four-year-old, an eight-year-old who insisted on walking behind us on principle and a shifty young man following at a discreet distance. I almost expected someone else to join in behind, like in one of those children's books where the mother, the children, the old pig and the chicken all dance down the road together chasing the big pancake.

In the shop, after some deliberation, Jake chose a plate with a picture of a sailing ship on it – not exactly tasteful, but not awful either. Daddy would like it, he said, because he loved reading *Captain Pugwash* aloud and doing all the voices and this ship was just like the ship in *Captain Pugwash*. That should go down well, I thought, relieved. Hannah, ever the pragmatist, settled on a barbecue cookbook and a mug. 'Angie is always telling Dad they should have more people round for dinner,' reasoned Hannah. 'Now they can have a barbecue.' I declined to comment on that one. Hannah is always throwing me a line to make negative remarks about Angie and David's relationship and lifestyle. I fell for it the first few times, but now I'm wise to it. Of course, I was secretly delighted to hear that Angie, like me, had to struggle with David's unsociability and his desire to have her to himself all the time, but I knew I mustn't let Hannah see it. Yes, indeed – now they could have a barbecue and jolly good luck to them.

Our shadow had disappeared by the time we reached home – either that or he had found a less visible vantage point from which to watch the house. I wanted to ring Robin to ask him if he was still getting his phone calls, and if he had any ideas about clients who might fit the bill, but there wasn't time, and anyway the chances of him being in on a Friday night were remote.

David collected the children at half past six. It had been a scramble to get them both ready, but at least the presents were safe and wrapped in their bags and the birthday fiasco was over for another year. After I had seen them off, I glanced up and down the road again, but there was still no sign of the man in the green jacket. Maybe he too was tired of the game now and, like the storybook characters chasing the pancake, had gone home to have his tea.

Chapter Thirteen

It was my favourite kind of theatre – old-fashioned, with a steeply raked auditorium, six lavishly decorated boxes and a domed ceiling ornamented with extravagant swirls and twists of gold. We were in the best seats – at least, I think they're the best – in the second row of the circle, right in the middle. It was Saturday night and I was sitting slightly nervously beside Pete, waiting for the lights to go down. He had put on a shirt and tie – despite my having told him the tie was unnecessary – tied back his hair and had an extra-close shave. His aftershave smelled lemony and expensive. Sitting back on his chair, his dark eyes roaming restlessly round the auditorium, he looked like an usher at a Mafia wedding. As well as looking round, scrutinising the rest of the audience, he kept twisting in his seat, trying to find a comfortable space for his long legs without wrapping them round the neck of the woman in front of him.

'Which part is your friend playing?' he asked finally.

I pointed out Steve's name in the programme. 'He's playing Eddie Burton, one of the husbands. Are you ever going to keep still?'

'It's these seats. Not much room, is there?'

This had seemed like a good idea about a week ago. Since Steve wanted me to see the play and Pete had been talking about us going to the theatre, I thought it was the perfect opportunity to kill two birds with one stone. But Steve had presented us with the free tickets on the condition that he got to meet Pete afterwards and I didn't like the twinkle in his eye as he said it. Pete was highly dubious about the subject of the play, as well he might be. It was about three couples who rent a house together in France for the summer holiday. The blurb read like a health warning that should probably be mandatory in every rent-a-*gite* holiday brochure: 'As they sit round the dinner table drinking wine, with their children tucked up in bed, the bonhomie turns to conflict, bitterness and despair. Neither the friendships nor the marriages will ever be quite the same again.'

'Is it a musical?' asked Pete, reading the synopsis over my shoulder.

Fortunately, the lights went down as he said it, so I didn't have to find out whether or not he was joking. But I had a feeling that this could be a testing evening for our relationship.

The play was everything it promised to be – wordy, harrowing and compelling in the same way as motorway accidents – you know you shouldn't look, but you do because the horror is mesmerising and you are so relieved it is someone else's misfortune rather than yours. Steve was tremendous as the loud, fatuous Eddie, whose ribald comments and sexual innuendoes mask the fact that he has become impotent. The pain in his face when he discovers that his wife has told everyone about the problem and made him a laughing stock brought a lump to my throat.

I stole a glance at Pete to see how he was taking it. He looked deeply engrossed – an illusion that was instantly shattered by him leaning towards me and saying in a voice which was audible at least two rows back, 'Can I stay at your place tonight?' I made a face and hushed him. He took this as a 'yes', grinned and slipped an arm round my shoulders.

It was hard to concentrate fully on the angst on stage with Pete so close. There is something very sexual about being in a theatre and the touch of his fingers through the thin material of my blouse was enough to set my thoughts off in another direction.

Pete, restless and bored, started to muzzle my ear. I pushed him off and whispered, sharply, 'Watch the play!'

'I'm watching! Nothing's happening. They're just talking.'

'Shhh!' hissed a man from behind.

At the interval, Pete and I drank cool beer and, as if by mutual consent, silently contemplated our own thoughts rather than attempt a conversation about the play. I wanted to listen to the comments of the people around us. I always marvel at the pretentious comments people feel driven to make in the interval of a play – myself included. One woman behind us described the play as 'Pinter without the Pinteresque', which could mean something very deep or nothing at all. A middle-aged man announced cheerfully to his companions that the whole thing reminded him of a holiday he had taken with his first wife and a group of their friends – they divorced, he said, shortly afterwards. The comment I most relished came from a debonair young man who told his friend, with some authority, that 'the fat one' was the only decent actor in it, which – though Steve might balk at the reference to his paunch – still gave me a proud rush of pleasure.

We met Steve afterwards in a smoky pub round the corner from the theatre, where other members of the cast also gravitated to wind down after the performance. Pete jumped up when Steve came over and offered to buy him a drink. Steve thanked him and asked for a pint. He rubbed his hands and asked anxiously, 'Did you enjoy it?'

'You were wonderful.'

'It was great,' agreed Pete. 'Mind you, the bloke who wrote it either can't add up or he's a pervert.'

Steve and I both looked at him dumbly.

'What do you mean?'

Pete sighed. 'When the blonde one – your wife – is telling that story – '

'Shelagh – '

'Shelagh, right – she says, like, I was four years old and I was playing doctors with this kid in the back garden when we won the World Cup. So it was 1966 and she was four years old. But then later, you – Eddie – say you met her at college and had a quick one in a Mini and it was 1973 which would make her, by my reckoning, only eleven.'

Steve's jaw dropped. 'I never noticed that.' He laughed. 'Wait until I tell the others!'

I caught Pete's eye, gobsmacked. So he had been paying attention, at least some of the time. He grinned, pleased with himself.

'You do the same part every night, then,' he said to Steve.

I held my breath, hoping Steve would not make a cutting reply. But Steve was still smiling about the inconsistency in the play. 'That's right,' he said mildly. 'But you do it a bit differently every night, to keep it interesting.'

'A pint?'

'Of bitter. Thanks.'

Steve raised his eyebrows at me when Pete was at the bar. 'You old cradle-snatcher. Sharp lad. Very handsome.'

'Steve – ' I warned.

He raised his hands, all mock innocence. 'What did I say?'

'He's not a lad.'

He tapped his lips with one finger and smothered a smile. 'Not a word, I promise. What did you think of the play really?'

'I thought it was a bit much, but you were terrific. Best thing you've done for ages.'

Steve nodded. 'I think so too.'

He was insecure sometimes, but never falsely modest. I repeated the comment I had heard at the interval and Steve patted his stomach. 'Bloody cheek,' he said, but he was obviously pleased.

*

219

If I was uncomfortable about the idea of putting Pete and Steve together, I needn't have worried. Within five minutes, they had discovered a mutual interest in football. How do men get sport into the conversation so early on? It happens so quickly you miss the link. Steve supports Oldham – a legacy from his boyhood – but he is also a devoted fan of the Italian league. Pete supports Arsenal, as well as an obscure Italian team from the same town as his family. The play was quickly forgotten in favour of reminiscing about memorable matches from the last World Cup and the poetry of Roberto Baggio's goals. I found the conversation supremely boring, but I still looked on contentedly as their politeness warmed into friendly argument about who should be picked for the next Italian team.

They argued about it as we threaded our way out of Soho towards the Westway, but by the time we reached the turn off to Shepherd's Bush, Steve had hit upon another topic which interested Pete profoundly – building security. It started with Steve asking Pete what he could do to make his flat more secure – he had been burgled twice in the past year. Pete took him through the options, sparing him no detail. I couldn't believe that either of them could be so boring. I yawned as I drove, starting to feel the day catching up on me. We had agreed to go back to my place for a drink, but when we got to Acton the only space I could find was outside Steve's flat. This gave the two men the perfect opportunity to continue their analysis of alarm systems.

I said I would meet them back at my house. I might as well be opening the wine and helping myself to peanuts. I walked back home feeling contented that, against all the odds, the evening was turning out to be a success. The air was sharp with the scent of dank earth, hyacinth and car fumes, the aroma which signals spring in the city. The road was quiet for a Saturday night, but it was still before midnight and the rowdier elements didn't usually roll home until after one. A couple strolled past me, locked in each other's arms, and a stray dog scuttled by, nose to the pavement, heading, no doubt, for the takeaways in Churchfield Road.

I ambled through my front gate, not bothering to close it because of Pete and Steve. I was just reaching into my bag for the key when I was distracted by a rustling in the front garden by the bushes. Without thinking, I stepped off the path onto our small patch of grass, expecting to see a dog or a cat dart out from under the hedge. Instead, the figure of a man loomed out of the darkness towards me. I gasped with surprise and turned to run. He reached out to catch my arm. 'Wait!' he whispered.

In my haste to get away, I stepped back, stumbled and fell against the sill of our bay window. I recovered my balance, but not quickly enough. He sprang forward and placed both hands flat against the wall of the house, one on each side of my head. His body smelled sickeningly of stale sweat and greasy fish and chips.

'I wanna talk to you.' The voice was familiar, but I still couldn't see his face. He loomed over me in the darkness. I tried to stay calm, sidled under his arm and started edging my way along the wall towards the front door.

'Don't touch me,' I warned. 'I've got two friends coming and they're both experts at Tai Kwondo.'

It would be news to them, but my attacker didn't know that.

'I said I just wanna talk.'

He put his hands on the wall again, this time at the level of my shoulders, to block me from moving any further. He was small, but powerfully built. I put one tentative hand on his arm to gauge his reaction. I sensed his nervousness through the soft leather of his jacket, and I knew that it could erupt at any moment into violence. He was twitching like a racehorse ready to go. Any move to escape could set him off. I stopped moving and became quite still. He probably didn't believe me about the two friends, so it might be better to wait and let them surprise him.

I strained my ears for the sound of Pete and Steve

approaching; I thought I could just about hear their voices, but they didn't seem to be getting nearer. How long could it take to explain a burglar alarm? About as long as it takes for a violent psychopath to drag me into an alleyway and rape me, I thought bitterly. He stepped right up to me and pressed his chest close to my body. As he did so, the light from outside my front door caught the left side of his face. Large eyes peeped out from beneath a baseball cap. I glimpsed a fleshy nose and thick, puffy lips. It was Richard Thornley.

'Richard!' Lucky I remembered his name. 'What are you doing here?'

'Like I said. Wanted to talk to you.'

I thought quickly, trying to marshal the tools of experience. He was fifteen years old – not a boy, not quite a man. His father was a bully; his mother a victim. His father had been killed recently and violently. He was angry; he was frightened. Everything suddenly became clear – the phone calls to the clinic, the boy following me, even perhaps the intruder in my house. This was a troubled boy who desperately needed an adult to talk to. I was sure he didn't want to hurt me, but I needed to move carefully to give him the right message – that I wasn't scared of him and I understood what he wanted.

'I don't know about you, Richard, but I don't find this the most comfortable place for a conversation,' I said briskly. Use his name, I told myself. Make it sound like you're calm and in control. 'Step aside, and then you can tell me what's on your mind.'

He hesitated for a moment and then moved an inch or so backwards. His body was still between me and my front door, but it was a start.

'What did you want to talk to me about?'

'You upset my mum!' He pointed a finger into my face. 'You're going round asking all these questions!' His voice was cracked with pent-up anger. 'What d'you upset my mum for? What's she ever done to you?'

'Nothing,' I answered gently. 'Tell me what she told you.'

'You're sticking up for Miss Pearson,' he spat. 'You're in it with that tart Cynthia Marsh – and Patel too probably. You won't get away with it. My Uncle Geoff's fixing Patel, so whatever he's promised you, you ain't going to get it.'

'Richard, I'm confused. Rajesh Patel hasn't promised me anything. I hardly know him. Why is your mother upset?'

'You know why!' he cried. 'He says he saw me, but it's all lies. He just wants the money. Leave my mum alone, or you'll be sorry!'

My head was reeling. Me, Patel, the money . . . I wanted to unravel it, but I knew I had to be careful. The most trivial thing might set him off.

'I can see why you're upset,' I said, keeping my voice low and calm. 'I expect your mum relies on you quite a bit. Even more so now your dad's not there.'

He thrust his hands into his pockets and scuffed at the grass. I was starting to make contact. She probably made you her ally against your father, reasoned my counsellor's voice. She makes you soft. Is that a problem for you, I wonder, now you're in a tough school, trying to find a place for yourself?

'I'm sorry if I upset your mother. I wonder what sort of questions you think I'm asking her . . . '

'Just stay away from her, and tell your friend to do the same.'

'If you want to talk to me, Richard, we could find a better time and a better place – '

I was interrupted by the sudden sound of voices. Pete and Steve had just turned the corner of the road. The boy froze when he heard the voices. He looked at me enquiringly, trying to gauge if I knew them.

'Don't call out,' he whispered.

'It's okay,' I answered him in a normal voice.

They were almost at the gate now, Steve's voice rising above Pete's, telling a story I had heard many times about the time he came home in the afternoon and disturbed a burglar. When the boy realised they were approaching the house, he suddenly made the connection with what I said about two friends. His eyes were wide with panic. He bent down and reached into his shoe; I knew what he was after.

'Richard, no! They're friends. They won't hurt you.'

Too late. He moved to the side of the path and flattened himself against the bushes. I saw the glint of the knife in the sodium glare of the streetlamp and my heart started to bang against my ribcage.

'Don't shout,' he rasped again, 'or I'll use it.'

Great, I thought. We were getting on fine until the cavalry arrived.

We stood quite still for what seemed like minutes but was, in reality, seconds. The possible scenarios flashed through my mind. Steve coming through the gate. Me shouting a warning. Richard running off. Or stabbing Steve. Pete grabbing the knife and hurting Richard. Or me yelling a warning to both of them before they got to the gate and the boy knifing me instead. I thought back desperately to my self-defence training – how on earth were you supposed to disarm a man with a knife? You weren't; you were supposed to run. But then I reminded myself not to overreact – the boy simply wanted to get something off his chest. The thing to do was to move slowly and let him feel in control. I would tell him clearly what I was going to do, so he didn't feel threatened or caught off guard.

'I'm going to warn them that you're there, Richard, but I won't let them hurt you.' I waited for that to sink in and then called out. 'Pete! Steve! Stay where you are for a moment.'

The footsteps stopped.

'What's wrong?' Pete's tone told me he sensed danger.

I tried to keep my voice steady, hoping they could interpret my counsellor speak, hoping they wouldn't rush in and do an SAS. 'There's a young friend of mine here who's very upset. I've told him you won't hurt him. He's just behind the hedge.'

'Are you okay?' Steve's voice now, sounding very macho and butch. The deep ringing tones probably put the fear of God into the boy, imagining a six-foot-three bouncer with biceps like balloons.

'I'm fine.' Then I added, just loud enough for everyone to hear, 'Richard, put the knife away.'

It was enough to make Pete and Steve appear simultaneously at the gate. I moved into the light of the house so that they could see I was free and unharmed. Pete was inching forward, but Steve laid a restraining hand on his arm.

'Shall I call the police?' asked Pete.

'No!' Richard and I answered simultaneously.

Try to involve him in the decision, counselled my inner voice. He's not a child. Get him to face the problem and help you solve it.

'What are we going to do about this, Richard?' I called out. I could hardly see him against the dark. I felt like I was talking to the hedge. 'It's late and I'm tired. I'm willing to talk to you inside the house if you want, but you'll have to get rid of the knife first.'

I heard Pete muttering to Steve, 'In the house? She's mad!'

'I have to know that you're able to keep control of yourself,' I continued. 'If you're not sure about that, maybe you should go off home and come back some other time.'

The hedge rustled. 'Tell your friends to piss off first. Then we'll talk.'

'Pete and Steve were coming to my house for a drink. They're not going to change their plans because of you. What's it to be? Do you want to talk, or do you want to go home?'

'Talk,' he mumbled.

'What about the knife?'

There was a soft thud in the middle of the grass. I could just see the handle, bone-white in the shadows.

'Steve and Pete can go in first,' I said, not wanting any mishaps. 'Then we'll go in together – okay?'

I motioned for them to come forward. Pete was muttering furiously. Steve had his hand on his shoulder. They came slowly through the gate. Pete strained to catch a glimpse of

Richard, but Steve steered him onwards. I stood aside and motioned for them to pass. Everyone was safer now we were by the door, because the boy had an escape route if he wanted it.

'What are you playing at?' demanded Pete, *sotto voce*. 'You can't let him in the house!'

I found his anxiety both annoying and touching.

'Leave it, mate,' said Steve quietly. 'It's her job.' Then, to me, 'Where's the key?'

I handed it to him gratefully. 'There's beer in the fridge,' I said.

'For fuck's sake,' said Pete, but the protest was less adamant. He took a long look into the darkness, then followed Steve into the house.

'I wonder if you'd like a beer too, Richard,' I said to the shadow which still lingered by the hedge. 'I know I could do with one. You gave me a fright.'

There was no reply. It was odd that he had stayed and opted to talk. Most other adolescent boys I know would have legged it and come back when there weren't any men around.

A few seconds later, he shuffled out, like a small boy who has hidden in the cupboard because he's done something naughty. He inched towards the door, blinking in the light. The scowl of his mouth was contradicted by the beseeching look in his eyes. Automatically, I checked for signs of the influence of drugs and noticed again the rash around his mouth and nose. He looked uncared for and desperate.

'Come in,' I said, steeling myself against the odour of grease and sweat as he pushed past me into the house.

The words started slowly and then, oiled by a can of lager, spewed out like a hot geyser, hissing with the steam of frustration. I had heard it so many times before, but it never fails to move me – the desolate raging of a rejected teenager who wants nothing more than to be loved and accepted as a person. My strategy was to listen, to let him talk himself out, no matter how irrelevant it seemed. He said he didn't want to talk about his father. He didn't miss him, didn't care about him. He didn't mind at all that his father never liked him. Not at all. He, Richard, was into body-building right now. Mason at the gym thought he was good. No one would mess with him at school by next term. Not even that fucking Granger kid. His father had meant nothing to him. His mum was better off without him. She said so all the time. He most certainly did not want to talk about his father. What was the point? He was dead and he wasn't coming back. He, Richard, was taking his mum on holiday this summer – to France. They couldn't go abroad when his dad was alive because he hated foreigners. Things were good. Great. Terrific. It was his body that bothered him. He wanted to be bigger. His shoulders were too sloping – had I noticed that? His chest could do with another four inches at least. His arms were pathetic, but they were getting better. And his neck – what did I think of his neck? His calves were okay, but not his thighs . . .

Slumped on the sofa, legs apart, clutching a can of lager, he looked like his father's son, but less complacent. He had a nervous habit of sniffing, flexing back his shoulders and jerking his chin. His thumbs pressed at the lager can as if impatient for that moment when the beer was gone and they could crumple it to the size of a ping-pong ball. I searched my exhausted mind for some entry point that would move him off body-building and on to whatever it was he really wanted to say.

I decided to call a halt at the stomach muscles to ask about his mother. Somewhere, at the back of my mind, a question loomed, but I couldn't quite get hold of it. He said his mum was okay, but she didn't approve of the body-building at all. She didn't see the need. He tried to explain that he needed to build up his strength but she didn't seem to understand.

'You said your mother was upset because of the questions I've been asking. Do you want to tell me more about that?'

'Patel wants to get Pearson off because they're both

coloured. And he wants his money. But you're white and so is your friend. You should keep out of it.'

I tried again to deconstruct the logic, but either I was too tired or I hadn't got hold of the missing link.

'I've been following you,' he added.

'I know. I've seen you. You broke into my house, didn't you?' He nodded.

'Why?'

'Just wanted to tell you to keep away from my mum.'

Too simple to telephone, I suppose. A young man wants a chat, so he breaks into your house at three in the morning, then changes his mind and walks out. Maybe he did it with the help of chemically induced courage, or paranoia.

Light suddenly dawned about Robin's mysterious phone calls. 'You've been calling Robin too, haven't you?'

He nodded again, surprised that I knew. 'It's just mum and me now and we're all right. We don't want people like you messing it up for us.'

'You should have come to see us at the clinic, Richard,' I said quietly. 'We would've been glad to see you.'

He blushed awkwardly, sniffed and flexed his shoulders again. My heart went out to him.

One more glug of lager and he was off again, describing his training schedule. Monday – a couple of hours on the pecs, half an hour on stomach, a few press-ups; Tuesday, legs – an hour on each set of muscles. Mason said if he kept this up, he'd look wicked by the autumn.

As he rambled on, I wondered if the sainted Mason might be supplying the boy with anabolic steroids. That might explain why he was so keyed up. They help build up muscles, but they can also make you wired up and violent. They make your balls shrink too, but poor Richard probably hadn't discovered that yet.

I decided to come at the subject of his father obliquely. I interrupted the training schedule to remind him of what he had said to me when I visited the school – he asked if I was one of his father's women and then decided I was too ugly. Was that another reason for following me? His father was pretty successful with women. How did he feel about that?

With hindsight, I should have foreseen that the one thing that would light Richard Thornley's fuse was some reference to his sexuality in relation to his father. It seemed obvious when I analysed what happened next, later, with Robin, but at the time all I saw was an arc of beer as those mighty thumbs squeezed the beer can flat and his face crumpling into fury. One minute he was sitting on the sofa; the next, he was sitting on my chest with his hands squeezing the air from my neck.

I had only a split second to cry out, but Pete, thankfully, had not completely closed the kitchen door as I asked him to and he sprang into the room just as coloured lights were starting to dance in front of my eyes. I attempted a scream, but it came out merely as a gurgle. It was at that inopportune moment, when Richard Thornley's stubby fingers were pressing painfully into my throat, that I finally got hold of the question I wanted to ask. He said Rajesh Patel had seen him – seen him where? His face, contorted with hate, swimming in and out of focus, answered the question for me. Patel had seen Richard Thornley at Arkwright High School, the night his father was murdered.

'Get off her!' Steve's booming voice came from somewhere behind Pete.

It caused Richard to loosen his grip just long enough for Pete to reach from behind and hook his arm round my attacker's throat. I grabbed his wrists and wrenched his hands away from my neck. With Steve's help, Pete dragged him off my chest and the three of us struggled to subdue him. But Pete's intervention seemed to give him renewed strength. He managed to beat us off and struggle to his feet. Putting a chair between him and us, he reached behind him onto the shelf and started hurling at us anything he could lay his hands on – plates, books, photos and finally, a metal car transporter, courtesy of Jake.

'Richard, stop! Calm down.'

'You fucking bitch!'

I ducked to avoid a decorative pot given to me by my aunt. I was glad to see that it shattered. I was not so happy when it was followed by a framed photo of Hannah as a baby.

'For fuck's sake, Sara, why did you let him in the house?'

Thanks, Pete, I thought, I'll answer that one later.

'I'll call the police,' said Steve.

'No wait,' I said.

There was no point in calling the police immediately – if the fight continued, the neighbours would probably do it soon enough and it didn't help with the immediate situation. Luckily, Richard was nowhere near the window, so he couldn't smash it and make a run for it. I judged the distance between him and us and tried to remember the training I had had as a social worker in physical restraint. There were three of us. He was strong, but he wasn't armed. We should be able to contain him.

'If you don't stop throwing things we're going to have to stop you, Richard,' I said, trying to keep my tone natural, as if this happened every day. 'I don't want to call the police.'

Another missile smashed behind my head – a table lamp. I sensed that Pete and Steve, standing on each side of me, were poised like cats, ready to pounce. My throat was throbbing from where he had tried to throttle me – I would have some prize bruises there by the morning.

'Pete, you take one arm, I'll take the other,' I murmured. 'Steve – get his legs. Now!'

At my signal, the three of us moved forward in a line.

'Calm down, Richard,' I said. 'We're not going to hurt you.'

He moved back as we approached, searching frantically for something else to throw. I carried on talking, urging him to stop throwing things and let us take control.

'Keep away!' His cry was frantic.

We got him just by the wall and managed to grab an arm

each. Steve lunged himself at his legs and held on for dear life.

'We're just going to hold you until you're calm,' I muttered between gritted teeth.

'Fuck off! Wankers!' He thrashed his head from side to side and aimed his head at Pete, trying to bite him.

'Bite me, shithead, and you're dead,' warned Pete, who was clearly exploding with frustration at the 'softly, softly' social-work approach.

We held on tight as he struggled. Gradually, the curses turned to moans and then the moans became full-blown sobs. I motioned to Pete and Steve to relax their grip. They were dubious, but experience told me the crisis was over. I loosened my hold on Richard's arm and slipped the other arm round his shoulders. He was howling like a baby. I sat him beside me on the sofa and held him as his body heaved with emotion. My own thumping heartbeat started to subside and my head cleared. It suddenly occurred to me that Richard Thornley was the only suspect whose alibi depended on another suspect. His mother had told the police that her son was at home when she got in, but we had only her word for it. What if he had actually come home much later, in a half-crazed state, and confessed that he had just murdered his father? How many battered women would turn in their own son?

'Your mum protected you, didn't she?' I said finally.

He lifted his face from his hands. There were smears of dirt across his cheeks and forehead. The tears were still spilling from his eyes, making clean tracks of pink through grime. There was fear in his eyes, but also relief. He lowered his gaze to his stubby hands, turned upwards and resting on his lap.

'There was so much blood,' he whispered. 'It was all over me. But it was dark and raining. I stuck to the back streets and no one saw me.'

'Except Patel.'

'That was before, not after. He must have seen me coming in as he drove away. He can't prove nothing.'

But you've just told me in front of two witnesses, sonny.

That was why he had been pursuing me and Robin – to off-load the crushing weight of his guilt. It must have been unbearable. Not only had he killed his father, but his mother knew about it. Just as he was trying to grow up and become his own man, she had bound him to her by the terrible secret of what he had done.

My arm was still round his shoulders. I was beginning to feel the effects of shock now, but I hoped I could control it long enough to encourage Richard Thornley to spill out the whole story of his father's murder. There was no going back. Pete and Steve were standing behind the sofa like statues, afraid to move in case they broke the spell.

'Why did you go to Arkwright that night?'

'She was scared to go home.'

'Your mum?'

He nodded. 'She never liked to be there alone with him. She liked me to stay in with her if she didn't have one of her meetings.'

I was torn between repulsion and sympathy. This great brute sobbing beside me had murdered his father and tried to murder me. But how could you blame him? He had been manipulated by his mother into being her shield, held up to protect her from the bully she lived with.

'So you wanted to have it out with him?'

'I knew he'd been at her the night before – I heard them. So I waited for him outside the school. I told him – lay your hand on her one more time and you'll be sorry.'

I pictured the scene. Thornley, smarting from his lack of success with Mona, strutting out of the door only to be confronted by his son.

'I suppose he didn't take you seriously.'

'He–he laughed at me.' His back straightened with the memory and he clenched his fists. 'Told me to mind my own business and if – if I ever got a girlfriend I might understand...'

So his father and I had something in common after all – we both managed to cast aspersions on his son's sexuality.

Thornley did it deliberately and died for it; I did it accidentally and nearly suffered the same fate.

'He was laughing and laughing. I told him to stop. I warned him. But he still carried on.' Foolish man. 'I had the knife in my jacket – '

'You got it from Mona's office.'

'I nicked it after school.' He caught the look on my face. 'Only 'cos it was good one! I fancied it, that's all. I didn't mean to use it. It's just for protection – I always carry one.'

Save it for the judge, Richard. He'll love it.

'I didn't know what I was doing. I–I was out of it.' His eyes filled again and his head dropped back into his hands.

'Je-sus,' breathed Pete from behind.

'Mum hid the clothes and told me to go to bed, act like nothing had happened. Then the police turned up and told her about Dad and she cried like she really meant it. They said they'd arrested Miss Pearson. And Mum, it was like – she really believed Miss Pearson did it. She said to me, "Don't talk about it any more. That woman did it." Like I can forget it and pretend. But I can't.'

Turning to me imploringly, he caught sight of Pete out of the corner of his eye. He had moved round to the side, to get a better look at Richard's face. Richard made as if to stand up and screeched, 'What you fucking staring at?'

'Richard! Relax. It's okay.' I laid my hand on his arm and gently sat him down again. Pete moved back to where he had been before.

Richard shook his head. 'I keep seeing his face. When he was there on the ground, with the knife sticking in him, he called me "son". He never did that before. "Why?" he kept saying. "Why?" He knew why. The bastard.'

The boy buried his face in his hands. He started sobbing again and his shoulders shook. I shot a warning look at Pete not to move. Steve was immobile, caught up in the drama, probably expecting a director to intervene at any moment and ask us to do the scene again. I kept thinking of Frances

Thornley, who was willing to see an innocent woman imprisoned for years for the sake of her son. I wondered if I would ever do that for Jake. I hoped I wouldn't. No wonder she had been so jumpy about Robin and me asking questions.

'Tell me about Patel,' I prompted.

Richard sighed and raised his head a little. 'Mum said we were rich. We could go abroad – do anything. Then Patel tells Mum that my dad cheated him. He says he saw me at the school and if he doesn't get his money he'll tell the police. I told Mum – he can't prove it. But she was scared.'

'So she went to your uncle . . . '

'Yeah, that wanker.'

Did no one have the Richard Thornley seal of approval?

'She didn't tell him about me – only that Patel wanted money and she didn't want to sell Dad's shares after all.'

So Geoff Thornley wasn't part of the cover-up. Pete would be glad about that. He wouldn't want his hero mixed up in this.

'How did you feel about Mona Pearson being arrested?'

'I felt bad of course! She's all right – she's fair. The other school wouldn't let me in, but she said I could come to her school if I made a bargain with her. I had to write it down and sign it. I didn't want her to go to prison.'

'You must have had a bad few weeks, Richard.' But not as bad as Mona, I added silently. I drew apart from him and turned to face him on the sofa. 'But now you've told us this, what do you want us to do about it?'

The question threw him completely. He made eye contact briefly, then looked away. His lips were parted and drooping at the corners. I reached onto the floor for a box of tissues that had fallen there in the fray and offered him one. He blew his nose noisily.

'I could go off somewhere and you could say you hadn't seen me.'

He said it in a half-pleading way, drawing the back of his hand across his face and smearing a line of snot from nose to ear. The silence from the three adults in the room was deafening.

'You're going to tell the police, aren't you?' He was petulant now.

The late hour and subsiding adrenalin were making me feel exhausted. I tried to stay patient. 'Richard, I didn't ask you to come here. You've brought the problem, now you help us solve it.'

'I'm not sorry I killed him. He deserved it.'

'But does Mona Pearson deserve to have her life cut short, to suffer for what you have done?'

'She won't get that long, will she?'

As I struggled to stop myself hitting him, Steve moved round slowly into view.

'Can I say something?'

No one protested, so he crouched down by the wall.

'I've got a son your age, Richard – a bit older. He's eighteen now. He lives in France. When he was sixteen, he nicked something from a shop.'

'Yeah. So what?'

'It was a part for his motor bike,' continued Steve. 'Worth a lot of money. It's a small town. The guy in the shop knows Eric and couldn't believe he'd nicked it. So he blamed his assistant. He fired him.'

Richard was listening, though pretending not to. 'Lucky for your son.' There was a pause, and then he asked, 'So what did he do?'

'He confessed.'

'What for?' Richard sneered.

'I asked him that just a few weeks ago. He said, "You reach a point when the guilt becomes worse than the consequences of confessing." From what I've heard, you seem to have reached that point.'

Richard said nothing and looked away. The room was completely silent for a while, and somehow everyone's eyes drifted to the telephone, which had been pushed right to the edge of the table. Richard stood up. I half expected him to make a run for the door, but instead he shuffled on unsteady legs towards the phone. He reached out his hand and picked up the receiver. His finger hovered over the dial and he looked up at us with a puzzled frown.

'Is it an emergency?' he asked, deadly serious.

Epilogue

Mona Pearson did not go back to Arkwright High after her release. She considered it. Staff and parents pledged their support and the governors gritted their teeth and added their voices to the rest. She took sick leave and thought about it; had some counselling, saw the psychiatrist a few times to finish piecing together the broken shards of what had happened on the night of the murder. In the end, she decided not to go back, but to study full-time, with a view to starting a new career as an educational psychologist. She said she needed time to come to terms with what had happened – to reinvent herself, to discover the person she might have become if she had not shut herself off so completely from her childhood.

I saw her many times after she was released from the nightmare of custody, but only once on her own. She dropped into the clinic for a cup of tea and a chat. Her calm, assertive manner had returned, but there was a brittle edge to it now. It was more like a shell that she had lived in for years to protect the soft body of her feelings. She had retreated back into it for a while, until she got the courage to come out again. She looked older. Her skin had lost its chestnut sheen and her hair was thinner and flecked with grey.

'I haven't had a chance to thank you properly.'

'For what?'

'You stood by me. I'll always be grateful.'

'I'm glad it's over.' We shared a knowing smile. 'That part of it anyway. Now comes the hard bit.'

'The counselling is very helpful.'

'Good.'

We both took a sip of tea.

'Have you heard the news?' said Mona. 'Bridget's taking early retirement, so they've got two posts to fill now.'

'Have you spoken to her?'

Mona shook her head. 'I can't.' She sighed and her gaze drifted over to the window. There were deep lines under her eyes, a telling reminder of what she had been through. 'I knew she hated me, but I was so arrogant I thought I could handle it. There's a great temptation to blame other people – Bridget, the Thornleys, Rajesh Patel. But in the end you have to say, "I did it. I got myself into this mess. Now I have to claw my way out of it."'

It sounded like a harsh judgement to me, but Mona was a tough person. Nothing I could say would make any difference to the high standards she set for herself.

As for Richard Thornley, his case ground its way slowly through the criminal justice system. The latest news is that the charge might be reduced to manslaughter, for which he might get a year or two in a young offenders' institution. Frances Thornley and Rajesh Patel will get off scot-free – there isn't enough evidence to charge them with anything. I have heard no more of Cynthia Marsh, except a small piece in the local paper which said she had been elected to the local education committee. All I can say is, if she's still there when Hannah goes to school, I'll be sending her to a different borough.

Robin said nothing more about his relationship with Mona and I didn't ask him. Even I can curb my nosiness when I really try. I heard they had stopped seeing each other; then that they had started again. I noticed that Robin went through long phases of being irritable and unapproachable, and that he spent more time with Clancy, having long chats after the clinic was closed. But late one Friday afternoon in autumn, as I glanced out of my office window to the road, which was bathed in orange light, I couldn't help but notice Mona and Robin leaving the clinic together. They walked off up the road in the direction of Acton High Street, deep in conversation. And – yes – I leaned out of the window just to confirm it: they were holding hands.

Also of interest:

Anne Wilson
Truth or Dare
A Sara Kingsley mystery

Caroline Blythe has always seemed the epitome of success. A journalist, wife and mother, she is confident, assured, sophisticated and self-contained. So why should she suddenly turn to Sara Kingsley – an overworked, underpaid community counsellor – for help? And what's behind her concern for a 'friend' who's involved in a dangerous affair with a married man?

Unconvinced by Caroline's story, Sara insists there is nothing she can do. Then Caroline is found dead of a drug overdose – and questions start to surface. Who was the 'friend' Caroline had been so anxious to protect? Was her death suicide or murder? And is Sara herself partly to blame? Despite the pressures of work and single motherhood, Sara feels impelled to undertake a perilous investigation that, if she dares, may bring her closer to the truth . . .

Crime Fiction £5.99
ISBN 0 7043 4461 0

Ellen Hart
Robber's Wine
A Jane Lawless Mystery

Winner of the Lambda Award 1997 for Best Mystery

'Filled with wicked deed, fast pacing and memorable
characters . . . this brightest of lesbian detective series burns
ever brighter.' *Booklist*

Jane Lawless and her irrepressible sidekick Cordelia Thorn set out for
the sleepy shores of Pokegama Lake to escape the urban swelter and
visit their old friend Anne Dumont. But hopes for a little rest and
recuperation disappear fast as a mysterious death in the town's most
prominent family triggers a bizarre series of events. As Jane and
Cordelia investigate, hot weather incites even hotter tempers, and the
explosive qualities of twisted family values keep them moving two
steps forward and one step back – all the while wondering if their
next step may be their last.

'A storyteller who more than keeps you guessing.'
Katherine V Forrest

'A classic whodunnit with an inventive twist in the tail.'
Sunday Times

'The psychological maze of a Barbara Vine mystery.'
Publishers Weekly

Crime Fiction £6.99
ISBN 0 7043 4558 7

Alma Fritchley
Chicken Run
A Letty Campbell mystery

'Julia was watching me carefully. "Well?" I said, "What gives?" Before she could answer, the inner sanctum of Steigel Senior's office was revealed and Steigel Senior herself appeared in the doorway. Julia leapt to her feet and in that sudden movement all was revealed. Julia was wonderfully, newly, ecstatically in love, probably truly for the first time in her life, and who could blame her? Steigel Senior was a cool-eyed, blond-haired Lauren Bacall, complete with Dietrich's mystery and Garbo's gorgeous accent . . . "I'm principal director of Classic Cars," Julia said. "The firm was shaky over last winter and I bought them out. It took every penny I had . . . I've made a few, erm, errors of judgement lately and I need the deal to get me back on track." "What's the catch?" I asked.'

When Letty Campbell warily agrees to let her land be used for a classic car auction, she has no idea what lies ahead. Why is her gorgeous ex, Julia, really so desperate for the auction to happen? Is the new love of Julia's life as suspicious as she seems? And why does Letty have a horrible feeling that she should never have got involved?

At least she has the farm, her irascible chickens and visits to Manchester clubs to take her mind off her worries – not to mention the newly appreciated charms of an old acquaintance who lives in the village . . .

Crime Fiction £6.99
ISBN 0 7043 4515 3

Abigail Padgett
Moonbird Boy
A Bo Bradley thriller

A child-protection investigator in the San Diego juvenile court system, Bo Bradley is courageous, compassionate, unique. She also struggles with manic depression.

'Gripping . . . powerful and suspenseful . . . an unusual heroine.' *Publishers Weekly*

Bo is sent reeling back into depression when she is suddenly bereaved. And her recovery at Ghost Flower Lodge – an innovative psychiatric healing centre – is appallingly interrupted when her friend and fellow-lodgemate is found horribly murdered.

'Sensationally fine . . . breathtakingly well told.'
Los Angeles Times

Who would want to kill the wealthy young comedian Mort? Where is bizarre Old Ayma whose mysterious disappearance coincides with Mort's murder? And who is trying to drive Bo over the edge with anonymous messages taunting her about her loss?

'Truly original . . . by a daring and obviously gifted writer.'
Chicago Tribune

As Bo sets out to track down Mort's killers – and find a home for his now-orphaned son, Moonbird Boy – she uncovers a motive more monstrous than even she could imagine . . .

'Truly exceptional . . . fast-moving suspense to keep one reading very, very late into the night.' *Mystery News*

Crime Fiction £6.99
ISBN 0 7043 4513 7

Carole laFavor
Along the Journey River
A Renee LaRoche crime novel

When irreplaceable Ojibwa artefacts are stolen from the school
on the Ojibwa Red Earth reservation, the community turns to
Renee LaRoche – a 'two-spirit' whose dreams give her a special
insight into the lives of her people. Her investigations rapidly
reveal a long list of suspects: white racists from a neighbouring
town; Billy Walking Bear, a financially troubled eighteen-year-old
who has been spending too much time with alcohol and
marijuana and too little time with his wife and child; Gerald
Peterson, the county medical examiner, known for his greed and
his bigotry; John Anderson, a building contractor who has
suspiciously appeared on the reservation shortly after the thefts;
and Jed Morriseau, the tribal chief, who has rejected Ojibwa
traditions in favour of making a quick buck. Then Morriseau is
found on the river flats – a bullet in his back.

Before she knows it, Renee is in the midst of a terrifying mystery
which must be resolved even as she struggles to deal with being a
lesbian in a cross-cultural partnership, maintain her relationship,
find time for her daughter, and sustain her commitment to her
community, where she is not always among friends . . .

**'Illustrates the injustices of racism, heterosexism, and
environmental degradation while illuminating Indian
spiritual values through the vehicle of a fast-paced
thriller. The dialogue is excellent, the sense of place vivid
and memorable. A fine novel.'** *Lambda Book Report*

'A unique mystery, filled with authenticity.' *Megascene*

'First-rate.' *Washington Blade*

Crime Fiction £6.99
ISBN 0 7043 4521 8

Joan M Drury
Silent Words
A Tyler Jones mystery

Tyler Jones, San Francisco newspaper columnist, is reeling from
the death of her mother and shaken by her mother's dying words
– that there are skeletons in the closet of her family history and
that now is the time to uncover the truth.

Returning to her childhood home is a strange but also poignant
and comforting experience as Tyler renovates the beautiful but
neglected house she has inherited, reconnects with family friends
and begins to wonder whether her old life in the city will ever
regain its appeal. Could she – a busy writer and lesbian feminist
activist – adapt to this life for ever? And, even if she could, is
there something beneath the surface here that isn't as
wholesome as it seems? Could the warm and good-natured
people of the town really have something terrible to hide? As
Tyler begins to uncover the truth she discovers just how far the
living will go to protect the secrets of the dead – even if that
means erasing the lives of women of the past who did not fit in
to the patterns prescribed . . .

**'A cut above the rest . . . will leave readers hungry for
more.' Lambda Book Report**

Crime Fiction £6.99
ISBN 0 7043 4522 6